TOGETHER
TEA

TOGETHER TEA

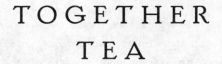

Marjan Kamali

An Imprint of HarperCollins*Publishers*

TOGETHER TEA. Copyright © 2013 by Marjan Kamali. All rights reserved. Printed in the United States of America. No part of this book may be used or reproduced in any manner whatsoever without written permission except in the case of brief quotations embodied in critical articles and reviews. For information address HarperCollins Publishers, 10 East 53rd Street, New York, NY 10022.

HarperCollins books may be purchased for educational, business, or sales promotional use. For information please write: Special Markets Department, HarperCollins Publishers, 10 East 53rd Street, New York, NY 10022.

FIRST EDITION

Designed by Suet Yee Chong

Library of Congress Cataloging-in-Publication Data has been applied for.

ISBN 978-0-06-223680-7

13 14 15 16 17   OV/RRD   10 9 8 7 6 5 4 3 2 1

THIS BOOK IS DEDICATED TO MY PARENTS
FOR ALL THEIR LOVE

TOGETHER
TEA

PART I

1996

CHAPTER ONE

TEA AND QUESTIONS

ina was half-asleep when her mother, Darya, called to say that she'd found the perfect gift for her twenty-fifth birthday. "His name is Mr. Dashti," Darya said, almost breathless on the phone. "Two degrees, a PhD and an MBA. He's a descendant of the third cousin of Reza Shah. He lives in Atlanta. Has perfect health. The nicest teeth. He'll be here on Sunday afternoon for tea and questions. Please, Mina. No tricks this time. I've done the numbers. And wear the lavender dress with your new belt."

Mina put down the phone and slid back under the covers. Another potential husband. Another Sunday afternoon spent nodding at a strange man, with her parents in their best clothes, aiming to please. She didn't want to get married. She wanted to quit business school and move to the mountains to paint all day.

But she had to prepare for her Operations Management exam.

Mina forced herself up and went to the kitchen. She boiled water and then brewed tea the way Darya had taught her, balancing the teapot on top of the open kettle so that steam from the boiled water underneath would gently simmer the leaves. She covered the teapot with a cloth so no heat could escape. Half Earl Grey, half mystery leaves. Darya's brew.

The phone. Again.

"Yes, Darya." For the past few years, Mina had been calling her mother by her first name, a small way of controlling the control obsessed.

"Mina, this is your maman."

"The new man over for tea on Sunday, I know. I won't meet him."

"Don't be silly, Mina—of course you'll meet him! No, I just wanted to extra remind you that I'm hosting math camp today. And I have a cold, which is why I've spent the morning eating raw onions. Your father says it's nature's antibiotic. I'm not contagious though. I'll see you at four fifteen sharp . . ."

Darya's voice was replaced by tiny sniffles. Mina imagined her mother dabbing her nose with the lemon-embroidered handkerchief that her mother, Mamani, had made years ago in Tehran. Darya mumbled that she had to go, but that Mina really should come over for tea.

"Together tea," Darya said in her Persian way of speaking English. "You come, Mina, and we'll have together tea."

Every Saturday afternoon, Darya's two friends, Kavita Das and Yung-Ja Kim, joined her for tea and math camp. All three of them lived in Queens and adored mathematics. Lately, Darya especially loved entering values into spreadsheets so she could spit out charts and graphs. When Darya was a young girl in Iran, she'd excelled in arithmetic. She had wanted to become a math professor, but then she got married, had three kids, and moved to America after the 1979 Islamic Revolution. Mina's father, a doctor, had worked at a pizza shop stirring tomato sauce when the family moved to New York in 1982. He couldn't practice medicine with his foreign license. He studied at night for over a year and surrounded himself with medical journals as he patted dough and sliced green peppers, then took his American medical license exams. He finally succeeded in being a doctor again: practicing internal medicine on Long Island, treating gastritis and ulcers, massaging gallbladders, and examining intestines. He was content with his patients, his medical library, and his daily turkey, tomato, and corn chip sandwiches. But above all, he wanted his wife to be happy. When he saw how miserable Darya was after their first few years in America, he suggested that she start her own math group.

"You have to do what you love, Darya," Baba said one night at dinner. "You can no longer just push it away! Don't you see? You say you love math. You say it's your passion. But where is it in your life? If the mountain won't come to Mohammed, Mohammed must go to the mountain. You have to focus your energy on mathematics. *Seize* it!"

As he said these last few words, he leaped out of his chair and punched his fist triumphantly in the air. Mina and her two older brothers, Hooman and Kayvon, quietly chewed their stuffed eggplant. In the late eighties Baba had discovered the tapes of a life-improvement guru and had become obsessed with self-esteem and self-confidence. He quoted the guru daily.

"But I haven't done math in years." Darya swirled her fork listlessly in eggplant sauce. Since arriving in America, she had worked at a dry-cleaning shop, tailoring clothes.

"No matter!" Baba punched his fist in the air again, then clapped his hands forcefully. He had learned the motions from the free seminar video that came with the audiotapes he'd ordered through the Home Shopping Network. "The past is not your dictator! If you believe it, you can give birth to it! You have to use your inner volition to make your life resplendent!"

Darya stared at him through tears and nodded like a child as she put down her fork. That night Baba and Darya worked together on various strategies for bringing more math into her life. Mina, Hooman, and Kayvon watched as their parents sat at the dining room table. Baba scribbled on memo pads, Darya brewed pots of tea, and they brainstormed. Baba paced up and down, occasionally bursting into an energizing set of jumping jacks. His favorite kind was the scissor jumping jack.

Mina and her brothers walked quietly around their parents to go up to bed.

The next morning at breakfast, Baba tapped his tea glass with a spoon. "Listen up, children! Listen well. From now on, Saturday afternoons will be different around here. Your mother will be pursuing her passion then. She will meet with her friends to do mathematics. On Saturday afternoons, they will immerse themselves in their work. During those hours, the dining room will be a mathematics think tank. You will respect your mother's space and her group. You will not run around or scream or argue during that time. If you wish, you are more than welcome to participate in the workshop, but only if you come prepared, having completed the problems and proofs due that week. No noise during that time. We must all support your mother as she takes targeted action to live with passion. *Fahmeedeen?* Understand?"

Hooman, Mina's oldest brother, who was a senior in high school at the time, grunted yes, then left for basketball practice. Kayvon, the middle child at fifteen, said, "Cool," and kissed Darya on the forehead before turning up the volume on his Walkman. Mina heard the muffled beat of a Tears for Fears song through the foam of Kayvon's headphones.

"Mina," Darya said in a squeaky voice. "Will you comply with these new rules so that I can, um, live with . . ." She turned to Baba. "What was it, Parviz, that I'm supposed to live with? Obsession?"

"Passion." Baba looked encouraging.

"Oh yes, Parviz. Passion," Darya repeated.

Mina took in her mother's hazel eyes. Darya actually looked vulnerable.

"Of course I will." Mina picked up her backpack and left for school. As she walked down the block, she thought about Baba's solemn speech and Darya's request for compliance with the new rules. She thought about math camp, the idea of inviting friends every Saturday to do equations together, and she wondered again, as she often did during her years of adolescence, what her parents would have been like if they hadn't moved to America.

Her small black address book in her lap, Darya parked herself by the phone later that evening and called all her friends. Of the dozen or so people she called, the only ones who agreed that spending every Saturday afternoon working on algebra and calculus was a fun idea were Kavita and Yung-Ja, two of Darya's oldest friends in America and immigrants themselves. From then on, every Saturday afternoon, they met over tea. They started with the basics, since they were all rusty. Mina could understand some of what they were doing at first. But together the women whipped through one textbook after another, and pretty soon it got too complicated for Mina. Not that Darya didn't try to include her. "Please join us, Mina Joon," she would say, using the affectionate term "Joon," which meant "dear" in Farsi. "You don't know how beautiful math is." For Christmas (which none of them celebrated, as they were a Muslim, a Hindu, and a Buddhist), Baba bought each of them a financial calculator. Darya cried when she untied the wrapping to find the small machine, the photo of which she had fingered longingly in technology catalogs. After that, the women whizzed through their work. Within two years Darya applied for a job at a local bank branch in Queens. She told Mina she loved punching in the figures and getting the right answer. She loved the whir of the paper as it slid out of the calculator. She loved how numbers added up to what you expected them to add up to.

MINA FINISHED HER TEA and got some peanut butter from the fridge. Her tiny apartment was on the Upper West Side, close to the Columbia Business School campus. Darya loved the idea of Mina's getting a master's in business administration, even though Mina wanted to be an artist. The pursuit of well-respected, high-paying professions was the duty of the Rezayi children. And since Mina had already ruled out medicine, engineering, and law, her only option was business. The Rezayis had to rebuild their wealth and prestige and, most important of all, stability in this new country. Art wasn't going to fit into that mold. Art, Darya said, meant standing on the street corner hoping to get noticed. With your nose running and no-good shoes. It was for the flighty, flaky, and feckless. Not for the daughter of immigrants who had given up their country, time spent with grandparents, and the best pomegranates in the world to come to America.

Mina ate the peanut butter out of the jar with a spoon. She put it back in the fridge next to the rows of neatly stacked Tupperware that Darya had dropped off: *olivieh* chicken salad, potato quiche cut into triangles, oval meat cutlets sitting in rich tomato sauce, stuffed grape leaf *dolmeh*, barberry rice, and the sweet-and-sour walnut-pomegranate dish called *fesenjoon*.

Mina was relieved that there were still so many lunches and dinners left for her in the fridge. Nothing was quite like the food Darya's skilled hands had patted into being.

IN THE CAR, MINA TURNED ON the news. "Iran" was mentioned in the same breath as "terrorist" and "rogue." Just once, Mina wanted to hear the name of her old country mentioned in the same breath as "joy" or "freedom" or "gentle goodness." She switched to the oldies from the sixties and seventies station, and John Travolta whooped out "You're the One That I Want."

The first time she'd heard that song was with Bita, when they were both nine and living in Tehran. A dozen times they'd danced to it. In the living room, in the kitchen, on Mina's bed, and by the rosebushes in the yard. They'd played that song everywhere but out in public, where they could've been arrested. Mina had wanted to marry John Travolta. His photos were all over her room. Bita kept a photo of his dimpled chin tucked under her headdress. A hundred times they'd listened to that smuggled cassette sound track. A thousand times they'd sworn to be best friends for life. A million years had passed since then. Mina swerved into a different lane, and the driver behind her honked. She had no idea where Bita was now. Best friends forever had turned to be best friends until revolution and war made one of us flee the country. Best friends until one of us became American and the other remained trapped in Iran.

Mina crossed the bridge from Manhattan into Queens. The last letter she'd received from Bita had come a year or two after Mina had moved to the U.S. The onionskin paper was covered with scratch 'n' sniff fruit stickers. If she scratched one of those stickers now, would it still smell of sweet summer strawberries? Mina turned off the radio.

DARYA STOOD OUTSIDE THE FRONT DOOR in her pink housedress, her red hair gathered in a bun, her hands on her hips.

"Are you feeling better?" Mina called out as she pulled into the driveway.

"Yes, but don't kiss me. I'm all oniony," Darya said.

Mina walked up to Darya and kissed her anyway.

"What is wrong with your hair?" Darya asked, as always.

AT THE DINING ROOM TABLE, Kavita and Yung-Ja sat drinking tea and eating baklava. Kavita was small and plump, with dark hair that used to shine and hands that were rough from years of scrubbing tubs, untangling her daughters' hair, and raking dirt so she could grow flowers in the stubborn soil of her Jackson Heights garden. Yung-Ja was thin and petite, always dressed beautifully, always made up—Mina had never seen her without heels and nylons. Mina could tell that all three women were on a high from some calculus. Kavita's frizzy hair was a mess, and Yung-Ja's kohl-lined eyes were shining. They greeted Mina with hugs and kisses, pinched her cheeks, and laughed.

"We did some more integrals today," Kavita said in her high voice. "Just reviewing basics. Applying integration to find total cost from variable cost!"

"Yes, but we also factor in fixed costs." Yung-Ja talked quickly in her broken English, like a runner who'd just successfully finished a sprint. "No forget, we also factor in fixed costs."

"It was beautiful, Mina," Darya said. "Beautifully beautiful."

"Now come, Mina." Darya took Mina's hand and pulled her toward the stairs. "Up to my office. I've made charts on Mr. Dashti. They came out so *precise!*"

Kavita and Yung-Ja waved their hands above their heads without looking up from their calculators as Mina reluctantly followed Darya. At the top of the stairs stood Baba, feet apart, huge goggles on his head, a drill gun in his right hand.

"*Salaam*, Mina Joon!" Baba engulfed Mina in a hug and kissed her on both cheeks. Various objects from his tool belt dug into Mina's ribs. "I'm off to caulk the bathtub! A homeowner's work is never done!" He saluted.

Mina saluted smartly back and watched her father march into the bathroom, his tools bouncing around his waist.

In Darya's bedroom "office," the sight of her two-drawer metal filing cabinet drained Mina's energy. She knew what woe those alphabetized folders held inside.

"Let's see now." Darya sifted through a file drawer. "Mr. Jahanfard. Mr. Samiyi. Mr. Bidar . . . Mr. Ahmadi . . ." She flipped through folders labeled neatly in Farsi. "Ah, here he is!" Darya swooshed out a bright yellow folder. "Mr. Dashti!"

A deafening drilling noise from the bathroom blocked out Darya's voice for a moment.

"Look!" Darya pulled out a piece of paper from the folder and held it up. It was a neatly typed CV. "Your father's aunt's friend in Atlanta faxed me his résumé after speaking to Mr. Dashti's uncle's wife. Look at *this*. He studied chemistry at Yale, got a bachelor's and a PhD. He then received a master's in business administration from *Stan Fohrd*! He likes Persian music and he plays the sitar. He has a very good job with Kodak in Atlanta now, running his own research department. Mr. Dashti decides the balance of the chemicals for each roll of film!" Darya folded her arms across her chest, then added quickly, "His mother was quite pretty."

Mina stared at the wallpaper. She realized she really hated wallpaper.

"Look at this, Mina!" Darya pointed to another sheet of paper titled "Family Background and Health Issues." "This took me hours to research. No history of disease in his family. Everybody healthy. One sister got divorced a few years ago, but I'm told it was for the best. You have to behave next Sunday at tea, Mina. You must. I talked to your father's aunt and to her friend in Atlanta and everyone agrees: he's the one!" Darya handed Mina the folder. "Spreadsheets don't lie!"

Mina plopped onto the bed. The sound of Kavita and Yung-Ja discussing integrals floated up from the dining room. Baba's drilling had stopped. Darya loved to calculate the statistics of available Persian bachelors, factoring in their attributes, family histories, education, the probability for divorce. She had her very own system of assigning numbers to certain qualities. Five for good teeth. Minus 10 for having only a bachelor's and no graduate degree. Plus 20 if it could be proved that they were kind to their mothers. Plus 7 if they didn't hold their forks like shovels. Darya was so proud of her knowledge of Excel, fond of making graphs. Where was the mother Mina used to know in Iran? A magician had made that mother disappear over the years and replaced her with this chubby, red-haired meddling matchmaker. The mother she knew back then would never have done this. Find someone who knew someone who knew a well-educated man. Do the research. Make the calls. Send a photograph of Mina, if requested. And then, bound by some ridiculous obligation to their own meddling matchmakers, these men would board trains or planes or get in their cars and come to tea.

"Darya, I don't want to have tea with Mr. Dashti next Sunday. I don't want to meet him. I don't want to get married. You know that."

Darya opened her mouth to say something, but her lips froze in the shape of a perfect zero. Then she turned and talked to the bedspread.

"My daughter says she doesn't want to get married. Interesting, no? What makes her say this? Youth. Youth and complete lack of knowledge!" Her hazel eyes shone when she turned to Mina. "Mina, I want you to meet Mr. Dashti. Do you know the percentage of divorce in this country? The probability of women over thirty getting married? Mr. Dashti's spreadsheet is very hopeful. Forget Jahanfard. Forget Bidar. Forget all those oafs who came over and made you bored and who you conveniently avoided any eye contact with and spilled tea on. I'm forgiving that, forgetting it.

Whoosh! Gone. Who cares? But this time, Mina! This time, I've computed *statistics*."

"You don't even know him!"

"I'm your mother, Mina. I know *you*!"

"Did it ever occur to you that I'm a lesbian?"

"Lesbian?!" Darya snorted. "Don't think I don't know about lesbians! We had lesbians in Iran. You know how we knew they were lesbians? From their lovers! You don't even have a girlfriend, Mina! You're no lesbian."

Mina sighed. She wasn't a lesbian but she also didn't want to marry someone just because his GPA had been graphed by her mom in Excel. She stared at the wall, at the paintings from India that Kavita had given Darya after visiting her soon-to-be sons-in-law there. Kavita raised her daughters in Queens, then received a phone call from her father in New Delhi and went over to meet her daughters' suitors. The new husbands moved to New York to be with their Indian-American wives. Darya had told Mina they were sweet, charming men who listened well. She told her that these new husbands had adjusted remarkably well to the culture shock of moving to America.

"Darya, I'm still trying to get through grad school. Why would I even want a husband now?"

"Everybody in this life needs a partner."

"I don't."

"You need someone. What's going to happen when I die? Who's going to take care of you? When you're all alone and old? Your brothers? Who'll wipe your nose when you're sick?"

"I'll wipe my own nose! I'll call a friend! Hire someone—I'll put signs on tree trunks for a nose-wiper!"

"You need someone, Mina. You need to have . . ."

"Everything you didn't have?" Mina finished the sentence for her.

"No, Mina," Darya said quietly. "Not everything I didn't have. Everything I *had*. I want you to taste life the way I have. To give you a fraction of what I was given. I want you to have a passion. I want you to fall in love like I fell in love."

"Your marriage was arranged."

"It wasn't arranged. It was . . . *encouraged*. I got to know your father. I took the time. I loved my mother. I knew she wouldn't do me wrong. Because my mother . . ."

Darya broke off and cried silently into her hands. Her mother had been killed by a bomb during the Iran-Iraq War. She had been buying pomegranates at the greengrocer's downtown when the bomb blew the grocer's wooden stalls into shreds. Darya often cried when she talked of Mamani.

Mina's body grew slack as she remembered asking Mamani for those pomegranates years ago. But she forced her body up straight. Darya's tears over Mamani were nothing new.

"Because . . ." Darya looked up, her face wet but suddenly calm. "Because, Mina, my mother gave me a gift when I was nineteen. Don't you see? She gave me a gift, and at the time I was young too and foolish and couldn't appreciate what she'd found for me. I attended my own wedding only because in those days we didn't refuse our parents' choices. It took years for me to realize what she had done for me. The happiness that she placed into my hands."

Mina thought of the man in the bathroom next door, sitting on his knees and squeezing putty onto pink tiles. She thought of her father's few wiry hairs, his uneven teeth and self-help tapes, his bulging stomach, and the way he listened to American songs on the radio, hearing the lyrics all wrong. That's the gift Mamani gave her? That's the happiness Darya was talking about?

"It's ridiculous," Mina said. "You can't pick a spouse for someone else. How do you know what's right for them?"

"It's been done for centuries. This, the way they do it here, *this* is ridiculous. You can't pick a spouse for yourself. How does one person, one *young* person know what's right for them? When you were fifteen, did you think the way you do now? Well, when you're thirty, you'll look back on today and laugh at your thoughts. It's like anything else when you're young. Vegetables. Cod liver oil. A jacket on a seemingly warm day. Your mother says take it, it's good for you. You refuse, it seems unnecessary. Then you realize she knew you better than you knew yourself. That's why she's your mother."

Darya's red bun bounced as she talked. "Don't you think I know how you feel? I cried like you cry by yourself at nights now. I didn't want to get married, didn't even find Baba attractive. I wanted to get a PhD in mathematics and become a professor. I always thought I would contribute something huge to academia, that I would be remembered for a theorem or proof or *something*. I never thought I'd be sitting with Kavita and Yung-Ja on Saturdays solving equations no one would ever see. I couldn't even imagine not being a famous mathematician back then. When my mother introduced your father to me, I hated him. I hated her for pushing him on me. I spent several months, years even, resenting the marriage."

"So? What happened?"

"What happened is I grew up. What happened is your father.

He gave to me. Consistently and unselfishly worked to make me happy. One day I woke up and looked at him and my house and my swollen stomach and realized I was happy and didn't even know it. I heard about a woman receiving a prize in mathematics and I laughed. I didn't care. When my mother died, I couldn't have survived it without your father. No professorship in math would have saved me then."

Darya absently picked up her hairbrush and twirled it in her hand.

"Besides," she continued. "Remember when you were eighteen and we went to the mall and I bought you that denim shirt? Remember how you didn't want to get it? How you hated it then? Now, you wear it almost every day."

"Mr. Dashti is not a shirt!"

"He wears nice shirts!"

"Darya!!!"

Mina felt a tiny tickle in her stomach. A quiver worked its way down to her toenails and her mouth burst open. She couldn't stop laughing. The insanity of their conversation! Mr. Dashti wears nice shirts. Her father as a gift   Mina imagined a huge red bow tied around Baba's bald head. She snorted like a pig as tears soaked her cheeks. She thought of the graphs, Mr. Jahanfard, Mr. Bidar, Mr. Dashti, the slopes of the lines Darya calculated. Her sides began to hurt.

She thought of the gift, her poor dead grandmother's gift.

Mina couldn't speak anymore. She was doubled over on the bed. Her cheeks hurt and her stomach was tight. Through her tears, she caught sight of her mother. Darya stood in her pink and white housedress, her pudgy feet pointing out, the Dashti folder in one hand, her hairbrush in another. Her roots showed, the fiery red dye was in need of a touch-up. When they left Iran, Darya had vowed to dye her hair red if she could ever reach a country where she didn't have to wear a veil. On one of those first mornings in New York, Darya had disappeared into the hotel bathroom for thirty minutes. When she emerged from the bathroom with her hair in a towel, Baba had clapped loudly for her, whistling and cheering, urging Mina and her brothers to join in. Mina could see Baba now, the pride on his face as Darya shyly removed the towel from her wet hair, how he went to the bathroom and cleaned the walls that had been stained crimson, just as he had cleaned her grandmother's body after it had been stained crimson from the bomb at the grocer's those years ago.

Silence replaced Mina's laughter. Her body hiccuped slowly a few times as she got up. Darya was quiet, her eyes confused.

"Oh, Maman," Mina said as she took the hairbrush from Darya's hand and sat her down on the bed. "Do you think I should wear the lavender dress with a cardigan or just by itself when I meet Mr. Dashti?" She placed the hairbrush at the gray roots on Darya's head, and slowly brushed her mother's hair.

CHAPTER TWO

THE MAN IN THE
BEIGE SUIT

The following Sunday, Mina took the subway to her parents'
house because her car needed repair. She rang the doorbell as though she were a guest. Baba opened the door, freshly
showered and dressed in his best three-piece suit. He had on his
Metropolitan Museum of Art turtle tie. His Old Spice was over-
powering. Darya ran to the door in the tailored bright skirt-suit
that made her hazel eyes look green. Her hair was in a perfect
bun, her lips glossy. She frowned at the sight of Mina's jeans and
white shirt with the lavender cardigan tied around her waist, but
she didn't say a word. Mina registered the scent of steaming basmati rice and fragrant *ghormeh sabzi* herb stew coming from the
kitchen. Tea with Mr. Dashti had changed to lunch.

At exactly 1:15 p.m., the doorbell rang again, and Darya
dropped her ladle into the sink and rushed to the door. She took

a few deep breaths and patted her bun into place before swinging the door open. On the doorstep stood a short, chubby man holding a bouquet of pink and white flowers. He wore a beige suit and a brown tie. He was clean shaven and had almond-shaped eyes. His few strands of hair were strategically combed across his head but suddenly blew straight up with a strong gust of wind.

"Mr. Dashti! My goodness!" Darya exclaimed in Farsi, as if completely taken by surprise to see him there. "Well, well . . . welcome! Please come in, come in!"

Mr. Dashti bowed deeply. "It is my pleasure to meet you, Mrs. Rezayi. It is truly my joy. Please excuse my boldness and impudence in making myself such a nuisance to you. I have inconvenienced you. I am a burden to you and your home. You must forgive me."

"Oh, Mr. Dashti, how could you say such a thing? Please, you have made us so very happy. You have brightened our day. You have lit up our eyes! You have embarrassed us with your generosity. Please come in—you who are filled with so much grace!" Darya bowed her head expertly with her reply. They were playing the Persian game of *tarof*, a verbal tradition stressing exaggerated politeness and formality in interactions, a ritual filled with flowery flattery, endless displays of respect for the other, dramatic self-effacement, and indirect answers to unnecessary questions. Darya and Baba relished this communicative art, though Mina had spent years resisting it.

". . . you have truly bestowed upon us a great pleasure," Darya continued. "Please, please come in."

With that Mr. Dashti entered the house and looked nervously

around. When he saw Mina, he looked away, at the stairs, then the wall, then his shoes until he was saved by Baba's booming voice from behind the front door, which was still wide open.

"Mr. Dashti, sir, I am very happy to meet you." Baba stepped into view. "You are most welcome in our home." He extended his hand and pumped Mr. Dashti's vigorously as Mr. Dashti expressed his rapture at meeting Baba.

Darya closed the front door, turned around to face Mina, looked confused, and then cried, "Well, my goodness, Mr. Dashti! Please! This is our daughter, Mina!"

Baba turned around too, and both Darya and he stared at Mina and then at Mr. Dashti as if it was indeed so strange that their daughter, Mina, should be standing there in the living room on such a day when good Mr. Dashti had come by for a visit. What a coincidence!

Mr. Dashti pivoted in Mina's direction but didn't look directly at her. Slowly, from the bottom of his neck, a deep pink blush crept up to the top of his bald head. He bowed. "I am fortunate to meet you," he said to his shoes.

Mina looked desperately at Darya, then at Baba. They prodded her on with their eyes until Darya's slight jerk of the head forced Mina to answer.

"Me too," Mina said as Baba motioned to the sofa. Mr. Dashti waddled his way across the rug and sat down with a heavy plop, underestimating the height of the seat. Darya offered Mr. Dashti some nuts and dried chickpeas, and Baba started chatting. Mina noticed tiny bubbles of perspiration on Mr. Dashti's forehead and chin. Baba asked about his trip, whether his flight was comfortable, how he found New York, how he liked Atlanta, how his family was, and commented cheerfully on New York weather and the immense ineptitude of taxi drivers in the city.

"Well, they're all immigrants now, aren't they?" Darya chimed in as if she herself were a descendant of the *Mayflower* cluster. Mina didn't say anything, just sat there, waiting for lunch. *We'll eat, then we'll have the requisite tea, then he'll go home.* She had accounting notes to review. She had a finance case to prepare. As Mr. Dashti folded and unfolded his legs, Mina saw that his beige suit was far too tight for him. He was much heavier than Darya's charts had indicated. Mina could picture long straggly hairs on his toes. He most likely wanted a baby within a year and a boy at that. He seemed like the kind of man she could never talk to in the middle of the night. He'd ask Mina to write to his parents in Iran once a week, in Farsi, with a fountain pen and only in blue. He probably liked his stews served steaming hot and wanted their son to do surgery on brain neuromas or become a famous engineer in Maryland where he'd live with his wife, Mina's daughter-in-law, who would go to aerobics classes while Mina watched the grandkids.

Mina didn't want to watch the grandkids. She didn't even like Maryland.

DELICATE ROWS OF SAFFRON-SOAKED RICE adorned their plates at lunch. The *ghormeh sabzi khoresh* was a perfect blend of lamb and red kidney beans mixed with the *sabzi* of parsley, coriander, scallions, and fenugreek. Mina bit on a dried Persian lime and a rush of tartness filled her mouth. By the time lunch was finished, Mr. Dashti, Baba, and Darya had talked about politicians (they're all charlatans), the weather (the sun gives light but not enough warmth in this part of America), business (it matters), medicine (it really matters), chemistry (they knew the same genius organics professor), immigrants (they're ruining Queens), cable TV (it's a massive commercialized wasteland), and especially the Food Network (it's a fine concept, but the cooks really should clean their utensils more often and not cut up vegetables on dirty counters). Mina had said a few words, like "good" in response to how is school, "interesting" in response to how she found her studies, and "yes" to would she like more rice. All of the above questions were asked by her parents in their attempt to get her to talk. Mr. Dashti was tongue-tied every time he looked in her direction. Dark spots of perspiration spread in the underarm areas of his beige suit, and he continuously wiped his forehead with a scrunched-up napkin held in his doughy hand.

Finally, Darya and Baba got up to clear the table, and Mina jumped to help. But Darya said through a tight smile that Mina must sit, and no, they didn't need assistance in the kitchen. It was clear then that Mina couldn't escape the dreaded time alone with Mr. Dashti. She sat in silence across from him, as Darya and Baba clattered about in the kitchen. The grandfather clock ticked loudly by the banister.

"Miss Mina," Mr. Dashti said finally. "Um, how is it going?"

Mina looked up, surprised. So far, everyone had spoken Farsi. His accent was not the familiar singsong her brother Kayvon could imitate so well when he did his "Irooni" accent. It was quite American.

"It's going," she said in English. Mr. Dashti's smooth forehead gleamed under a strip of sunlight from the window. "I mean, it's going well, thank you."

He nodded. The dishwasher turned on in the kitchen. Mina could imagine her father washing the copper pots by hand while Darya prepared fresh tea.

Mr. Dashti bit his lip and studied the Persian miniatures on the wall. For the first time in all the husband-setting-up meetings, it occurred to Mina that he was just as uncomfortable as she was.

"So, how did you like getting an MBA?" she asked.

His eyes lit up, and he smiled. Well, one thing was right about what Darya said. He did have good teeth.

"My MBA? Yes, well, I liked it, Miss Mina. It was a good program and very useful for me. I enjoyed it." He looked in her eyes for the first time. "It's a lot of work, but in the end, it is all worth it."

"Yes," Mina said. She nodded unnecessarily. Something about the way he talked made her feel she should help him along instead of childishly making it more difficult for him. After all, who knew what kind of Darya he had back home? Who knew what busybody relative of his had talked him into getting on that plane and coming to Queens for lunch? They were both victims of the same curse. Mina knew they'd never see each other again, so she decided to try and make the remainder of their time together at least relatively pleasant. *Poor guy. Wearing that beige suit and everything.*

"It's quite a program!" Mina said, a little too loudly. "I'm learning loads!"

"It's true. You learn . . . heaps," Mr. Dashti said.

He nodded and looked again at the Persian miniatures on the wall. Mina studied the tablecloth.

"Here is tea!" Darya bounced in holding a tray with four *estekan*, small hourglass-shaped glasses, filled with dark tea. Baba carried a silver bowl of sugar cubes in one hand and a platter of baklava cut into diamonds in the other.

"May your hands not ache, Mrs. Rezayi," Mr. Dashti said. "I apologize so much for the trouble I have given you."

"Oh, it was no trouble at all," Darya said.

"This baklava is divine," Mr. Dashti said. "I am embarrassed at the trouble I've given you."

"Well, you see, the secret lies in the consistency of the almond paste." Baba rubbed his fingers together to demonstrate how to achieve that consistency. "It's all in the kneading, sir. All in the kneading."

Mr. Dashti leaned in and listened to Baba's recipe. Mina knew that Mr. Dashti deserved someone decent and sweet. She wished him well and felt a small twinge of guilt that she couldn't be that someone. Baba continued to talk about soaking almonds. And then, in a sliver of a moment—when Mr. Dashti broke his baklava in two and Baba's glasses fogged up from a sip of tea—Mina exchanged a glance with Darya. She knew her mother could read her face, and instantly Darya registered that Mina would not be trying on bridal dresses anytime soon. There would be no *sofreh* bridal silk cloth laid out for a wedding.

It was over.

The tea glasses were empty now. Darya gave out a long sigh and folded her napkin into smaller and smaller squares on her lap. Mr. Dashti thanked everyone again for the wonderful food and the lunch and the tea and the baklava.

"It was no trouble at all, Mr. Dashti. We hope you've enjoyed New York," Darya said tersely.

Now everyone at the table knew that Mina and Mr. Dashti would not be getting married.

"We hope your trip back to Atlanta is comfortable and without hassles," Baba said. And with this it was clear that Mr. Dashti would not be coming back. Darya raised her tea glass. "We wish nothing but the best for you, Mr. Dashti. God willing, you will find nothing but continued success in the future."

And they all sipped their tea and sucked on sugar cubes as the afternoon fell and sank around them. Mr. Dashti's head was low and his shoulders drooped but he repeatedly thanked Darya and Baba for the delicious lunch and the tea. Mina noticed that his face was not so damp with perspiration anymore, even though he'd been drinking steaming tea. As Mina reached for the baklava, so did Mr. Dashti, and their eyes locked for a moment. Mina saw the expression on his face quite clearly. He politely withdrew his hand and smiled, showing his perfect teeth.

When Mina got up to take the tea glasses to the kitchen, she knew that the expression she had seen on Mr. Dashti's face was not one of dejection or rejection, but actually one of exasperated, glorious relief.

CHAPTER THREE

A PUDDLE OF FOLDERS

Fatty," Darya said. "He was a fatty. He needs to exercise. God knows he has a PhD. You'd think he'd know not to eat so much baklava in one sitting. And what *was* that suit?" She crinkled her nose.

"*Basseh.* Enough. Stop it, Darya," Baba said.

They were in the kitchen, putting away the lunch dishes. Darya's forehead vein throbbed, the way it always did when she was upset. Mina noticed that her bun was coming undone.

"It's just that . . . well, it didn't work out. And sometimes the information that comes to me from *some* of my sources is a little biased. All I'm saying is . . ."

They had stood in the yard as Mr. Dashti's sleek, silver car had backed out of the driveway and disappeared down the street. The three of them had waved perfunctorily, continuing to move their hands back and forth even after Mr. Dashti's car had gone.

"No matter!" Baba said as he dried a tiny spoon. "Onward!"

"Yes, of course. On . . . with it, or whatever it is you say. You know it's not at all important, right, Mina Joon? He was a fatty." Darya picked up a frying pan to dry.

"Please stop. Stop with the name-calling. Just stop with all of this. Stop inviting men, stop graphing them. Stop humiliating me. And them. Just. Stop. *Please*," Mina said.

"What on earth's the matter?" Darya shoved the frying pan into Baba's chest. "Come upstairs with me, Mina. Come on!"

Mina felt as if all this were happening to someone else, in someone else's family. Somebody else's parents invited all these men over, not hers. Not the mother she had known growing up, who had driven them to English classes in Tehran and taught them *ghazal* of Persian poetry, not the father who had calmly tied her shoelaces on mountain hikes and taught her how to count tadpoles in the rain and play chess by a campfire.

Pulled by some invisible rope between her and Darya that she wished she could slice in two, Mina followed her mother upstairs.

The bedroom smelled of green apples and lotion. The bureau was freshly polished and shone. The desk was in perfect order. The only thing out of place was the filing cabinet: it was open, and Mr. Dashti's yellow file stuck out. Darya must have done some last-minute reviewing this morning.

"I really didn't like the way he slurped his tea is all I'm saying, Mina. It was very peasant-like." She crossed her arms. "Surely you can do better than that!!"

Dear God above, help me, Mina thought. "He was your idea. Remember?" She tried to be calm. She tried to be reasonable and *businesslike.* "Aren't your twenties supposed to be when you take time to figure things out, have fun, find out who you are? Why fast-forward to husband-and-kids. I'm already in business school, aren't I? Crunching those equations that you love?"

"Oh please, Mina, don't give me this garbage. This extended childhood that you Americans glorify . . . 'finding out who you are'? That's psychobabble. Mumbo. *Jumbo.* You want to know who you are? I'll tell you who you are. You're my daughter!"

Mina plopped onto Darya's bed.

"All this 'adjusting to the real world' charade that people here talk about. You know what it is? *Laziness!* A way to delay responsibility. It doesn't take a decade to 'figure things out.' Figure what out? How long do these people expect to remain children?"

Mina stared at the folder. Did Darya think that a man would be the last piece of the Mina math puzzle? The final variable to complete the spreadsheet? Was she after the perfect formula to solve Mina? What did it take to create Darya's ideal of a "whole" Mina? If only Darya would just dump these folders. Mina would then ask her why she'd thrown them all away. Darya would probably say because it's not worth the aggravation I go through to set up these meetings. You don't cooperate. I give up! She'd give her martyr-mother sigh and Mina would be left swimming in her familiar pool of guilt.

"We're done with this setting-up thing, right? It's not worth it anymore, is it, Darya?" Mina asked out loud.

"It's not that it's not worth it," Darya said quietly. "It's that you are worth more."

A car drove by on the street below, loud rock and roll blasting through Mina's skull.

"All of this." Darya's hand waved over the folders and filing cabinet. "It's *here* that there's so little I can do. There, I was in my element. We had dignity. A solid life. We were established. Not foreigners having to scavenge for foreigners. I could have given you everything."

Mina thought of Darya *in her element*. She couldn't imagine herself in any element she could call her own. That other country, was it a dream? When Mina pressed her face to the plane window that first night when they were about to land in New York and took in the glittering jewellike city lights, did the other country cease to exist? Was Mina a foreigner here? She thought she was an American. Darya always called her one.

The setting sun created pools of light on the Persian rug. Twilight fell. Mina and her brothers had to hold up the fragile web of the new life they'd created and make sure that not one thread got unraveled because they had left a place of horror and this— the secure house, the freedoms, the convenient food markets, the peaceful streets—this is what they had come here for, and they did not need to argue. They did not need to disrupt this safe American life that they had somehow pieced together and built from scratch.

"I'll set the table for dinner." Mina walked carefully around the filing cabinet and went downstairs.

THEY HAD LEFTOVERS FOR DINNER. The rice had lost most of its saffron grains and the *tahdeeg*, the crunchy bottom-of-pot rice, was gone. The phone rang.

"It's Yung-Ja," Baba called out.

When Darya took the phone, she mumbled "yes," "no," and "well, you know my spreadsheets do have a margin of error."

Mina knew she should go back to her apartment in Manhattan. She had a huge finance case to prepare for the morning. But she felt stuck. Imbalanced.

She crept up to Darya's bedroom after dinner. How could a person spend so much time trying to find a mate for someone else? Did Darya really worry so much about Mina's spending her life alone? Or did she just get a thrill out of the charts and graphs?

Mina pulled out folder after folder containing data on accomplished men. She spread the résumés on the floor. Darya's handwriting was all over the CVs. "Mother forgot to give his brother the polio vaccine, brother got polio," Darya had scribbled in the margin of Jahanfard's résumé. Then in an angry red she'd written the word "CARELESS!!" In another manila folder Mina found notes about a thirty-three-year-old banker who, according to Darya's handwriting, "smoked for ten years but has now quit." Next to that note, in red, Darya had scribbled, "Check on this. Make sure."

When Darya appeared in the doorway of the bedroom, her bun had completely fallen apart. Even in the tailored suit, she looked defeated. She stepped over the folders that Mina had strewn on the floor. She said nothing, but just slid down and sat on the floor across from Mina. Darya drew her panty-hosed knees to her chest and blew her red hair away from her eyes, and for a moment she looked young again. In that minute, she looked like the mother Mina remembered from prerevolutionary Iran. The mother who would laugh at the idea of suitors being graphed and who had more important things to do with her time than drawing charts of potential husbands. That old young mother.

Mina thought again of Mr. Dashti. He was actually a nice enough man, but the day felt as if it had revolved around a monster.

"I used to laugh at people who set up meetings with suitors. Did you know that?" Darya lowered her head onto her knees, surrounded by the puddle of folders. "I used to laugh."

When Darya bent her head, Mina could see the gray roots.

"Have you prepared your finance case, Mina? Don't you have a big assignment coming up? You shouldn't be wasting your time on suitors, you know that, right?" Darya's muffled voice spoke into her knees.

CHAPTER FOUR

PILLOW TALK AND
ADULT EDUCATION

Darya couldn't wait for the day to be over. Her heart beat too fast against her drawn-up knees. Lately nothing worked out. And "lately" meant since the revolution. For fifteen years, her life had been on hold. For fifteen years, she'd been waiting for the regime in Iran to change. So she could go back to her normal life. To her green house in Tehran, just a few blocks away from where her father and mother had lived before her mother was killed. To go back to that life where it didn't matter what an MBA stood for or where Atlanta was. But here she was. The kids were getting older. Sassier. Sometimes, she was convinced, even stupider. The lunch with Mr. Dashti hadn't been all that different from the lunches and teas with other men. But there was something about his shiny face and perfect teeth and calm demeanor that made Darya feel embarrassed for having him over. It was as if he had telegraphed with his white smile the folly of the whole experiment. Darya felt done in. As if she'd had the last straw with this one. For what? What the hell was she doing typing up résumés and making graphs on some two-cent men who didn't even deserve her daughter?

Things had happened the way they happened. The revolution had changed her world. What is done cannot be undone.

Parviz walked in then. Parviz now had on his sweatshirt and jeans, no more suit and turtle tie. Though he still smelled of Old Spice. Ever since they had moved to America, he'd smelled of that cologne. He hadn't stopped splashing it on since the day he brought her to this country with its candy canes and carousels and carefree attitude about everything and anything.

"Darya Joon, I'll drive her home," Parviz said.

"You don't need to drive me. I took the subway today. I can take it back," Mina said.

"It's late," Parviz said.

"I'll be fine."

"Okay then, just to the station."

"Go with your father. Let him take you to the station." Darya lifted her head. "Off you go, then. Off you go." Mina, sulky and sullen, waved, and Darya wished her daughter had more oomph. More confidence. Where had Mina's confidence gone? And her gratitude. Say thank you to your father for driving you, for goodness' sakes. Hadn't she taught her anything?

Once she heard her husband and daughter back out the driveway, Darya sank onto the floor. She stretched out her body and closed her eyes. In Iran, the ceilings of their home had been so high. Making them feel freer inside. Here, in this "cape" style house as Parviz called it, she always felt as if the walls were closing in on her. Her sons could barely stand up straight in this room. Even she felt as if she could bump her head if she stood on her nyloned tippy toes.

She thought of her mother's garden: the fat crimson flowers, the lemon trees, the smell of the leaves and the dust after her father watered the bushes, the sound of the beet seller's wagon going by.

"*Khoobi?* You okay?" Parviz reappeared in the doorway as if by magic. The ride to the subway had been so short. Or maybe she'd lost track of time.

His familiar, warm hand folded over hers as he slid onto the floor and lay down next to her. The first time she'd touched his hand, back when Mamani presided over their courtship, she'd been surprised at the thick strong veins on the back of it. Now she loved those veins. They lay side by side on their backs, staring up at the ceiling.

"*Khoobam*, I'm fine," Darya said. Darya closed her eyes again and thought of their old life in Tehran. There it hadn't been just Darya, Parviz, Hooman, Kayvon, and Mina. There had been Mamani, and Darya's father, Agha Jan, Darya's sister, Nikki, her children, Parviz's parents, his four siblings, their children, Mamani's five sisters, their children, all the cousins and aunts and uncles and the extended family that stretched from Tehran to Mazandaran by the Caspian Sea. Darya had loved that connected life. She would throw birthday parties, and about a hundred people would show with gifts and kisses and kind words and gossip. There were friends too, the friends that Darya and Parviz had made at the university: a rowdy, jovial group who might as well have been family. She missed them all so much.

Parviz grunted. Was he sniffling? Maybe he was missing their old life too, missing that stability that had vanished once the revolution and then war blowtorched their country and tore them all apart. Maybe he was remembering the day of that awful bombing that killed Mamani.

Darya opened her eyes and looked at her husband.

"Oh my God, Parviz, are you doing *ab crunches*? Is there ever a time when you're not trying to optimize the moment? We're . . . I thought we were talking!"

Out of breath and slightly sweating, Parviz let out a puff. "Just a few pelvic . . ."

"Oh, for God's sake!" Darya got up. Her panty hose was cutting into her ever-expanding middle. What was the use? Parviz was happy to be here. He didn't miss anything about Iran. He was always seizing the bloody moment.

Darya couldn't wait to rip off her tight panty hose. Couldn't wait to just put on her pajamas and collapse into bed.

"And fifty!" Parviz let out a triumphant exhale and bounded up.

LATER THAT NIGHT, AS PARVIZ SNORED peacefully, Darya lay awake next to him.

Parviz let out a long, satisfied snore. Darya turned toward him. How could he not ever want to go back? How could he not miss his parents' home in downtown Tehran, where the bathroom was outdoors and Persian cats roamed by the pond in their garden?

Darya nudged her husband gently. He made one loud snore, then startled awake.

"Are you sleeping?" Darya whispered.

"No, just doing scissor jumping jacks, dear. Of course I'm sleeping! What *is* it, Darya? Just forget about that Dashti fellow. Just let it go. Go to sleep."

"Parviz, do you ever miss your parents' house in downtown Tehran where the bathroom was outdoors and Persian cats roamed by the pond in the garden?"

"*What?*" Parviz mumbled.

"Do you miss it?"

"No."

"Why?"

"Because it was in downtown Tehran and the bathroom was outdoors and cats roamed in the garden. That's why! Darya, are we replaying the 'I miss my homeland' record? You know you have to live in the present. You know you can't go back to the past . . ."

"Oh please, no self-help rubbish right now, okay?" Darya turned her back to him.

"You wanted to talk!"

"I just get homesick, that's all. I never thought I would be graphing men's grade point averages for Mina. I thought . . . I thought it would be different when I was middle-aged. That I'd be accomplished."

"You *are* accomplished, Darya. You have three beautiful children. You have re-created a life and a home in a brand-new country. Hooman is a doctor. Kayvon is a lawyer. Mina is in business school. We got out of Iran. We're Americans. You're even working as a bank teller now. What more could you possibly want?"

Darya sighed. "Good night, Parviz."

Within a few minutes, Parviz was snoring again. Even his sleeping was efficient. He was right. The kids had turned out well.

That was most important. She was indeed a bank teller, which was far better than the dry cleaner's seamstress she'd been when they first moved here. Darya thought back to her university days. Back then, unlike now, not too many girls had attended university in Iran. Female enrollment in universities had actually increased *after* the Islamic Revolution. But before the revolution, she'd been one of five girls in her whole class. How the men had vied for her attention! The flirting. The drives to the cinema. The *proposals*. Darya had tried so hard to concentrate on her grades. The math classes were the most fascinating, the most challenging, the best. The numbers in her mind had felt like numbers she could hold— squeeze between her fingers, roll around, even toss up in the air, and rearrange in perfect new order. The satisfaction when she slotted those numbers into place. Nothing felt like that. Well, maybe some things.

Those Iranian men of her youth had driven her around in convertibles and taken her on hikes in the mountains. In a Tehran that felt new and modern and on the brink of excellence. They were modernizing, the king had said. They were improving. They were onto something great. Once upon a time. Darya remembered the *possibilities* that had stared her in the face at every turn. Parviz had been only an afterthought then. All spindly arms and awkwardness, acne scars on his cheeks. His bass voice was all he had going for him. And his kindness. He'd held her hand and helped her as they hiked in the mountains. She had never thought she would marry him. But Mamani had insisted.

Darya watched her husband's nostrils flare with each snore. She pulled the comforter over his vibrating belly. Mamani had seen something in Parviz that she'd liked from the very beginning.

And that had been that. What is done cannot be undone.

Three kids later, here they were.

When her sons were little, Darya was bewildered by their manic energy. As they wrestled each other on the living room floor, destroying the *khatam* boxes and nut bowls that she'd so carefully arranged, she'd dream of having a daughter one day. In her fantasy, she saw herself as an older, wiser woman eating *chelo kabob* at a restaurant with a young lady who was her grown daughter. They'd chat and eat, gossip and share. Darya would listen and advise as her daughter confided in her. They'd burst out laughing at silly little things. After lunch, they'd shop for silk together, then go home and swap dress patterns. Darya would guide her daughter's hand along bolts of fabric, teach her how to cut just right, instill in her the sense of strength and inner confidence that her own mother had given her. On her daughter's wedding day, Darya would watch her dance, feeling pride in a job well done. That was how she had imagined it when she was a young mother of two sons who fought at her feet. Then it had happened. After hours of pushing and a pain that felt as if it could blind her, a wet, purple kitten-like baby had been placed in her arms. A girl. And Darya felt the joy infused with terror that only comes when a long-held dream is finally realized.

And sometimes she still felt that joy infused with terror, the pain that could blind her.

Some dreams had come true. Others had not.

Darya closed her eyes. She should let Parviz sleep. But she managed to somehow throw her hand across his face. Managed to because she wanted to wake him.

"What? What is it?" Parviz shook awake again.

"Parviz, did I wake you?"

"Um . . . yes. Did you just slap me?" Parviz rubbed his cheek.

"No, sorry. Look, I just can't sleep. I just . . ."

"Darya, forget about the men. I told you. Just go to sleep." Parviz nestled into his pillow.

"Do you think I made an error in inputting the data? Is that why Mr. Dashti didn't turn out as planned? I thought I was doing everything right. But maybe I'm not . . ."

Parviz sat up. "That's it! You want to improve your skills! And I know just the thing. I saw something the other day . . ." He was awake now all right. Within seconds, the comforter was thrown off. *I've done it,* Darya thought. *He's in his Let's Solve This Problem by Taking Action NOW! Mode.*

"Let's grab life by the throat, Darya Joon! Let's take care of this right now!"

Parviz walked over to the bedroom desk and started rifling through a pile of mail and papers. He held up a booklet.

"Look, it's 1996, okay? The solution to every problem can be found. You just give me a minute, my lady. You just give me one minute."

Darya watched as Parviz flipped through the pages of the booklet. He was now fully in his hyperactive mode. She lay back on her pillow and pulled the covers over her. This was not what she had been looking for.

"Ah-ha! Perfecto! See what I found for you, Darya Joon? Would you look at this? Huh? Come on! And it's perfect timing. Just come over and look at this!"

Darya flung the covers back and got out of bed. She went and stood behind Parviz in her pajamas. He was holding the Adult Education Community booklet that had arrived in the mail earlier in the month. He had opened to the Queens Public Library page. She squinted to read the fine print.

"Would you look at that! A class, my dear. A class that will take care of your yearning for more knowledge and know-how and will better your ability to manipulate percentage probabilities. Look at that, Darya Joon. It's made for you!"

Darya's eyes followed Parviz's hand on the page.

"Forest Hills Adult Education Fall Class Schedule." Parviz's huge forefinger glided down the page to "Spreading Spreadsheet Specs. Intermediate/Advanced class on all things spreadsheet."

"Oh," Darya said.

"That's what I'm saying! Oh! indeed. It's like it was meant to be. What do you say? Let's get this done!" Sounding just like his go-getter guru, he ripped out the registration form at the end of the booklet and started filling it out with a pen. He quickly wrote in her name, their address, their credit card number and expiration date. "In the mail tomorrow morning, I promise. Your first class starts next week. This will help you. Done! Now, let's get some sleep!"

With an excitement and zeal that only Parviz could muster for the simple act of having filled out a registration form for an adult education class that Darya didn't even want to take, he jumped back into bed, snuggled in, and, before long, was snoring again.

Darya stood there staring at the filled-out form. The air around the desk still smelled of Old Spice. The scent clogged her brain. Spreading Spreadsheet Specs. Had she said she wanted to take a class? Is that what she had said? No. But that's what he thought would make her feel better.

Well, the solution was simple. She'd get rid of the form before he could send it in. She simply wouldn't go. Silly class in some library at night taught by who-knows-who. Who said she had to go?

CHAPTER FIVE

SPREADING
SPREADSHEET SPECS

Darya walked to the Queens Public Library under streetlamps festooned with banners for an upcoming neighborhood carnival. She stopped and hesitated in front of the redbrick building. Against her better judgment, and because Parviz was absolutely convinced that improving her Excel skills was her key to happiness, she'd come. But in truth, she'd come because, of course, Parviz had woken up early and mailed in the registration with full payment before Darya could get rid of the form. When she had called a few days later to cancel her registration, they'd said the fee was nonrefundable and now Darya needed to talk her way, face-to-face, into a refund.

Going down the musty steps caused a sharp twinge in her right knee, which probably meant the beginning stages of some form of arthritis. Lovely. Middle age and all its new aches and pains. Darya followed signs on yellow paper featuring a hand-drawn arrow and the words "Miranda Katilla's Spreading Spread-sheet Specs!" until she arrived outside a room with an opaque glass door. She turned the knob and walked in. Was she late? Because the teacher was already talking and people were already seated on folding metal chairs, taking notes as if it mattered. Darn it. Now she couldn't talk privately to the teacher till after the class was over. Darn it, darn it. It was too late to go back. She'd already walked in, and all eyes were on her and the teacher motioned for Darya to sit with a huge, welcoming smile. Darn. It.

Miranda Katilla was the kind of chipper that came about from overly caffeinated bad coffee. Darya eyed the Styrofoam cup in Miranda's hand. How rude. People here always ate and drank in front of others, *when the others weren't eating and drinking*, which in Persian culture was considered beyond uncouth. She hated herself for being so judgmental, but she'd lived long enough and had seen enough to know a few things. For example, already Darya knew that Miranda was the kind of woman who never ironed anything.

Miranda Katilla was talking about the importance of spread-sheets in everyday life. "Not just for work. Not just for accounting, per se. But for everything. Your groceries. Your home budget. A way of measuring and keeping a record. Documenting. Adding up."

Darya sat a little straighter. She did like the sound of this. Perhaps she would sit through this one class, then ask for her re-fund. Poor Miranda Katilla. Teaching this class at night instead of having a real job. Yes, Darya decided, she would be more *open-minded*, as Mina would say, and give this fool a chance. There, she was getting better at being less judgmental already.

Darya rummaged for a pen in her handbag.

"Here you go," she heard a whisper.

A man was handing her a pen. He was about Darya's age, slim, with brown hair and deep laugh lines around his mouth. He wore a flannel shirt that looked like a second-rate lumberjack's.

Darya took the pen and murmured, "Thank you." She held it in her hand. It was a fountain pen. Who on earth came to a spreadsheet class with a fountain pen?

Miranda's curls (unnatural, forced into shape by chemicals, Darya had already surmised) bounced as she continued to extol the virtues of Excel.

"Sam, was it? Sam, can you tell me one thing you think spreadsheets could help you with? In your own life?"

The man next to Darya looked up. "Well." His voice was much deeper than it had been when he was whispering. "For my music. Lesson plans, student names. Grades. Especially grades."

"Teachers need spreadsheets more than anyone!" Miranda said, apparently delighted. "Now. If we all turn on our programs, I'd like to review some Excel basics, then take you all to another level."

Parviz would really like Miranda Katilla. She spoke his language: "another level" and all that. Darya realized she didn't have a computer. Of course she didn't. She had only come to get her refund and leave.

Sam's chair was suddenly closer to hers. "Share?" he said and flipped open his laptop.

His chair had made no noise. Darya looked down and saw that all four legs ended in yellow tennis balls. She looked around and noticed that all the chairs had tennis balls attached to the bottom of their legs. So that's why Sam's chair had sidled so silently next to hers. Darya found herself enchanted by this trick of tennis balls.

Sam smelled of soap and tea, a bergamoty smell. Not of Old Spice. His eyes were kind, and he pulled his chair even closer and tilted the screen so she could see. His kindness reminded her of Parviz.

When Miranda Katilla asked them if they really appreciated the difference between columns and rows and if they truly understood how mastery of the program could do no less than "change their spreadsheet lives," Darya couldn't help but snort.

Sam raised his eyebrows at her and smiled. He didn't smile the way a classmate smiles at another classmate in the basement of the Queens Public Library during an adult education community class. No, he smiled at her the way those boys of her youth had smiled at her, back when she hiked in the mountains with them, back when she had suitors, back before she got committed to the gift her mother gave her, and before she signed up for the strict columns and rows of adult life.

WALKING HOME FROM THE LIBRARY that night, Darya felt that the evening air was a little sweeter than it had been on her way to class. When she opened the front door and saw Parviz sitting on the couch, eating pistachios, and he asked, "How was it, Darya Joon, how was class?" Darya felt almost guilty when she said, "It was so wonderfully wonderful."

She hadn't asked for a refund. Maybe she could use more spreadsheet knowledge. It would help her at work, wouldn't it? Maybe she could even get a promotion with this training.

"Was it interesting?" Parviz asked.

"Yes." Darya again felt guilty saying this to Parviz as he sat there shelling pistachios. She put down her handbag. It was just a smile from a middle-aged man in a class taught in the basement of the public library by a woman who never ironed anything. But during that smile, Darya's round middle had whittled down, her wrinkles had been erased, her skin firmed, her legs toned, her knee pain vanished, and she didn't need her reading glasses. Her daughter's eye rolls no longer broke her heart, and she wasn't in chronic grief for the mother she'd lost to the bombs that fall and kill at random. For that brief moment, within those musty library walls, Darya Daneshjoo felt herself again. Her old, young self. The self that stood at the top of the mountains of Tehran and laughed because she felt free. That self.

"So, you liked it, Darya Joon?" Parviz asked.

"I did," Darya said.

"Highlights?"

"Hmmm?"

"The class, the teacher, the students. Anything stand out?"

Darya fluffed her hair. "There were tennis balls at the bottom of the chairs."

"Tennis balls?"

"Tennis balls."

Parviz held a pistachio in midair. He seemed to be thinking. Darya got ready for more questions. She stopped him before he could ask more. "To keep the chairs from scraping the floor when you move them."

Parviz nodded as it dawned on him. Then he popped his pistachio into his mouth and clapped his hands in the air. "Genius!" he cried. "What will they think of next?"

And with the clap of his hands, she was back. Back in her living room in Queens, no longer on the mountaintops of Tehran. No fountain-pen-wielding, lumberjack-shirt-wearing, deep-voiced music teacher was smiling at her. Her right knee started to hurt. She asked Parviz if he wanted some warm milk before bed.

"With honey, my honey," he called out.

He did not just say that, Darya thought.

But of course, he did. He always did.

CHAPTER SIX

SAMOSAS AND KIMBAP

S amosas and mango chutney for you ladies, made by yours truly." Kavita handed Darya a plate covered with a dish-cloth. "I told Shenil that if he doesn't learn to appreciate the virtues of his domestic goddess soon, he'll find himself with a ghost of a wife in search of a bon vivant Clark Gable for romantic times tout de suite!"

Darya let Kavita in and led her to the dining room. It was their third math club since Darya had started her spreadsheet class at the library. In class, she and Sam sat next to each other. They'd talked a little. She'd learned that he lived on his own, had no kids, and that he liked fly-fishing. She had no idea what fly-fishing was. Catching fish with flies? He was so . . . American. They chatted before class and sometimes after, and during "break" they went outside while others smoked or ran to get coffee from Starbucks.

Darya and Sam never got coffee. They just stood together under the starless New York sky, and Sam told her about his students. He taught guitar. Not violin. Not piano. Not Persian sitar, which would've been really impressive. But guitar. That wasn't a "high-class" instrument in Darya's book.

"I do believe you have wafted to the fjords!" Kavita said in her high voice. "My dear, what has gotten into you? What puts you so deep in thought, darling?"

"Oh, nothing! I love your samosas, you know that!"

Kavita arched her overly tweezed eyebrows. "I do believe, Darya dear, that our guitar hero with whom you are so besotted has convoluted your mind and gotten you in a tizzy. What tomfoolery! Who would've ever supposed that math-obsessed Darya would find her heart flying out to a children's music instructor, ey? The world does not cease to amaze *moi*!"

Darya had confided in Kavita and Yung-Ja over equations and samosas and *dolmeh*. Confided wasn't the word. She'd *shared*. Wasn't that the expression? So American, so Sam. They had asked her about her new class, and she had answered. Only unlike Parviz, who believed that her fascination with the class lay in mathematical precision and tennis balls on chair legs, Kavita and Yung-Ja had caught on that there was a certain someone whom she liked to sit next to and read her xeroxed handouts with. She'd insisted that it was nothing more than that, but Kavita and Yung-Ja had chuckled and giggled and snorted and wheezed. They were convinced that Darya was "besotted," as Kavita called it, with American Sam.

Well, they were wrong. It was nothing like that. She loved her husband. Sam was just different, that was all. A "laid-back" person who was always "mellow." Darya didn't know too many mellow people in the Persian community.

The bell rang. It was Yung-Ja, holding a Tupperware dish filled with kimbap, or "Korean sushi" as Yung-Ja described it. Over the years, math camp had turned into math camp with food. Which none of them minded because they all loved to show off the cuisine of their homelands and, more than that, they all loved to eat.

"It's the early onset of menopause that has me all aflutter," Kavita said. "My face is burning half the time, and sometimes I truly feel as though smoke is emanating from my ears. When Shenil smirks at me, I am tempted to take my hand and slap the side of his face for no reason whatsoever other than this rise of feminine hormones that plagues us all at this stage in the wild charade that we call life."

Darya sighed. Yung-Ja looked confused. Yung-Ja's English, even after years in the United States, was still not that strong, and half the time she could barely understand Kavita. Darya was used to Kavita's unique excessive verbiage, her British English sprinkled with French, her constant references to her husband as some kind of menace when he was actually a charming, sweet biology professor and hardly thoughtless. Kavita loved to joke about cheating on Shenil, although her only points of reference seemed to be Clark Gable, Gregory Peck, and Spencer Tracy. Kavita now focused on who American Sam looked like.

"Humphrey Bogart?" Kavita asked eagerly.

"Who's that?" Yung-Ja said.

"No, no. Not Bogart."

"Jack Lemmon?" Kavita quizzed.

"No. I saw a movie from the video store the other day—wait,

what was it called? *Crimes of the Heart.* He looks like the man in that movie. Sam Shepard, I think is his name," Darya said.

"Who's that?" Yung-Ja asked.

"Never mind," Darya said. "Let's just do math."

As Darya placed the samosas and kimbap on the table and got out the math workbooks, she wished that she had never told Kavita and Yung-Ja about Sam because they were making it out to be more than it was, when it was actually nothing. But part of her also enjoyed having friends to chat with about something so silly. She couldn't tell Parviz, of course, because he might think it was actually something, when it *wasn't,* and she couldn't tell Mina or her sons because, well, that just wouldn't be right. So, grateful for the company of Kavita and Yung-Ja, and for the equations they were about to tackle, and for the smell of spicy samosas and sweet kimbap, Darya sharpened her pencil and asked her friends to take a seat.

FOR A SOLID FORTY-FIVE MINUTES, they lost themselves in math. That was their rule. To stick to the project at hand for forty-five minutes, no veering, no break. They were allowed to talk, but only about the math problems. No one could go off topic. And they stuck to that rule strictly because all three of them loved rules, and all three of them had deep disrespect for people who broke them. That's what brought them together. Strong convictions about math and life. Love of numbers. A need to solve. They scribbled and thought and broke things down and built them back up. They showed their work and argued about how to arrive at the answer. Darya had even invested in a big white dry-erase board. She loved the squeak of the markers on the board, loved seeing how the solutions all made sense. When they were finished with their work for the day and reemerged into the real world around them, it was as though they had been swimming underwater and were now coming up for air.

And they were starving. The samosas had an excellent kick, the kimbap hit the spot, and Darya's handmade baklava was the perfect accompaniment to tea. When Darya hosted, math camp always ended with tea. She had even succeeded in stopping Kavita from putting milk in hers.

After math, they were allowed to talk about anything. Usually, they talked about their children and husbands. Occasionally, they discussed politics. Darya and Yung-Ja competed over who had suffered most in the twentieth century: Iranians or Koreans. Whenever Darya brought up dictatorship, military coup, torture, war, Yung-Ja said, "Ya. Korea had that." To which Kavita would say, "Yes, but do you two ladies have a country that has been artificially manipulated into two based on nothing more than the false gods of organized religion and the fallacies of fatuous farts in office who wish to portend great power and prestige?"

And then Yung-Ja would be silent because she didn't understand what Kavita had just said, and Darya would get up to open a window because when Kavita discussed "The Division," as she called the topic of India and Pakistan, she got overly animated and menopausey and before long would be dripping with sweat and asking Darya for a glass of water and a wet washcloth for her forehead.

Today's math camp ended with a short discussion about their respective children's inability to truly understand the gifts of America and how they were all so sheltered in New York because they knew neither war nor bombs nor true poverty. "These children of ours do not know the pain of prolonged prostration under the piddling paucities of pauper politicians turned princes," Kavita said.

That was another thing. Sometimes the combination of calculus and menopause made Kavita extra alliterative. Made her "mull over the messy and malleable morphings required to manage magnificent mathematical mountains from mere marginal molehills."

At the end of math camp they did the dishes together. After that, Yung-Ja, who was the best at calculus, reviewed the best way to answer some of the harder equations. Then Yung-Ja took her Tupperware dish, Kavita took her empty samosa plate, and Darya kissed her friends good-bye.

Whenever math camp was over, Darya felt a certain emptiness. She loved these afternoons with her friends. She loved being in her dining room with two women who, unlike most Americans (and this included Sam), knew a thing or two about war and dictatorship and "the pain of prolonged prostration."

CHAPTER SEVEN

ACTION, NOT REFLECTION

Y ou are in the right place at the right time. You are the best
and the brightest. Your future is filled with wealth and op-
portunity."

Mina bit into a slice of greasy pizza as she sat in the business
school auditorium listening to Dean Bailey's monthly "Question
and Answer Lunch Bunch!" which had been advertised all over the
B-school buildings.

Mina knew that Dean Bailey couldn't answer any of her questions. Like whether she should just quit business school and once
and for all focus on being an artist. But there was free pizza.

"You will go to Wall Street and create wealth. This economy
is going nowhere but up. Financial success is yours for the taking.
The first decade of the 2000s will be phenomenal. Unstoppable.
And *you* will be at the helm."

A drop of oil slid off the pizza slice onto Mina's white shirt. She watched as it soaked into the cotton fabric.

"You will go further than any previous generation. But remember: This school is a place for action. Not reflection. Reflection is for the MFA students."

Some students laughed.

But Mina reflected. She thought of all the pizzas she'd had at B&K's Pizza where her father had pounded dough when they first moved to America. She reflected on her lunch with Mr. Dashti. *It isn't worth it anymore.* That's what Darya had said finally. *You are worth more.* Mina wanted an end to her mother's graphs and charts, an end to the parade and charade of men over for tea. She certainly wanted that. But now what would happen?

As Dean Bailey droned on about the excellent promise of the stock market, Mina fingered her pink coral necklace. It had been a gift from her best friend, Bita, given in a rush on her last afternoon in Iran. Where was Bita now?

Just after Mina left Iran, Bita had written about how she and her family shelled peas in the bomb shelter, and about what a vermin Saddam was for bombing them. How she had to wear a mouth guard at night because during the bombing she ground down on her molars. In the last letter that Mina had received from Bita, she said how good she looked, indoors, of course, with her new bob hairdo. Outside, she had to cover her hair like everyone else.

After the first few years, the letters stopped.

"And remember when the recruitment officers are here, the worst thing you can do is renege on an offer. We do not renege. No reflection. No reneging," Dean Bailey said into the microphone.

With the hand that wasn't holding the pizza slice, Mina sketched strawberries and veiled women in the margins of her notebook.

LATER THAT DAY, PROFESSOR VAN HEUSEN, her finance professor, lectured from the podium, water bottle in hand. Mina never understood how he knew which student to call on. He rarely looked up at them, preferring instead to stare straight down at the floor as he lectured. She hoped he wouldn't call on her today. She was completely unprepared.

"Who can review for me the CAPM formula and equity versus debt?"

Chip Sinclair, the finance superstar and first-class jerk, raised his hand. Mina listened to Chip review the formula as she plugged her laptop's internet adapter card into one of the newly installed internet connection sockets. After a few minutes, she was connected to the web via dial-up and a website about oil paintings popped up as her homepage. She pulled out her legal pad and copied down Professor Van Heusen's formulas from the whiteboard.

What is r?   It is the cost of capital, the
                            sacrifice involved. It is the
                            WACC.

WACC   Weight of that company for its
                            cost of debt plus cost of equity.

WACC $alphaKD+(1-alpha)KE$

Discounted Cash Flow $PV=C1/(1+r1)^1+C2/(1+r2)^2$
                           $+C3/(1+r3)^3\ldots\ldots$

Darya would be breathless. She'd be up there in the front row, her hand high up in the air. "Oooh, oooh, pick on me, Professor, pick on me." She'd tell Professor Van Heusen the value for alpha KD. A hundred times over. Her financial calculator would click the fastest of all. The financial calculator was a specialized machine that Darya said made all normal calculators feel like toys.

"If I get in an interest squeeze, am I going to fall off a steep cliff into oblivion or is it a bump in the road? Meaning, is it a big drop or a little drop?" Professor Van Heusen talked into his water bottle.

Chip Sinclair bedazzled with a labyrinthine answer. Mina copied down more formulas from the whiteboard.

"Competitors: Are you dominant? Are they dominant?" Mina's laptop screen showed the artwork from a recent gallery show in Marblehead, Massachusetts. In a painting of a lone china teacup, white and blue mixed perfectly. Mina copied down the brand of oil paint the website recommended, even though she hadn't done a real painting herself since college, which now felt like a very long time ago.

"Are these supply sources relatively flexible? If you get into trouble, are they going to help you or liquidate you?"

Mina remembered the mixture of blue and white on the dome of the mosque near her grandparents' house in Tehran. She wondered what it would be like to go back there. She typed "Tehran" in her search tab. Photos of universities and buildings popped up, none of which she recognized. Which university had Bita gone to? Had she gone to university? Was she being set up with Mr. Dashti types over there? Maybe she was already married and had a few kids.

"Are your dealers loyal?" Professor Van Heusen asked. "Will they desert you?"

Mina clicked through photo after photo. She had not been back to Iran in fifteen years. She often thought of what would happen if she ever went back. Would she see what she had left behind? Would it still be there?

A girl in a camel cashmere cardigan a few rows down typed as if her life depended on it. A tall redheaded boy next to Mina wrote diligently in his notebook.

"The higher the coverage, the more sensitive you are to interest." Professor Van Heusen's marker squeaked as he wrote on the whiteboard. Some students nodded with understanding. They'd solved the problem. Mina had the germ of an idea: if she went back to Iran, she could figure out what her family had been, what they'd lost, what they'd gained. She could expel this sense of never belonging, feeling lost. She could "find herself," like every character in every book she'd ever read about immigrants going back to the homeland.

But more important, she could find Bita.

Mina was excited about her new plan.

"What is the point at which debt starts to interfere with operation?" Professor Van Heusen asked the floor. "Ms. Rezayi, could you tell us, please?"

Mina stiffened at the sound of her name. The students up front turned around and looked at her. Mina had no idea what the question meant. She fumbled through her backpack for her calculator. Where the hell was it? She turned to her laptop only to see her screensaver staring back at her. She looked at her notebook. It was filled with formulas she'd copied down, the name of that brand of paint the artist from Marblehead used and endless strawberries and women in veils.

Professor Van Heusen blew into his water bottle. It made a hollow, whistling sound.

Mina's face grew hot. Her underarms grew sweaty. Chip Sinclair's hand shot up. A few others did too.

"Ms. Rezayi?"

Perspiration slid down Mina's forehead. Why hadn't she been paying attention?

"We are waiting, Ms. Rezayi."

Mina had no answer. She pressed her keyboard. The screensaver disappeared only to be replaced by pictures of Tehran. It was pointless.

Professor Van Heusen tapped his foot. "Ms. Rezayi, I can't wait till the new millennium. Surely you were working hard to arrive at your answer?"

A small icon flashed at the bottom of Mina's screen.

"Check your mail," the redheaded boy next to her muttered.

Mina quickly clicked on her mailbox. She had half a dozen new messages, with more coming in. She opened one of the messages. There in front of her was the answer to Professor Van Heusen's question, along with a formula for how to arrive at the solution. She clicked on the next e-mail. The same. Her classmates were sending her the answer.

"Ms. Rezayi?" Professor Van Heusen's voice was loud.

The screen blurred in front of Mina.

"Do you have the solution?"

"Yes." Mina spoke up. "I do. I have the solution right here. And the method of arriving at the answer. It's all right here, in front of me."

The redheaded boy next to her breathed a sigh of relief.

"But I can't explain because I wasn't working on the case. I hadn't even read it."

Stunned silence. One did not admit to not reading Professor Van Heusen's case. One did not admit to not knowing in his class. One feigned knowledge or stayed up all night trying to attain it so that one's grades were high enough for a stellar investment bank or consulting firm to offer one a job. Starting salary: 100K minimum, plus signing bonus, plus perks. Mina knew all that. She knew Dean Bailey's lectures by heart. This was the school for the best and the brightest in finance. These were the good times. The year 2000 was just around the corner. Nothing could go wrong. Competition, Mastery, Success. Doubt was weakness. Action mattered.

"Well," Professor Van Heusen finally said.

"To tell you the truth, I don't really know what I'm doing here. I don't really belong here."

More students turned around to stare at Mina.

Professor Van Heusen looked up from his water bottle and squinted in Mina's direction. His face was surprisingly small when he actually lifted it up. The clock on the wood-paneled wall ticked loudly.

"Well, Ms. Rezayi," Professor Van Heusen said. "I don't know where you *belong*, but I understand that you have not been with us." He cleared his throat. "However, in business school, as in life, honesty is always the best policy. And that's a message for all of you. Let's walk through this problem again together. So everyone can arrive at the solution by actually knowing what it is they're doing. Shall we?"

Chip Sinclair groaned. A few emboldened students actually raised their hands and asked new questions. The girl in the cashmere sweater turned around and gave Mina a thumbs-up sign. The classroom went back to work. Fingers tapped on keyboards, pencils scribbled, calculators clicked.

Mina concentrated on the problem. She scribbled and struggled her way to the solution. And she suddenly felt better than she had in ages. Part of her had always been hovering in midair over the place that she had left. What if the country and history her parents loved was still buried there? What if she could find it? Could Mina go back and see what Darya meant when she said she wanted Mina to have "everything she had"? Mina had always wished that she could have known the Iran Darya had grown up in, instead of the Iran she herself had escaped from. Could she find it and piece it together if she went back there as an adult?

You will go to Wall Street, Dean Bailey had lectured. But first, she would go to Number 23 Takesh Street in Tehran, Iran. She would land firmly on that street and take in that other world again.

CHAPTER EIGHT

LIFE ON THE HYPHEN

The river reflected the streetlights, and all Mina could hear was the passing traffic on the Drive. As she jogged along Riverside Park, Mina saw Mr. Dashti's doughy hands holding his tea and his look of hesitation when their eyes met. Of course he was like all the other men: well educated, polite, careful. But there was something different this time. Maybe it was the palpable *relief* she saw on his face when they didn't click. The sense that he was equally lost in this messy matchmaking business. He didn't want it either. Poor Mr. Dashti was just as stuck as she was.

Mina's sneakered feet hit the tarmac. How would she tell her parents about her decision to return to Iran? They would be so worried about her safety. She hadn't been back in fifteen years. What if she was accused of being an American spy and detained? The political situation there was unpredictable. Anything could happen. But Mina had to go. She wanted to know what Agha Jan was doing every day without Mamani to cook him his meals, talk to him, sing for him Googoosh's songs and recite Rumi's verses. She needed to know where Bita was. What was she doing? Over the years, Mina had put that world out of her mind. Stuffed it away, just as she had shoved her oil paints into plastic storage boxes and slid them under her old bed in her parents' house. She hadn't had time for reflection as the dean put it. To reflect on the place where her mother had grown up *in her element*. Because Mina was busy building, busy striving, busy making.

After her run, she practiced the karate kicks that her brothers had taught her when they were children. After all these years, she still loved doing those kicks. She raised her leg, put it in chamber position and leaned back the way Kayvon had taught her. Then she kicked out. Imagine getting Bruce Lee in the knee, the groin, the "precious place" Kayvon had drilled into her. Don't be afraid. Kick! Mina kicked over and over again at her imaginary opponent, then jump-switched to work her other leg.

Back in her apartment, she showered and got ready for bed. But she couldn't sleep. Maybe she was crazy for wanting to go. What if she could never come back to her life here? She turned on the TV. A late-night talk show host swayed in his suit and made fun of the president. The audience laughed. Mina still felt a twinge of danger when Americans said negative things about their leaders. But you could get away with it here. And now she was going to go someplace where the rules were vastly different. She had to call her brother.

"How did your lunch with the latest greatest suitor go?" Kayvon asked.

"Ridiculous. Embarrassing. As always. I can't keep doing this, Kayvon," Mina said.

"Don't worry, kiddo. Mom will find a new hobby soon. This spreadsheet thing is getting absurd."

"I know." Mina sighed. It was a relief to talk to Kayvon. She had always been closer to him than to Hooman. Maybe it was because she was only three years younger than Kayvon and six years younger than Hooman. But it was also because of her brothers' different personalities. Kayvon was more easygoing, more relaxed. He could usually make Mina, or anyone for that matter, see the lighter side of things. Hooman was more serious. And now that they were all adults, Hooman's schedule as a doctor didn't leave him much time for small talk. Ever since he got married, he had even less time.

"She never did this with Hooman. Or you. Right? I mean, Hooman's married to an American. Your girlfriend's from Brooklyn. Why do I have to be matched with the perfect Persian? It is such a double standard."

"You're her favorite, that's why. She just wants to see you settled. Happy. She's obsessed."

"Isn't it enough that I'm in business school? You know, Kayvon, I've been thinking. I have this idea. I really want to . . ."

"Oh no, not this again," Kayvon said. "Mina, you know you can't be an artist. Don't sweat it so much. We all have childhood dreams and then we grow up. I wanted to be a professional soccer player, but I'm a contracts lawyer! That's life. We all make choices, but it's for the best, you'll see. Now get some sleep."

Before Mina could even tell Kayvon about her plan to go to Iran, he'd said good night and good-bye.

So much for her buddy brother. Mina sighed and reopened the photo album she'd taken out before her run, the only one they'd brought from Iran. Darya had cleverly hidden photos of herself behind pictures of the kids so that the customs inspectors wouldn't confiscate the photos with no hijab. Darya in her bikini was hidden behind Hooman in a high chair. Darya with long flowing hair, her arm linked with Baba's, was stuck behind a shot of Kayvon playing soccer. And photos of Darya at university, in her cotton blouse and billowing skirt, books hugged to her chest, were behind snapshots of Mina's early artwork.

The album helped link Mina to a past that felt almost glamorous. There was the mother she'd once known. Her hair black, not red. Her hazel eyes bright, hopeful. Darya looked happy, confident. Not tired and foreign. The Darya dressed in Jackie O jackets and pillbox hats was such a very different woman from the Darya of Queens. There she was standing by a fountain in Isfahan, her black hair blowing wild, a tiny Hooman and Kayvon by her side. There they all were on a London double-decker bus, waving. They didn't need visas back then. The world at that time didn't confuse them with terrorists. Mina pulled out an older photo: Darya in a hospital bed holding a scrunched-up newborn wrapped in a Mamani-knitted receiving blanket. It was their first moment on camera together. When Mina held the photo close, she noticed that Darya looked completely exhilarated and overwhelmed.

In America, the mother, father, brothers, and previous self that Mina had known before the revolution slowly melted away and evaporated. They became like characters she'd read about in a book, people who lived in a different land, long ago.

"You know we're going back," Baba would say some mornings

in those early years as he ironed his pizza apron. "As soon as this revolution thing dies down." Hooman would concentrate on his cereal and mumble, "That's what you said a year ago." Mina would think of her blue suitcase under her bed, ready to be filled with her clothes and paint set so she could return home to Bita and Agha Jan and Aunt Nikki and all the rest of her family and friends at any given moment.

When the TV host delivered his punch line, the studio roared with laughter and Mina was jolted back to the present. Young women in the audience clapped and flipped back their hair. Big men in baseball hats guffawed and hooted. What had she missed? What was so funny? What did those girls in the air-conditioned California studio do after the show? Go to a bar and sit on skinny stools and order drinks? Mina knew about the ancient Persian poets: Saadi, Rumi, and Hafez. She knew about bombs in Tehran in the 1980s. But she couldn't name more than one cocktail. She had never been comfortable inside bars. Darya and Baba found the bar culture unseemly. Wouldn't want her sitting on a skinny bar stool swinging her legs. Mina knew how to study and work very hard. She knew how to swing her legs on that hyphen that defined and denied who she was: Iranian-American. Neither the first word nor the second really belonged to her. Her place was on the hyphen, and on the hyphen she would stay, carrying memories of the one place from which she had come and the other place in which she must succeed. The hyphen was hers—a space small, potentially precarious. On the hyphen she would sit and on the hyphen she would stand and soon, like a seasoned acrobat, she would balance there perfectly, never falling, never choosing either side over the other, content with walking that thin line.

But to now jump off the hyphen and return to Iran required vaulting over a few hurdles. She had to get her paperwork straight and trust that despite some horror stories of Iranian exiles going back and being imprisoned, she'd be safe. More important, she had to convince her parents that their daughter's going to the Islamic Republic for winter break was an absolutely brilliant idea.

CHAPTER nine

COFFEE SHOP NOTHINGS

G rab a coffee?" Sam asked.

"I am sorry?" Darya replied, taken by surprise.

"Wanna get coffee? After class." Sam shrugged. "Now that we've . . . we've . . . taken our spreadsheet knowledge to another level."

He was trying to seem relaxed, Darya could tell. Mimicking their teacher to make her laugh. He liked it when she sighed in the middle of class, when she found Miranda Katilla a little too ridiculous. She could tell he enjoyed her reactions. It felt like they were teenagers. It felt like the beginning of something, when really, if one thought about it, what beginning was left for her? Except maybe the beginning of an ulcer or a tumor or gout.

"I know a coffee shop around the corner . . ." Sam continued.

"Please do not say it starts with 'S' and ends with 'bucks' because . . . that place is not my cup of tea," Darya blurted. She didn't mean to be rude but the Americanization of traditional Italian coffee into something so commercialized had always bothered her.

"Oh, this place does not start with 'S.' It's a small mom-and-pop coffee shop. They serve other hot beverages too, you know."

Parviz was expecting her. What would she tell him? Is this what it had come to? Going to coffee shops with Sams from basement classes?

"I must call my husband," she said. "To let him know I will be late."

"Sounds good," Sam said. Cool dude, guitar man, laid-back Sam. Nothing seemed to rile him.

The pay phone receiver on Queens Boulevard was cold, and Darya didn't have a quarter so Sam had to dig deep into his front jeans pocket for one. She watched his hand, then looked away. She blushed as she took the quarter. She dialed the number, then heard Parviz's loud "ALLO!"

"Parviz Joon, it's me. I will be a little late coming home tonight. I'm going out with, with some classmates," she said in Farsi. Sam waited outside the pay phone booth, rubbing his hands together in the cold.

"Isn't that wonderful, Darya Joon? You're making new friends. I told you you would. Go. But I will pick you up. It'll be too late to walk home."

"No, no, don't pick me up."

"I will not have my wife walking home late in the cold. I will pick you up. How much time will you and your friends need? Nine thirty? Is that good? I will pick you up at nine thirty. Where are you going? To Starbucks, probably, no? I will pick you up at nine thirty at Starbucks?"

"Yes," Darya said because Parviz was so protective, and she knew he'd worry if she said she'd walk home and because her head felt dizzy and she didn't know what else to say.

SAM ORDERED SOME COFFEE that had about six names using the Italian words that seemed required in this godforsaken place. He'd only said "cool" when Darya told him that her husband insisted that they go to Starbucks and that he'd pick her up at 9:30. He ordered Darya some tea, and she pretended not to be disgusted by the leaf-filled bag floating in lukewarm water. They sat by the window, and part of Darya felt as if she were in a movie. *It's just coffee. It's just tea. It's just time after class with a classmate. Parviz is picking me up soon.*

Sam asked her a lot of questions. About her children, about Iran, about how they left, and even about the Shah. He seemed to know a lot. He obviously read a lot. He said his favorite poet was Omar Khayyam and that he'd had Persian food many times. "So delicious, so real," he said.

"Yes, real," Darya said. That lumberjack shirt was growing on her. Part of her brain felt guilty for liking his shirt, another part was wondering when Parviz would show up (he tended to be early), another part wondered why she'd said she was with "friends" and not "a friend" to Parviz on the phone earlier, another wanted to know what Parviz would say when he noticed there were no "friends" other than Sam. A small part of her brain surprisingly thought the tea was hitting the spot.

Was this what fun was? Sitting in a chain coffee shop with this man, listening to him tell her that Persian food was real? Why hadn't she done this before? Why hadn't she had a million coffees with Sams? A spreadsheet came to mind. She couldn't hang out with the Sams of the world and be Parviz's wife. It didn't work that way. It just didn't add up.

When the door opened, a huge blast of wind swept through the room. Parviz stood there in his hand-knitted scarf and hat, both the color of turnips. Mamani had knitted them.

"Allo, hello!" Parviz almost shouted. Darya saw him scouring the tables near her and Sam, obviously looking for the rest of her friends.

Sam turned around and paused at the sight of the bundled-up figure in the doorway. Parviz looked as if he had stepped out of *A Christmas Carol*. Darya felt both embarrassed by and protective of him. Her Parviz, in the doorway, all lost.

Parviz strode over to them and extended his hand in Sam's direction.

"Parviz Rezayi," he almost shouted. Darya wondered if he'd make his handshake extra firm, the way his self-improvement tape advised.

"Sam," Sam said. After an awkward pause, he added, "Sam Collins."

Parviz looked at Sam, then at Darya, then at Sam again. "May I sit down?"

"Of course." Sam got up and brought a chair from a nearby table.

Darya could not form words. Here was Parviz. Here was Sam. Here was a teabag in lukewarm water. There was the scarf her mother had knitted for the son-in-law she adored. He hardly ever wore that scarf. Why was he wearing it tonight?

"I am early, I know," Parviz said. He looked at Darya. "I just thought I'd give your other friends a ride too if they needed one."

She looked at her husband of over thirty years and felt ashamed. "It's just me and Sam tonight," she said finally.

"I can see that." Parviz forced a smile.

It was only coffee. It was only tea. It was nothing, really.

But it was, in that smelly, busy place, a moment when Darya felt chopped off from Parviz's love for just long enough to make her wish she could turn back the clock and not come here at all.

Persian politeness dictated the rest of the interaction. Parviz could not, would not, be small about this. He even went to the queue and ordered himself a whipped cream–laden cup of calories masquerading as "coffee." Darya could no longer bear to swallow her tea. Sam, though initially caught off guard, soon regained his relaxed cool dudeness. How could someone not like Parviz? It was what made his patients adore him. It was what made even the postal workers smile at him. Parviz was a genuinely kind person who did not think ill of others and who treated all people with respect. His behavior toward Sam was no different. He asked Sam questions, a lot of questions. First about the spreadsheet class. Then about his work. Then about his instrument.

It was as though Sam were one of the men that Darya had graphed for Mina. Darya realized that Parviz was so accustomed to talking with potential suitors that he was perfectly comfortable making conversation with strange men. Only this wasn't a potential suitor for Mina, and they both knew that. This was different. An air of awkwardness cloaked their table, their chairs, the way the knitted scarf cloaked Parviz's neck. They could chat and laugh and drink together and pretend it was all perfectly normal.

But it wasn't.

ON THE DRIVE HOME, PARVIZ was uncharacteristically quiet. He wasn't positive. He wasn't excited or zealous or passionate. He didn't spout his self-help guru psychobabble phrases like "the universe is unfolding as it should."

He just said, "I'm tired, Darya," when they returned home and brushed his teeth and went to bed. There was no honeyed milk, no long lectures, no reprimands, no questions.

Quiet Parviz, Darya realized, was worse than all the other self-help, positive, overbearingly silly Parvizes she'd ever known.

Quiet Parviz took her by surprise.

CHAPTER TEN

NO, NA, NON, NEIN, NYET

n o. *Na. Non. Nein. Nyet.* How many ways would you like me to tell you?"

Baba rubbed one hand on his bald head, a glass of tea in the other. Mina sat in her parents' living room. Baba paced and took deep breaths. Mina knew he was using "Stay Calm!" techniques from his latest self-help tape. He smiled extra widely at Mina as he handed Darya an *estekan* of tea. Darya sat perfectly still in the big armchair, her legs crossed.

"See now, Mina Joon." Baba spoke as if he were talking to a mental patient who could attack him at any moment. "See now, *joonam.* What you're suggesting is ludicrous. First of all, you're in school. Second, the political situation there is unpredictable at best. Third, I think you're just really tired. So let's just focus on the present." He stopped pacing. "You OWN today!" he said, but his voice shook. "The past is not your dictator!"

"It's for a visit, Baba. People go back all the time now. I just need to see it again. To be there . . ."

Baba laughed a high, nervous laugh. "Mina Joon, is it the stress of your graduate program? Are you worried about finals? Look, your mother—" He pointed to Darya who sat sipping tea serenely. "Your mother will talk some sense into you."

Why wasn't Darya more alarmed at Mina's announcement that she wanted to go back to Iran? Why was her mother so calm all of a sudden?

"Stay focused. On the task at hand. No crazy trip ideas." Baba took in a deep breath.

All day, Mina had rehearsed the conversation with her parents in her head, anticipating all the derailments. But even as she'd played out their inevitable discouragement, she'd still felt strangely energized. As if she had just finished skiing in the Damavand mountains. Or had chased Hooman and Kayvon screaming and giggling through their old garden. Or had smelled again the lemon trees at Mamani and Agha Jan's house. Just the *idea* of physically being back there again was exhilarating. She couldn't let Darya and Baba talk her out of it.

"Go ahead, Darya Joon, tell her," Baba said, nodding.

"Tell her what?" Darya asked.

"What do you mean?" Baba stopped pacing and studied his wife carefully. "Darya, what has gotten into you lately? Your daughter wants to visit the Islamic Republic of Iran. Hello? *Tell her*, Darya, why this is a ludicrous plan!"

Darya sipped her tea and sighed.

"Say something, Darya Joon!" Baba gave Darya a desperate look.

"What would you like me to say?"

Mina hadn't seen her mother sit up so straight in a long time.

"Excuse me?" Baba stopped. He looked up at the ceiling and held up a finger as if telling an invisible Almighty to just be patient and wait a minute while his wife caught on to the gravity of the situation. He turned to Darya. "I honestly don't know what is happening with you, Darya. MY LOVE, your daughter wants to take a hiatus from business school to visit Iran. Let's take a moment to see what's wrong with this picture . . ."

"Not a hiatus," Mina said carefully. "I wouldn't miss any classes. We have our two-week winter break coming up anyway. I've timed it all to go then."

"You have, haven't you?" Darya swiveled her perfect-postured head in Mina's direction.

Mina gulped and nodded.

"Oh, well then, I suppose it all makes perfect sense! Silly me!" Baba slapped his head. He took in more deep breaths, then put on the voice he used with patients when he delivered bad news. "Mina, you have not been back in fifteen years. You have an American passport. There are risks involved with returning after all this time. Risks that we cannot predict . . ."

"I still have my Iranian passport . . ." Mina reminded him.

Baba dropped the doctor voice and looked up at his invisible friend in the ceiling again. "She has it all planned out!" He laughed nervously at the ceiling.

"She does, doesn't she?" Darya said. But, unlike Baba, she seemed to be impressed, not annoyed.

"Tell her that this is all a fantasy!" Baba cried.

"And what, may I ask," Darya said, looking tired now, "is wrong with a little fantasy?"

"I beg your pardon, Darya?" Baba almost whispered.

"Seems to me like a truly wonderful plan."

Baba looked at Darya as though she were a dragon who had materialized out of thin air and appeared in his living room. "WHAT?"

"It would be during the semester break. She wouldn't miss any school. She would just be going back home." Darya listed off the positives on her fingers as casually as if she were reciting vegetables for a grocery list.

Mina stared from one parent to another. Now, like Baba, she too was in shock.

Baba stood frozen in the middle of the room, a half-crazy smile on his face.

"Perhaps it's not so strange an idea," Darya confirmed, pausing to pat her skirt. Then she looked straight at Mina. "But on one condition only. That if you go on this trip, you promise that when you come back you will simply buckle down and focus entirely on business school. Drop the whole 'I'm torn because I want to be an artist' routine once and for all. Agreed?"

Mina was so much in shock that she just nodded and said, "Sure."

"What? We can't set *conditions*, Darya. The whole idea is ludicrous!" Baba said. "Though it would be good, Mina Joon, if we could just get you to actually focus on your business studies. Without the monster of doubt tormenting you. Doubt kills achievement. It is the elixir that feeds that other monster negativity . . ."

"Good, then! It's all settled!" Darya interrupted. She looked out the window. "It has been such a very long time," she said softly. "And the answer is yes, Mina Joon. The answer is yes."

"Oh. I wasn't asking for permission . . . exactly," Mina said. "I was just letting you know . . ."

"No, I mean the answer is yes, of course I'll come with you," Darya said as if explaining the obvious.

Baba sank into a chair, holding his hand to his heart, air blowing out of his cheeks.

Mina sat there, speechless.

"You're welcome!" Darya smiled and held up her tea.

CHAPTER ELEVEN

DARYA'S DREAMS

Ever since they were born, all she'd ever wanted was to do right by them. To be done, in a way. Not that she hadn't enjoyed raising them. She had. She'd buried her face into their infant bellies, held them up and delighted in their perfection, laced her fingers through theirs while walking them to school. She had never known, nor could she have guessed beforehand, that her children would consume her so. Once each kidney bean–sized embryo formed inside her, her world was reconstructed. Once they were born, she had spent sleepless nights holding them close, rocking and singing while they cried their hearts out. Those nights had spooled into years.

Every toothache, every cough, every ear infection they had, had been hers too. She did not know she could stand so much love.

In those early days, she'd tripped over their scattered toys on the living room floor, not realizing that she'd soon be tripping over their unannounced friends, their political choices, their careers and mates.

When Hooman sank a basketball into the net, her own body extended. When Kayvon threw up at the new restaurant on Queens Boulevard, her own insides flip-flopped. And with every step Mina took, every head she turned, every drawing she drew, Darya held her breath, enchanted.

It was for them that Darya had come to America. It was for them that she had stayed. But not one day had gone by when she hadn't thought about the place she'd left.

But these children were no longer just hers. They were grown now. Hard as it was to believe. She needed to let them live their own lives.

It was her and Parviz now, more or less.

And ever since Parviz had shown up in his wool hat and scarf and had sat in that chair at the coffee shop with her and Sam, and ever since that quiet ride home, it was as if something tiny had broken between her and Parviz. She hadn't done anything wrong. Parviz, she knew, knew that.

That moment in that coffee shop, sitting there between Sam and Parviz, the air had been so charged. She couldn't place it. In the next spreadsheet class after the coffee shop incident, she'd still sat next to Sam. They'd still stood outside together during the breaks. Talking was allowed, wasn't it?

Darya's confusion was what made going back to Iran all the more enticing. To get away and to go back. Even though it had been so hard to come over here in the first place.

Those first few weeks in America, Darya had kept turning

around, expecting to see the extended family she loved right behind her. But no one was there. Every time she saw a woman her own age with someone who seemed to be her mother, Darya felt empty. Those grown women with their mothers by their sides—how jealous she was of them. She had been one of those women once. She'd had a mother. She'd had just about everything.

What is done cannot be undone.

In those early years, Darya waited in their house in Queens for relatives who never came. She even made tea. Brewed the leaves and placed a cozy on the pot. Tea glasses clean and ready. But no one came.

She'd give anything to throw the dinner parties she used to complain about. Her young, naïve self had dared to say, "We never have any time to ourselves as a family." What a fool she'd been. They'd floated as a family of five, alone, for so many years. And now here they were, down to two. Just she and Parviz.

Americans went about their business as if life were short and all their energy and efforts had to be spent today. Rushing around with gargantuan shopping carts and rushing off to appointments and errands and whatever was next on their schedules. They saw shrinks and doctors constantly, bought do-it-yourself home-repair kits, and believed self-esteem could solve problems. They acted as if every action they took were just for the sake of taking action. They acted as if everything were a race. As though the faster you moved, the more it mattered. As though by simply repeating something, you could make it true. And how was it that Parviz, her husband, a *doctor*, for God's sake, had bought right into it? Hook, line, and sinker. Parviz repeated mantras and took bloody action all the time.

But that's not how it worked. That's not how it added up. Not for one minute.

This much Darya knew: Life was cruel. Beauty passed. Children grew. Countries transformed overnight. Fundamentalists tortured the young. Mothers died from bombs. Why act as if a single bit of it were okay?

That's why she loved Kavita and Yung-Ja. Because they didn't buy into the hype. That's why there was something so intriguing about Sam. Because, though American, he seemed to have looked behind the façade and figured it out. He wasn't like the others. He didn't rush around in useless activity but was willing to sit quietly and listen. He seemed calm and at peace.

Part of Darya had always felt ashamed of her homesickness for Iran. How could she be homesick for a place filled with cruel laws and bottomless sadness? Because it was filled with so much more than that. Because her father was still there. Because her sister was too. Because the lemon trees and pomegranates were still there. Because the poetry was still there. Because her ancestors had cultivated a life and a legacy there. Because that place was home. Her home. Maybe not Mina's. Maybe not even Parviz's anymore. But hers.

So as Mina sat there and insisted she needed to go back to visit, Darya had to bite her tongue at first. Because how could she tell her daughter that she too had wanted nothing more than to go back all these years. How could she break Parviz's heart, Parviz, who so loved where he was, and let him know that she could not *wait* to go back? And how on earth could she let Mina go alone?

Go back, go back, go back.

Home.

It made sense. It added up.

CHAPTER TWELVE

HOVERING OVER AZADI SQUARE

Mina constantly checked that her scarves were safely tucked into her carry-on. She'd brought several in case one got lost or misplaced. Darya pushed up against her as they stood at the departure gate: bags crammed with gifts, headscarves, and raincoats. Darya held in her hand the same leather cosmetic case that she'd held when they left Iran. They had picked out their *soghati* souvenir gifts carefully. "I love NY" T-shirts and wallets for the nieces and nephews. Snow globes and gloves with different-colored fingers. Statue of Liberty figurines and American face creams. They made their way through security, waving to Baba and Hooman and Kayvon. Kayvon cheerfully blew them a kiss, but Hooman looked worried sick. Baba puffed out his chest and bravely made a thumbs-up sign. He was going to let the universe unfold as it should, he'd finally said. But even from a distance Mina could see he was sweating.

IN AMSTERDAM, THEY HURRIED ACROSS the airport to catch their connecting flight. Groups of women in headscarves and raincoats ate hot dogs and drank beer by the boarding gate for the Tehran flight.

"Getting in their pork and alcohol while they still can," said a plump old woman sitting by the gate. She smiled at Mina. "You may want to get out your headscarf. Once you board that plane, you're considered to be on Iranian soil."

Mina took out her raincoat and put it on. It was the closest thing she had to an official Islamic *roopoosh*. She got out her headscarf and tied it tight, wondering how many other first-timers would be on the plane. Exiles like her who hadn't gone back since the early days of the war.

After Darya put on her own headscarf and raincoat, they stood in line to board. Inside the plane, muffled voices mingled with classical music wafting from speakers. Female flight attendants in headscarves smiled politely.

"Well, look who I get to sit next to!" The old woman from the boarding gate waddled up to Mina and Darya's row. "Let the young one"—she pointed to Mina—"sit by the window. You"—she patted Darya—"sit in the middle. I must sit on the aisle. Swollen feet. Oh, but my bag is heavy. I am Badri Khanom, by the way." Mina helped put her Mary Poppins–looking carpetbag in the overhead compartment.

"Look at you all, so young and pretty!" Badri Khanom whooped out as a flight attendant passed by. "Remember when it was a job requirement for them all to be so young and pretty, even on the foreign airlines?" she bellowed as if taking a poll from the rest of the passengers.

"I remember, Khanom!" an older man's voice called out.

A few people laughed.

One of the young and pretty flight attendants flashed a smile. "Sweet?" She held out a basket filled with candy. Mina leaned over and chose a bonbon with a picture of a tiny lemon on its wrapper.

A squat male flight attendant in a crisp uniform strode down the aisle, standing on his toes to bang the overhead bins shut. Golden tassels dangled from his shoulders.

Badri Khanom covered her ears with each bang. "He thinks he's a general!" she said, looking straight at him. "Look at him. Thinks he's a general!"

"If he's a general, he's Napoleon!" a man shouted from somewhere behind.

"Yes, my uncle Napoleon!" someone else called out.

Mina caught Darya smiling.

"What?" she'd asked.

Darya shook her head. "Nothing," she said. "It's just . . . I missed this."

"You missed complete strangers lobbing insults at one another?" Mina asked.

"I missed this . . ." Darya paused. "Banter. No, that's not the word. It's the communal conversation. That's what I missed." Darya pulled out a magazine from the seat pocket in front of her and flipped through it. In a few minutes, she was giggling.

"What's so funny?" Mina asked.

Darya showed her the cartoon she was reading and pointed to

the thought bubble. "See? The politician's the donkey! Get it?" She chuckled into her hand.

Mina studied the cartoon in the Iranian magazine. She didn't get it.

Badri Khanom took the magazine from Darya and looked at the cartoon. She let out a big guffaw.

"He's the donkey! *Vay*, my God!" She laughed even harder when Darya showed her the caption under it and pretty soon she was dabbing at her eyes with the ends of her headscarf. Mina saw her mother touch Badri Khanom's hand. Badri Khanom was about Mamani's age. Or rather, the age she would've been now, Mina thought.

As Darya and Badri Khanom flipped through the pages, Mina caught glimpses of the ads. For detergent. Popcorn. Chewing gum. One for toothpaste featured kids in knit sweaters, smiling with superwhite teeth.

"So many ads!" Mina said quietly.

"What did you think? That we wouldn't have ads in our magazines? We are a capitalistic country despite it all, don't you know!" Badri Khanom responded.

"No, I just meant . . ."

Darya quickly changed the subject and began to name all of the places she wanted to visit on their trip. Each location elicited sharp, judgmental responses from Badri Khanom.

Mina looked out the window. What would it be like to be back there without Mamani? The government couldn't have changed everything. The smell of morning had to be the same. They couldn't remove all the roses and jasmine. Could they?

BADRI KHANOM SNORED LOUDLY for the last two hours of the flight. When the plane was about to land, Mina peered back out the window. In the midst of the brightly lit city below, she saw the curved winglike ivory pillars of the Shahyad, now known as the Azadi, monument. Suddenly, the memories washed over her: dancing with Bita around her room as they listened to music. The feel of the red vinyl seats and metal frames of Mamani's kitchen chairs, the clang of the pots and pans as Mamani worked her way from stove to sink, the smell of sautéed onions simmering in turmeric and salt and pepper. The beat of music from the stereo in the living room, the guests pouring into the house on the night of her tenth birthday party. The greengrocer's wife had a chador that was white with a pattern of small green and yellow flowers; their gardening water can was a shiny copper color; and the sky after the nightly good-night kiss from Darya melted from pomegranate red to a deep charcoal. Against the backdrop of those white pillars they had had their childhood. Thousands had then bled and died on the street, and the colors of their clothes had been struck to black and gray in one swift move.

The plane zoomed down and seemed to hover for a moment above Azadi Square. Mina's stomach did a somersault.

"In this place we once lived," Darya whispered as she leaned over Mina's shoulder and they both looked at the glimmering city below.

PART II

1978

CHAPTER THIRTEEN

DRAWINGS AND
DEMONSTRATIONS

His hair curls the other way, silly," Bita said. She leaned close to Mina. "Wow. That is really good."

Mina moved her pencil across the page. Recess was always more fun when she sketched in her notebook.

"*Afarin!* Bravo!" Bita's smile was huge. "Hey, *bacheha!*" she called out. "Look how she can *draw!*"

A few kids jogged over to where Mina sat and hovered around her. Farokh, a boy with thick eyebrows and broad shoulders, slapped her on the back. Mina lurched forward.

"I told you!" Bita said proudly.

"What's going on here?" Mrs. Shoghi strode over to them.

Bita held up Mina's drawing.

Mrs. Shoghi's eyes narrowed. "Hmmm. *Bah bah! Che gha-shang!* How beautiful! You've drawn our own crown prince. Mina,

I didn't know you had it in you. Such a good drawing for someone who's not even eight yet!"

Bita put her arm around Mina. "She's an *artist!*"

Mrs. Shoghi clapped, lacquered nails shining in the sunlight. "Get in line, children, get in line. Recess is over!" As she gathered the children together, her hand touched Mina's shoulder and stayed there for a minute.

"*Ba honar hasti,* my girl. You are 'With-Art.'"

Inside their second grade classroom, the Shah's picture hung on the wall and looked down at them as they worked in their notebooks, passed secret notes, and struggled to memorize sums, ancient Persian poems, and the importance of their country's greatest natural resource: oil. The Shah was crisp and stern in his white military uniform with rows of colorful ribbons on his shoulders. The tiny ribbons reminded Mina of Chiclet gum. She wanted to reach up and grab one and taste it. But they were inaccessible, shining under the glass, teasing her.

"I'M GOING TO MARRY HIM," Mina whispered to Bita as they dipped their brushes into the ink during calligraphy class. She'd drawn the crown prince almost every day for the past week and shown the sketches to Bita. Maybe she shouldn't have drawn him so much. He was royalty, after all. She didn't want to malign him.

Bita scowled. "*I'm* going to marry him!"

They glared at each other. A test of wills. Bita bit her lip, determined.

Without a word, Mina thrust her calligraphy brush into fresh ink and drew a dripping outline of herself next to her outline of the prince. "There!" she said. "See? That's *me!*"

Bita's standoff evaporated when she saw the ink on the page. The dark-haired girl with a wide jaw and a cocky expression created with a few deft strokes conjured Mina perfectly. Bita gave Mina one last glare, but the stoop of her shoulders conceded defeat.

They picked up their brushes again and wrote the words for the assigned verse from Saadi's poem. For a second, Mina held her brush in midair and looked at it as though she were seeing it for the first time. Those thin bristles dipped in ink had made Bita give in. They'd made Mrs. Shoghi tell her she was "With-Art." She looked at her ink-stained finger pads as though they belonged to someone else.

"NOT BAD," HOOMAN SAID THAT NIGHT after looking at Mina's drawing. "I mean for an almost-eight-year-old!"

"It's great, Mina." Kayvon grinned. "You should see how Hooman draws! Seriously, Mina, maybe one day you could be a great artist. Maybe one day we'll see your work hung up in galleries." He put his arm around Mina and squeezed her. "My little sis: world-famous painter!"

When Baba saw one of the drawings, he pretended to stagger backward in absolute awe. "*Bah bah!* Wonderful!"

Mina could only shake her head at Baba's reaction. He did the same thing whenever Kayvon imitated the greengrocer's nasal voice or when Hooman showed him pages from his science homework. He showed the same exaggerated appreciation when Darya brought out her platter of *tahdeeg* to the dinner table or when she dressed up for a party. Baba seemed perpetually delighted by all the unexpected gifts of his own family.

Darya was less effusive. She gently picked up Mina's paper between her thumb and forefinger and held the page up to the chandelier as if she were studying film negatives.

"I see," she said.

Then she marched to her bedroom and came back with a plain folder. With one of Mina's markers she carefully wrote "Mina— Almost-Eight" on the folder tab and placed the evening's artwork inside.

After a few weeks, the folder was stuffed and Darya prepared a new one. She stacked all the folders neatly in a drawer in her and Baba's bedroom.

Mina liked knowing the folders were there, safe and organized. At least her mother didn't use her artwork as scratch paper, scribbling "milk, eggplants, cucumbers" on the back and crumpling it into her handbag as she ran in her slippers across the street to the greengrocer's the way Bita's mother did.

"WHO'S THIS IN ALL THE DRAWINGS?" Darya asked after breakfast one day.

"The crown prince. I'm going to marry him," Mina said.

Hooman and Kayvon had already left for school. Baba was at his clinic, and Soghra, the housekeeper, was busy sweeping the sidewalk with her wet broom.

"When you grow up, you should marry whomever you fall in love with. That's what's important. And you can't plan it. It just happens," Darya said and sipped her sweetened black tea.

Mina nodded. Her mother's hazel eyes reminded her of the light green shade in her new paint set.

"Now hurry up so you're not late for school." Darya got up.

Soghra came in then, broom in hand. "Khanom, missus, this shooting pain in my back will one day cause my death. My hands are all twisted up. The city dust is not appropriate for my lungs. *Vay*, my breath is all caught up. O Great Big God—the fate you've given me. If my great-grandparents had not lost all their wealth, I wouldn't be reduced to servantry. Fate, you fiend! The foe that prevents me from being a proper lady!"

"Pour yourself some tea, Soghra Joon, and rest your legs," Darya said calmly. They were all used to Soghra's drama. "Mina, up you get! After school today, we're off to Book City."

Mina hugged Soghra good-bye. Soghra seemed perfectly fine now that she was seated and sucking on a sugar cube.

Mina grabbed her backpack and followed Darya out the door. Book City! They had the best books, the best stationery, and the best selection of colored pencils, markers, and paints. Mina couldn't wait to go and look at the big sets of colored pencils from Switzerland, the tubes of tempting oil paints stacked in rows, all the colors dizzying and delicious in that shop.

THAT DAY TURNED OUT TO BE Mina's last trip to Book City. A fortnight later, they couldn't go downtown anymore.

"Please?" Mina pleaded with Darya on a rainy Friday. She held her Snoopy handbag in one hand and the keys to the car in another.

"No."

"But why?"

"Because there are demonstrations going on, Mina. It's not safe."

Just then Hooman and Kayvon marched through the living room, their fists in the air. "Death to the Shah!" they yelled. "No more king!"

Mina's stomach started to feel strange.

"Boys, did you finish your homework? Stop this nonsense and focus," Baba said.

"We will not talk about kings or politics in this home," Darya said.

Her brothers stopped reluctantly. Baba collapsed into a chair, looking exhausted. Darya looked out the window, her eyes glassy and distant.

FOR MONTHS THE DEMONSTRATIONS in the streets continued. Baba would come home bewildered and mention that a cinema or a bank had been set on fire. Darya would receive the news in silence. Hooman and Kayvon sometimes cheered. They were slowly becoming prisoners in their own home, unable to venture too far outside.

It was Darya who said the word first. She said it at dinner, right after she passed a bowl of sautéed eggplants and smashed tomatoes to Mina. "There is a *revolution* going on. *Enghelab*." Mina hadn't heard that word before. *Enghelab*. It sounded so powerful. Hooman had to explain to her what it meant: a rotation that could turn the world upside down. This "revolution" was going on outside the walls of their house and yet, to Mina's disappointment, her parents were doing nothing to stop it. In fact, sometimes she even thought they liked it. Baba listened to the BBC on his radio constantly. Darya called her sister and asked where the demonstrations were taking place and how many people had shown up. Darya seemed torn, as if she didn't know whether the demonstrations would result in something wonderful or something horrendous.

Later that night, Mina scolded Hooman and Kayvon for yelling bad things about the Shah. She hated that they liked to imitate the demonstrators. Hooman and Kayvon ignored her and continued to repeat slogans as if they were in a pretend parade in the living room. Mina started to hit them and soon the three of them were on the floor wrestling. Baba and Darya stood there motionless watching the three kids fighting on the floor.

"Enough!" Baba yelled.

"They're saying bad things about the Shah," Mina said in a small voice.

"Look at that!" Hooman got up slowly. "Look how they've brainwashed her!"

Kayvon wiped his nose. A trail of blood trickled from his nostril, over his lips, and down his chin.

"Into the bathroom, now!" Baba said. "Both of you, *now!*"

From the living room, Mina heard the bathroom faucet turn on and could make out some of Baba's furious lecture. She heard him say "brothers," "fighting," "absurd," and "gentlemen." She heard Hooman mumbling. She could imagine Baba washing the blood from Kayvon's nose with Darya's yellow washcloth.

Darya turned to Mina. "There's absolutely no need . . ." She trailed off. "For you to worry. About this . . . stuff."

"Bita says the youth are going to kick the Shah out. Kick him out of the country and bring in a new leader for the people." Mina wasn't sure what a new leader meant, but she assumed it meant an evil king.

"Never mind, Mina," Darya said. "This king is far from perfect. He's done some horrible things."

Mina froze. Her own mother was like one of those demonstrators in the street. If the authorities heard her, they would accuse her of being a criminal woman. Mina's hands felt clammy as she remembered all the things that happened to people who spoke against the king. Torture. Execution. They had been taught in school about all he had done for the country—brought them wealth, created reform, made them modern and Western. The textbooks were filled with his accomplishments. One did not speak against him. But Darya had.

Baba returned with a glum-looking Hooman and Kayvon behind him.

"She said very, very bad things about the Shah," Mina whispered. She needed Baba to set her mother straight.

"She's right." Baba shrugged.

And Mina was left feeling suddenly alone.

CHAPTER FOURTEEN

PUMPKIN STEW

It wasn't easy leaving. They waited longer than most. Some families left when the Shah's tanks entered central Tehran. But Mina's parents said the upheaval might turn out to be a good thing. It could bring democracy. Freedom. Mina detected in her parents an actual desire for the monarchy to end, which she found blasphemous. Mina loved to watch the parades on TV celebrating the Shah and his wife, Farah. The king and queen looked absolutely fabulous—dressed in burgundy velvet cloaks draped over intricately embroidered silver coats, golden crowns encrusted with diamonds and rubies balanced on their heads. Their jewels sparkled. At the sound of trumpets, hundreds of men saluted. The music was majestic. Mina would leap up off the Persian rug to salute the Shah along with the masses. She couldn't help it.

Hooman bought posters of the new revolutionary leaders.

He listened to their speeches and tried to grow a beard. He put away his fancy polo shirts and wore simple peasant-style cotton shirts and baggy pants. Girls whom Mina used to see walking home from the university in their platform shoes and miniskirts, their long hair swaying seductively down their backs, began to don headscarves and stopped wearing makeup. Everywhere she looked, Islam was in, and anything that reminded people of the Shah or his Western ways was considered old, outdated, and plain uncool.

One day the Shah left and the world changed. The revolution's new religious leaders took over. People spray-painted the words "FREEDOM," "REVOLUTION," "ISLAMIC REPUBLIC" on street walls. People whom Mina had never seen observing the Muslim faith before started to become religious. Aunt Nikki's daughter, Maryam, emptied out her drawer of makeup and lipstick and filled it instead with prayer beads and prayer stones. Maryam threw out her skimpy dresses and tight tops and went to the bazaar and bought simple headscarves and Islamic uniforms.

It was hard to keep up with who was on which side. Revolutionary or anti-revolutionary? When Mina and her family went to people's homes, sometimes wine was served and other times sermons were given on the evils of alcohol. Sometimes one spouse served wine while the other angrily denounced it as it was being poured. Families were divided.

Every afternoon Baba used a stepladder to remove the pictures of the new leader that Hooman had put up in the house. With increasing fervor, Hooman climbed on top of bookshelves and furniture to tack the pictures back up.

"We have gotten rid of the dictator," Hooman said in his changing voice. "We have freed the country of his contamination."

IN THE KITCHEN, AUNT NIKKI WHISPERED to Darya while Mina eavesdropped.

"My kids are slipping away from me," Aunt Nikki said. "My kids tell me I'm wrong, old-fashioned, too Westernized. Sometimes it feels like my children aren't even mine anymore. It's become like they're *theirs*. Children of *their* propaganda."

Darya leaned against the kitchen counter, thinking. Then her face lit up. "Invite them over. They can't resist my pumpkin stew. I'll talk to Maryam. Parviz will talk to Reza. We'll talk some sense into their fanatic teenage skulls."

Aunt Nikki frowned at first, but then she thanked her younger sister. A time for the dinner was set. For the first time in weeks, Mina saw Aunt Nikki relax again. Darya said no need to thank her, they'd do their best.

Mina pretended Aunt Nikki was right to be so hopeful. Never mind that Darya hadn't been able to talk sense into Hooman's skull.

MINA AND KAYVON RAN TO OPEN the door to find Uncle Hamed standing there, hat in hand, his face weary. Aunt Nikki was still by the car, talking to the closed windows in a coaxing voice. After several minutes, Cousin Reza came out of the car. He looked taller than when Mina had seen him last. Though he was only sixteen, a little stubble had grown on his chin.

"Come, let me see you!" Darya rushed to give her nephew a kiss. But he shrank away from her.

A woman in a black chador followed Reza into the house.

"Say hello, Maryam," Aunt Nikki said.

Mina and Kayvon nudged each other. This was their glamorous eighteen-year-old cousin who only a few months ago had been giggling and flirting with the greengrocer's son? This was the Maryam who had worn high heels and tight blue jeans, her eyelids green from sparkly eye shadow? Mina stared at the new cousin in front of her.

"Tea?" Darya almost shouted, as though Maryam were hard of hearing because of her cover-up.

Mina and Kayvon scrambled to go help in the kitchen. When Mina came back balancing a tray of hourglass-shaped *estekan* filled with dark chai, she saw that Darya had plopped herself next to Maryam and was talking and laughing and gesturing wildly. Maryam was nodding politely, the way one nods at an older person who is losing her mind.

Baba methodically asked Reza about his studies. "I remember," Baba said, "when you were four years old and you'd beg me to put you up on my shoulders. Remember that? Remember we'd play hide-and-seek outside?"

Reza scowled.

At dinner, Maryam ate with one hand, grasping her chador tightly with the other.

"Maryam Joon, I told you already, while I respect that you are now a devout follower, we're all family here, you really don't need to cover your hair from family. You know that, don't you?" Darya's façade of good cheer was disappearing.

Aunt Nikki looked as if she might cry. Maryam loosened her chador a tiny bit. Reza growled about the deaths caused in prisons by the Shah. Hooman listened raptly to Reza's words. Darya's vein throbbed in her forehead. Baba kept asking Uncle Hamed if he wanted more wine, but in a half-whisper, when Reza wasn't looking.

When it was time to kiss the guests good-bye, Maryam hugged them all, but Reza didn't want to be touched. "But we're *family*," Darya insisted. Reza angrily said good-bye and then marched off to the car.

From behind the living room curtains, Mina saw Maryam walk to the car door and lift the bottom of her chador ever so slightly before climbing in, like Cinderella with her ball gown. Uncle Hamed and Aunt Nikki waved from the front seat with apologetic smiles. They drove off with Maryam and Reza expressionless in the backseat.

Mina and her family stood in the doorway, waving as the car drove away.

"That was . . ." Baba sighed. "A pumpkin stew I won't forget."

Hooman continued to look at the street, spellbound. "Reza said that if we are relentless in our demands, we can get revenge on . . ."

Suddenly Darya took Hooman's face in both her hands. "Listen. *Khoob goosh kon.* Listen well. I am your mother. You got that? You listen to *me*. The picture comes down. *Basseh!* Enough! Go brush your teeth. Go put on your pajamas. Go on, then!"

Hooman was quiet. Mina thought he almost looked scared.

"Go!"

Hooman walked toward his bedroom.

"Put your pajamas on and brush your teeth!" Darya yelled out after him.

Hooman pulled off his sweater as he walked.

"That's right! Go get ready for bed! I am your mother!! I'm sick of this *chart-o-part* nonsense!"

Mina heard the faucet turn on in the bathroom.

Darya turned to Mina and Kayvon. "You two as well. Go on! Get ready for bed. Nobody tells you what to do except your father and me. You got that?"

"Darya Joon, it's time for all of us to rest." Baba pulled Darya away.

Darya shook his hand off her. She continued to yell at Mina and Kayvon, "I am your mother. You don't follow anybody else's stupidity, EVER!"

"Come on, Darya Joon, come on." Baba led Darya away.

"They're not going to take them over, Parviz," Darya said. "They're just children."

That night Mina lay in bed thinking of Maryam and Reza. The cousins she once had were no longer there. Maryam and Reza behaved entirely differently now. While it was uncomfortable to think of how they had changed, what scared her more was seeing her mother yell like that. Ranting and raving, forehead vein throbbing; slowly morphing, it seemed these days, into a mother entirely new and strange.

MUCH TO EVERYONE'S RELIEF, HOOMAN'S revolutionary zeal was, in fact, a passing phase. But by then, the zeal of the other teenagers and men and women who had marched the streets to end the Shah's dictatorship had brought about a change of regime. And the smallest corners of Darya's and Mina's lives began to feel the weight of that change.

CHAPTER FIFTEEN

MAMANI AND RUMI

When Mina woke up, it was cold, and the snow outside looked like ice cream, the kind Darya drizzled with rose water. Darya was quiet in the car on the way to school. She drove Mina and her brothers now. It was no longer safe to walk. Even the fighting had stopped. There was silence in the streets, no more shouting. No more bloodshed. The Shah was trying to get to a place called America. Mina thought of him there. Would they treat him like a king? Would he go to Disneyland? Kayvon had once shown her pictures of that magical land. People were sitting in teacups. Enormous teacups that were pastel blue and pale pink and light green. In the pictures the Americans were laughing. "It's the Land of the Teacups," Mina had said in wonder. And Darya had smiled and in their family after that they always called America "the Land of the Teacups."

People began to disappear. Their neighbor was sleeping one night when the new government authorities banged on his front door, barged in, arrested him, and took him away. His daughters wore black now. Mina eyed them on the street and wondered what it was like to just have your father taken away. She worried about Baba. She didn't want him to show any signs of being anti-revolutionary.

OVER A YEAR AFTER THE REVOLUTION'S success, Mina stood in front of the mirror in her bedroom, a scarf in her hand. "Is this how I do it?" she asked. Mamani and Darya sat behind her on the bed.

"Here, let me show you." Mamani took the square piece of cloth from Mina and placed it on the bed, folding it into a triangle. Then she put the triangular-shaped cloth on top of Mina's head and tied a tight knot at her neck. Mina looked at herself in the mirror. A headscarf. She looked like one of her Russian dolls.

Darya tugged nervously at a baggy gray tunic that lay on Mina's bed. The sleeves were long and puffed out; the length was long. Buttons went straight down the front.

"This is your new uniform, Mina," Darya said quietly. "Your *roopoosh.*"

"My uniform for school?" Mina asked.

"Yes," Mamani said.

"Mark my words, before long they're going to change the law so that it's her uniform for going anywhere. They want to make hijab mandatory by law."

"We don't know if they'll succeed," Mamani said gently.

"Oh, they'll get their way. By force. You just wait."

Mina picked up the heavy *roopoosh*. With her tenth birthday coming up, she was approaching the dangerous threshold of adolescence. She looked at herself. All of this—the long hair under that scarf, her round bottom, the tiniest hint of developing breasts—was considered a threat now. She had to cover up for school by law. Her body had become a liability.

Mamani came up behind her and slid the *roopoosh* onto Mina's arms. As she buttoned her up, Darya sat on the bed, arms crossed, frozen.

"Don't worry." Mamani forced a laugh at her own daughter's pained expression. "Our history is filled with these extremes. Everything by force. When my mother wanted to walk down the street during Reza Shah's time with her chador, the police attacked and pulled it off her head. That's what they wanted to do then, make us Westernized, erase religion. Now they've decided we're too Westernized and should go back to our religion. The pendulum swings. One extreme to another." She sighed and stepped back from Mina. "It's always through the women that the men express their agenda. Now she has to cover up so they can feel like they're in power."

Mina was familiar now with "they." Everything was "they" since the revolution. They were the leaders who had replaced the Shah. The brand-new regime. The new authorities. They were the ones the people now feared.

Mina wanted to tell her mother that the gray cloth covering her head and body felt unusual, but it was okay, she could manage it, her mother needn't worry so much. It seemed as if Darya fought anger all the time now. She snapped at Hooman. Burned the bottom of the rice so that their *tahdeeg* came out all black and charred instead of golden brown and smooth.

THE NEXT DAY, MINA FOUND her mother at the dining room table leafing through yellowed sheets of paper.

"What's that, Maman?" All Mina saw on the page were numbers. Endless numbers, written in pencil, with unknown signs and symbols linking them. Why wasn't her mother cooking dinner? Why wasn't she patting meat into ovals for the *kotelet* dish they had on Wednesday nights?

Darya acted as though she hadn't heard her.

"What is it?" Mina asked again.

"Nothing," Darya finally said. "Absolutely nothing." She gathered up the papers.

On top of one page, Mina had seen the words "Darya Daneshjoo," her mother's maiden name. The numbers looked like something Darya had written a long time ago. Maybe something for school.

"You did lots of math before," Mina ventured.

"I did lots of things before," Darya said. "Your father and brothers will be home soon. We have to cook dinner."

They cooked together in silence. They sank their hands into the *kotelet* meat mixture. The ground beef, turmeric, salt, pepper, bread crumbs, cooked potatoes, and raw eggs oozed through Mina's fingers. She scooped up a small ball of the meat mixture and passed it to her mother. Darya pressed the ball between her palms and patted it into a perfect thin oval. She plopped it into the hot oil. They repeated that over and over again in silence. Mina wondered if Darya's head was with those number-filled pages. If she was still trying to solve those old-looking equations.

Mina stared at the pink ground beef in front of her and opened her mouth to say something. But Darya's posture was so stiff that Mina instead handed her a fresh blob of meat and watched as Darya made *kotelet* of all the same size and shape, as if manufactured by a machine. The meat sizzled in the oil.

From the kitchen window, Mina couldn't see Mamani's house, but she knew it was there. Across the street, behind the greengrocer's, past the roofs of the smaller homes with the wrought-iron gates. Three streets down and to the left. It was a comfort to know that back there stood the redbrick house her grandparents had lived in for almost half a century. Roses carefully cultivated behind its gates. Pigeons competing for bread crumbs outside their windowsill. The bushes shining with droplets of water from the garden hose. As their *kotelet* browned one by one, Mina imagined her grandmother by her own stove, frying onions and singing along with the pop singer Googoosh's (now outlawed) tapes. She pictured her grandfather lying on his side on the burgundy cushions on their living room floor, leaning on his elbow, his head resting on his hand, as he read the evening paper and sipped from his teensy-tiny tea glass.

Evening fell. The sun melted and dissolved into the opal sky, casting a reddish hue on the greengrocer's tin roof. At this very moment, Mina knew that Mamani would turn off the stove. Put aside her fried onions and whatever else she was cooking (eggplant stew tonight? *aush* soup?) and go to the bathroom sink. There, she'd splash her face with water and stroke her forearms and toes with wet hands. She'd graze her hairline with water. Perfectly perform the ablutions for the evening prayer. Within minutes, Mamani would be on her prayer mat, *tasbih* prayer beads in hand as she melted into meditation. Mina pictured her grandmother's face: white, feathery skin, eyes half-shut, lips moving. Mamani's toes always stuck out from under the prayer chador. Soon Mamani would kneel, facing Mecca. And the next day, at the same time, she'd be kneeling in the same pose, having performed the same ablutions, sitting in the same perfect peace.

Mina watched Darya remove a few *kotelet* from the pan and place them on a paper towel to absorb the oil. Mina tried, but she couldn't muster up a mental image of Darya praying. Her mother's straight body wouldn't even bend into the right positions. She wouldn't want to spend her time standing, kneeling, sitting, murmuring words to an unseen entity. She'd say, "Enough of this," pat her skirt, and go about accomplishing something. "It's a crutch," Darya repeated to the kids. "Religion is a crutch for the weak. An escape. An illusion. A means to get manipulated. Don't get sucked into the propaganda!"

But there was a certain beauty to something you could count on like religion, Mina thought, as she scraped the last bits of the meat mixture into a lopsided shape and handed it to her mother. At least you knew what you were doing. Like Mamani. It could be sunny or snowing, they could be in the middle of a huge party or eating watermelon on the beach, a revolution could be going on in the streets with people collapsing in pools of blood, or it could be the middle of a parade for the monarchy's bicentennial—and one thing would hold true. At sunrise, noon, afternoon, sunset, and nighttime, her grandmother would be on her mat, saying her prayers, facing Mecca. And that, Mina thought, didn't seem like such a bad thing at all.

The day before the Friday holy day, Mina visited Mamani. She wound through the narrow streets, not quite skipping. She followed the water ditches, *joob*, till she reached her grandparents' home. Even outside the front door, she could smell Mamani's *aush* soup.

Mamani's hands were red from seeding pomegranates when she greeted her with a big hug and kisses. Agha Jan lay on the silk Persian rug in his pajamas, reading a book. Mina went to him and kissed him on the cheek.

"How many pomegranates do you want, *azeezam?*" Mamani asked as Mina followed her into the kitchen.

"Give her as many as she wants. Don't even ask. They're all for you, Mina Joon," Agha Jan shouted from the living room.

Mina noticed the wooden box outside the kitchen windowsill. It still had bread crumbs for the pigeons.

Mamani stirred her *aush* soup. "I added extra noodles, *reshteh,* Mina Joon." Without turning from the stove, she yelled, "Agha Jan! *Pasho!!* Get up! Get the yogurt!" She smiled at Mina. Then yelled again. "*Beeya!* Come on! This poor child is hungry."

Agha Jan walked in and removed the yogurt he'd made from the fridge. Yogurt-making was his one contribution to the household cooking. Mamani did the rest. There was a certain distinctive taste to the cooking of the Daneshjoo women that Mina loved. Spices and recipes and secrets that Aunt Nikki and Darya now continued. Mina wondered if one day her stews would carry the same balance of turmeric and allspice. Would she be able to sauté her onions till they were perfectly translucent? Would she cut meat in the shape of diamonds, using the knife in that quick expert way? Mina watched as Mamani sprinkled cumin into the *aush*. She suddenly realized that her brothers wouldn't necessarily be folding *dolmeh*. She'd have to learn to carry on the works of art from her palette of spices just like the women before her.

After dinner, they ate pomegranates sprinkled with echinacea powder. Mina bit into the pomegranate seeds. The tart kernels burst into her mouth with a delicious rush.

"Do you like these pomegranates?" Mamani asked.

"Very much," Mina said.

"Then I will get some more for you."

"Ones just like these?"

"The best ones are at the *meeveh-foorooshi* downtown. I will get for my Mina Joon the pomegranates that she loves. Next time. Next time, I will go to the store downtown."

"Thank you, Mamani. Thank you."

THE NEWS THESE DAYS WAS ALL ABOUT deaths. Not from people dying on the streets—the bloody revolution was over. But now came word of executions. Killing behind closed doors. Executions of all those who were too close to the Shah, too close to the West, too similar to what spies might be perceived to look like, too *taghooti* and attached to the monarchy, too short, too tall, too fat, too rich, too loud—it didn't seem to matter anymore. The killing did not stop. Mina knew all this, knew that her country had turned upside down, that a revolution was revolving into something else. She'd been told. The conversations at home were all about her brothers' changing political views and her parents' frustration at the hopelessness of it all.

But her grandparents seemed immune from the drama play-ing outside the walls of their house. They were detached from it all. Mina wanted some of their calm. How did they stick to their daily routines so diligently when the rest of the country was con-fused and in a state of chaos? Back in the kitchen, Mina watched Mamani spoon the remainder of the leftover onion, cucumber, and tomato salad into a ceramic dish for storage. Agha Jan sucked se-renely on a lemon. Maybe their calmness was a reward of old age. Maybe this was the payoff for staying in the world long enough.

"How is school?" Mamani asked.

"Well, it's all girls now. Except for the janitors. And we have lots of new rules. You know. The hijab. And our new teacher said we shouldn't look at boys. Ever. Except our husbands once we've married."

Agha Jan winked and pinched Mamani. "Hear that? You're supposed to be looking at me!"

Mamani swatted his hand away. "*Basseh!* I've looked at you enough—forty-five long years, I've 'looked' at you!"

"Mrs. Amiri is always giving orders. Cover your body. Chant the death slogans. Don't be immoral. Don't be anti-revolutionary. Die for the cause if you have to. My friend Bita thinks that Mrs. Amiri is a donkey."

"I always liked that Bita," Mamani said.

"The nonsense they teach you these days! The nonsense these . . . what was it your friend called them?" Agha Jan raised his eye-brows at Mina.

"Donkeys," Mina said shyly.

"You have a good friend right there, Mina Joon," Agha Jan said.

At least they could joke about it. If Mina told Darya all this, Darya's forehead vein would throb overtime. But Mamani and Agha Jan just shrugged it all off.

Mamani got up and left the room. A minute later she came back with a book.

"This, Mina Joon," she said, "is my antidote to all the nonsense."

Mina knew that book well. It was small. Tattered. The blue leather cover was inscribed with faded gold lettering. The pages were worn, dog-eared, soft. Mamani's book of poetry. Inside were Mamani's favorite stanzas from the ancient Persian poets. Words she'd copied in her own calligraphy, in black ink with sweeping cursive letters.

"Come look." Mamani motioned for Mina to come and sit next to her on the carpeted cushions on the living room floor. "Come look at these beautiful words of your ancestors."

Mina snuggled in next to Mamani and rested her head on Mamani's shoulder. Mamani read out loud, without holding back, her voice full of expression. Agha Jan listened in silence. With the sound of Mamani's voice, Mina felt the stress of school and new rules slip away. She was content listening to Mamani read from the black cursive script of Rumi and Saadi and all the rest of the ancient Persian poets in the crinkly pages of the book. Mina wanted it to stay like that: her head on Mamani's shoulder, the smell of fried onions and mint on Mamani's dress, the gurgle from the samovar where tea was being brewed, the sun lowering gently in the crimson sky.

CHAPTER SIXTEEN

SCHOOL AND SADDAM

Darya marched through the living room, a roll of aluminum foil flashing in her hand like a sword. She unleashed the foil with a loud crackle that whipped through the air. Then she began pressing the foil over the living room window.

"What are you doing?" Mina asked.

Darya didn't answer.

Families had disappeared around them. One by one, they left. Most to America. And Europe. Some of Mina's aunts and uncles left without saying good-bye. They ended up in Germany, France, England, Canada, Sweden, and the Land of the Teacups. Los Angeles and New York. Mina heard these names whispered at the dinner table over minted cucumber yogurt. Every week a new family vanished from Tehran. Then suddenly the new government stopped letting them leave. And when that happened, everyone wanted to leave.

The front door opened, and Baba came in. After a hello and a quick wash of his hands, he helped Darya cover the windowpanes with silver sheets. When the living room was completely covered up, they moved on to the bedrooms. Mina trotted after her parents from room to room, observing this bizarre but apparently important action.

Olivia Newton-John's "I Honestly Love You" played on the cassette player in the living room. Mina had been with Hooman when he bought it from a street peddler's collection of pirated tapes displayed on an old rug on the side of the street. The street peddler had looked around nervously to make sure that no guards were watching, then pocketed Hooman's money.

The three of them in Hooman's bedroom now, Darya and Baba stood back from the Pink Floyd poster on Hooman's wall. Darya looked as if she would say something. But she didn't. A few months ago, it had been an ayatollah's poster. Pink Floyd. Ayatollah. Darya threw her arms wide apart as she stretched out another shining, crackling sheet of foil. Baba pressed it onto Hooman's window, attaching it with masking tape.

"Why are you doing this?" Mina asked.

"Because of Saddam," Darya said matter-of-factly. "Because of his bombs."

Baba cleared his throat. "Light travels into the . . ." he began in his let's-learn-science voice. "See now, there is a distance from which . . ."

"We're covering the windows so Saddam's planes can't see our lights, so they can't find the city and bomb us," Darya interrupted him. "That's why."

Baba paused. "Yes, well . . . that's another way of putting it," he said. He waved the aluminum foil in the air like a baton, and tried to whistle along to Olivia Newton-John for a bit. He gave Mina a reassuring smile. "Who's hungry?" he said. "Let's have some dinner!"

SADDAM QUICKLY BECAME A PART of life. He was everywhere. Mina saw an outline of his mustache in the clouds. In the sheen of the oily water of the city's sewer *joob*, she was sure she counted his fat fingers floating. Parts of the tufts of his hair appeared in her lentil rice. At night, the sound of his planes terrified Mina. His name was plastered on newspapers, splashed in spray paint on the streets next to the word "Death," and incorporated into schoolyard chants and recess songs. Always, his name was said with disgust. He had attacked Iran on a September day in the year 1980. And though it didn't seem possible, a new level of change had been reached.

They were now at war with Iraq.

School became drill oriented. They practiced running for cover, crouching down, and covering their heads with their arms. Bita was the fastest runner. She'd crack her gum while crouching, even though they weren't allowed to chew gum.

The whole city covered its windows with aluminum foil. But it didn't stop Saddam's planes from roaring above. Mina imagined the pilot looking for just the right place to drop a bomb. Just the right perfect spot.

Halfway through the night, in the middle of the sweetest of dreams, slowly Mina was nudged by Darya and then, in pajamas and with doll in hand, drowsily, she followed her family down to the basement and waited there until the bombing was over.

Mina would remember stumbling down the steps to go underground. Her teeth chattering as they waited, heart in mouth, for the bombs to end, the ground shaking beneath them. The numbers of the dead announced each day, printed in newspapers, anxiously pored over by locals.

It was in the basement that Kayvon decided to teach Mina karate moves. He painstakingly trained her while they took shelter under the ground for hours on end. Kayvon's favorite kick was what he called the "side heel thrust kick." He had learned it from watching Bruce Lee movies. He said he had perfected it.

"See, you stand with your toes parallel. In a sparring stance."

Mina tried to copy Kayvon's stance.

"Keep your feet shoulder-width apart. Pivot on your left toe. Now lift your leg into a chamber position. And kick out, strong."

Mina tried and tried and tried again, not quite getting it right.

"You almost have it," said Hooman, who was watching along. "You'll get it, Mina, with practice. But you have to concentrate."

WHITE. ORANGE. RED. COLORS THAT Mina had often used for chalky clouds, an emerging sun, big fat hearts.

The government found new use for them. When airplanes flew overhead, the towering speakers on the streets of Tehran, on supermarket signs, inside lima bean stalls, on top of police cars would begin to wail. There were three kinds of signals, named by color and altering in siren tone, for three stages of emergency.

White meant be careful but you won't die, orange meant better go to the basement, and red meant get to the basement now, lie on your stomach, put your hands over your head and pray.

Darya kept a deck of cards in the basement. They played gin rummy, nervously, knowing playing cards was outlawed now too. Anything to do with gambling was a sin. Sometimes Darya played solitaire. She silently mouthed a question before she started each game. They never heard her. Then she said, "The cards will determine the answer." They all knew the question. *Will we survive?*

Her games of solitaire ended in failure more than once. When that happened, Darya swept the cards up quickly and shuffled them into a tidy stack. The boys often took over then, making a house of cards. They placed each card onto another as though their lives depended on it. When the house of cards collapsed, as it often did, their faces fell and everyone's optimism was stifled. Still, they made it back upstairs. Each time they entered their house again it was as if they were entering it for the first time, and each time they were also acutely aware that it could be their last.

IN THE MORNINGS, MINA SLOWLY ATE the soft-boiled eggs her mother made. If she could delay going to school, she would. Darya brewed the tea carefully, making perfect potfuls—the china teapot snug within a tea cozy Mamani had sewn. Before leaving the house, Mina did one last check in front of the hallway mirror. She tucked every strand of hair under her headscarf and buttoned up the last button of her *roopoosh.*

Their new Lessons of Religion teacher, Mrs. Amiri, had appeared out of nowhere to teach this brand-new subject. Mrs. Shoghi and the other teachers were ordered to wear headdresses.

The old headmistress was asked to leave because she was too *Shahi*. A new headmistress came, holding a megaphone in one hand and a list of new rules in the other. Anyone who appeared with a bad hijab would be reported. Bita was constantly sent to the principal's office for signs of being "deviant."

The old textbooks with the photograph of the Shah on the first page were replaced with brand-new textbooks with a photo of the new leader inside. The drawings in their old books of girls feeding roosters and going to the market were almost exactly the same, except headscarves and *roopoosh* had been added to the girls' pictures.

In the new books, the Persian kings were no longer dynamic and amazing. They were corrupt and cruel. Mina had to relearn the "facts." She saw that the definitions of things like "history," "good," and "bad" shifted depending on who was in power. Mina realized that whoever had access to dispensing information drew and colored the world.

"Don't get brainwashed, Mina," Darya said at dinner. "Don't let *them* get to you. No one can tell you what to think. No one can tell you what to do. Except me. And Baba. But don't get in trouble either. They are ruthless. So just keep quiet. Keep your head low. Try not to talk back. It's not worth it."

On her walk to school, Mina avoided the eyes of the guards that stood watching. "Good girls don't look men in the eye," Mrs. Amiri would say. "Good girls don't raise their voice. No need to smile unnecessarily. Good girls do not provoke. Do not let your laughter be heard." One of the bearded guards shifted in position as Mina walked by him. Mina held her head down, able only to see the thick black leather of his boots.

At school, after morning prayers and twenty-five jumping jacks, they lined up for assembly in rows according to height. It was hard to imagine that just a short while ago, boys and girls went to the same school. The presence of opposite sexes, Mrs. Amiri said, caused mental, spiritual, and physical effects that only should be felt after marriage. Mina missed playing dodgeball in school with Farokh and his friends.

Farokh still came over to her house sometimes, and they kicked a ball in the yard, enclosed by high walls, unseen. Then they ate the apples and dried mulberries that Darya brought out for them, and teased each other quietly.

THE NEW AUTHORITIES TOLD THE CHILDREN to hate America. But most of the kids Mina knew loved America. They liked its music, its minty chewing gum, its freedom. Mrs. Amiri said that America was vulgar and greedy—that it had supported the dictatorship of the Shah with zero conscience and propped up an evil dictator. *But who's the one making our lives hell?* Bita asked Mina. *It's this new regime, not America!*

One day, during a particularly hot recess half hour, while the headmistress was busy arguing with one of the janitors and while Mrs. Amiri sat in the shade chewing on a green apple, Bita motioned for the girls to gather around. When Mina, Jaleh, and Sepideh were all comfortably seated on the cement floor, Bita beamed conspiratorially and fished out a small cassette tape from underneath her *roopoosh*. There was a photocopied black-and-white photo on the cover of a smiling man with dark hair and a dimple on his chin and a beautiful woman facing him, her hands on his shoulders.

Bita held up the cassette and looked at the other girls with an expression that invited stunned appreciation. The girls leaned in closer.

Mina instantly recognized the cassette's image and took it from Bita.

"This is Olivia Newton-John," Mina said. "Hooman wants to marry her."

"Yes, and you want to marry the crown prince, who's not even the crown prince anymore but some poor refugee boy in the middle of America," Jaleh sputtered. "What is it with your family and their obsession with marrying famous people? You'll marry who your parents pick, just accept it."

Mina wanted to pull Jaleh's hair. But it was well protected under her headscarf. "For your information, my parents don't believe in that old-fashioned nonsense!" she said.

"Can we stop this *chart-o-part* talk and look at the tape?" Sepideh grabbed the tape from Mina. "Can I borrow this? Please? Please?"

The other girls shouted in protest. Jaleh reminded Bita about the supershiny lip gloss she had lent her three weeks ago, which Bita had almost entirely used up. Sepideh told Bita that she would give her three sticks of spearmint gum that her uncle had sent all the way from America.

"I'm your best friend" was all Mina could come up with.

After several rounds of "rock, paper, scissors" (Jaleh accused Sepideh of cheating, and Sepideh insisted no, she wasn't cheating, that's how her hand formed a fist and so what if it looked like paper, it wasn't right to make fun of her double joints, and Jaleh said being double-jointed didn't mean you had to cheat at how you made a stone shape with your hand, and Sepideh looked as if she might burst into tears), Bita finally broke the conflict by saying, "Mina gets to borrow it first because she's my best friend!"

Mina ran straight home after school and slid the cassette into the player. She began dancing on the sofa. Jumping up and down and feeling free from care. This was happy music and she blasted it as loud as she could.

That night, she took out the paper insert in the plastic cassette case and found that on the inside, in Farsi letters, was the name of the singer-man who was facing Olivia Newton-John on the tape's cover. A certain Mr. John Travolta, from New Jersey.

By the end of the week her time with the tape (which she learned was the sound track to some movie named *Grease*) had run out, and she had to pass it to Jaleh (during recess, covered in a napkin, pretending it was a butter and chicken sandwich). By then, Mina had memorized most of the words to "Summer Lovin'," "Hopelessly Devoted to You," and "You're the One That I Want." She found the songs popping into her head at inopportune moments—during prayer time or chanting time, or worst of all, when Mrs. Amiri's heavily cloaked body roamed the classroom checking the contents of their notebooks. She knew that if Mrs. Amiri could hear half the lines dancing in Mina's head, she would send her straight to detention. *"Cause I'm losin' control, of the power you're supplying, it's electrifying."* Mina hummed the new English words as she walked home from school under the stare of the Revolutionary Guards. *"I'm outta my head, but I'm hopelessly devoted to you."* She didn't know the meaning of all the words, just the easier ones like "love" and "summer" and "want" that she'd already covered in the private English tutoring class that her mom signed her up for as an extracurricular activity.

"Bita," Mina whispered the next morning at assembly during chant sessions.

"What?" Bita's thick eyebrows shot up.

"I don't think I can change my marriage plans," Mina whispered as the new headmistress chanted. "But if, for some strange reason, the crown prince and I don't work out, then I think perhaps this John Travolta man might make a fine husband."

"May you enjoy many happy years together, Mina," Bita said and winked.

They tried not to giggle.

When Bita came over after school with a new copy of the tape that her brother had made just for Mina, they held hands and danced all around the room.

"Of course I won't marry him," Mina said later while they were doing homework.

"Of course you won't," Bita said, not looking up from her notebook.

"The crown prince," Mina said.

"I thought you meant John Travolta."

"I don't think I'll marry either."

"No, I guess you won't," Bita said quietly. "They're both in America and you're in Iran."

And they continued their work without saying another word.

THAT NIGHT MINA DREAMED THAT she was sitting by the beach with John Travolta, enjoying a cup of tea. The crown prince was flailing in the waves, trying to get her attention, but Mina was too busy chatting with Mr. Travolta. She could hear the crown prince screaming for help, yelling about sharks, but she found herself unable to help him. "Let him drown," John Travolta said. "He's useless, just selfish. Greedy too." Mina could only nod. "Be a doll and get me another cup of tea," John Travolta said. And Mina got up and poured him a fresh hot cup from the samovar that was on a Persian carpet on the sand. They sat together looking at the horizon, she and John, and sipped their tea through thick chunks of sugar that they had placed between their teeth.

Every now and then John Travolta would tilt his head back and close his eyes and wail a line from one of his songs in *Grease*. And Mina would look him straight in the face and quietly recite Hafez. They continued in this way until Mina heard Darya's voice calling her to wake up and get ready for school.

CHAPTER SEVENTEEN

BREATHLESS FROM
THEIR DISCO DANCING

For Mina's tenth birthday party, Darya measured and rinsed basmati rice all morning. She crushed strands of saffron, then soaked the cooked rice in dissolved saffron powder, delighting in each and every orange-yellow grain. Baba climbed out from under the dining room table after hiding wine and whiskey in a picnic basket under the tablecloth. Mamani came early to fry the onions. Soghra sat in the kitchen and dabbed her forehead with a rose-water-dipped handkerchief, moaning about all the work still left. Hooman and Kayvon swept and hosed down the front steps. Mina seeded pomegranates for her mother's walnut stew. Her stomach fell at the thought of her tenth birthday party. At any minute, the Islamic Revolutionary Guards could barge in, seize the illegal alcohol, arrest her parents for forbidden music and dancing, and detain everyone. Baba would be handcuffed, Darya would faint and fall to the floor, Hooman and Kayvon would get flogged by the guards, and Mina would end up crouched in a corner, a ball of misery. Mina prayed for the guards not to discover her party. She also prayed with her eyes squeezed shut for Saddam not to pick her birthday night to bomb the city.

Everybody helped. Relatives and neighbors gave Darya their ration coupons for meat and eggs. Aunt Firoozeh came over in her billowy *roopoosh*.

"Take my kerosene coupons, Darya Joon. Keep your house warm. Your uncle Jafar, as you know, lives like a horse and can't stand too much heat. Besides, he's been talking about rice pudding for three weeks now. I'm ready to hit him in the head. I keep telling him we don't have enough milk . . ."

"Aunt Firoozeh, don't say another word! Please take my milk coupons." Darya searched for her ration book.

"No, no, I wouldn't dream of it! I just mentioned it because . . . well, I couldn't take just a few of your milk coupons! You with those two growing boys, Hooman and Kayvon! And that Mina of yours, turning ten! No, I don't expect anything in return for *all* our kerosene!"

"Aunt Firoozeh, please, I beg you. Take it. I won't sleep at night until you do!"

Mina heard them insist with exaggerated politeness in the traditional style of Persian *tarof*. She remembered that a few years ago she'd embarrassed Darya at a family gathering because the hostess had asked her if she wanted a piece of cake, and she had said yes.

"Never," Darya had whispered in Mina's ear after pulling her aside later, "accept anything at the first request. Wait."

Mina had looked at her blankly, the spongy cake still filling her cheeks, a few crumbs on her lips, unable to speak or chew or swallow. She nodded instead and then observed, learning to master indirectness. With Darya's help, Mina learned how to use just the right amount of insistence and refusal, self-restraint and flattery. The next time they were at someone's home, she remembered the art of *tarof*.

"Do you want a piece of cake?"

"Oh no, thank you, I'm full. I wouldn't dream of having cake."

Then the hostess asked again. "Please, I would rather throw dirt on my head than have you not eat my cake."

"Oh no, I couldn't, you're too kind."

"You must. A big piece."

"That's far too big, you're embarrassing me."

"Please eat it. Look at you so skinny. You're too young to be on a diet."

"In God's name, no . . ."

"Here, may it feed your soul."

"May God prolong your life. I thank you."

Mina took the cake and ate it until a second piece was offered and the *tarof* started all over again.

THE GUESTS WERE TOLD TO COME at seven o'clock so Darya knew they'd come by nine. That's how it was in the City of War. Everybody was later than usual. It took time to get ready—time for the women to cloak themselves in the now mandatory Islamic uniforms and veils, for the men to organize the backseats of their cars with flashlights, battery-powered radios, and bottles of water. Time for everybody to stop in the middle of traffic, get out of their cars, and crouch in ditches by the street when Saddam decided to burst open a bomb.

Poor Mr. Johnson showed up at 7:06. Darya opened the door pretending he was right to be on time and everybody else was embarrassingly late and uncouth. She wanted Mr. Johnson, an old friend of Baba's who was a correspondent for the BBC, to feel at home. Despite the anti-foreigner slogans spray-painted on Tehran streets in bloodred, Mr. Johnson had not left. Mina had heard Mamani say that he was going to leave soon, though, and return to the orderly world of England. Mina wondered if he'd have fish and chips on his first night back. Mrs. Isobel, the Iranian-Armenian teacher Darya had hired to teach the kids English after school, often talked about fish and chips and tea and crumpets during lessons.

Mr. Johnson sucked on the ends of his glasses and smiled at Darya.

In her red, wrinkled purse Mamani kept a photograph of her sister's oldest granddaughter, Leila. At a previous party, Mamani had made sure Mr. Johnson saw that photo. Conveniently dropped it onto his navy lap. Cousin Leila was nineteen and beautiful. And Mr. Johnson, with his blond hair parted in the middle, his tall, slim figure, and the ease with which he spoke Farsi, was not married. Mina had sat on Mamani's lap as Mamani whispered into the phone, "Don't worry, Sister. I've found someone for Leila. If all goes well, she can leave Iran before she's twenty. She can study in England. She won't have to suffer here anymore."

KISSES AND HUGS AND HAIRSPRAY surrounded the guests as they arrived. Their house had one of the most coveted designs in post-revolutionary Iran: a big private foyer. Here, when the women arrived, they could stop and remove their heavy *roopoosh*, release their hair from their headscarves, and slowly transform themselves into the women they were—the women they had been before the revolution's new laws. The state's obligatory flat shoes were thrown off and feet slipped into stiletto heels pulled out of plastic bags. Flattened hair was fluffed and teased back into shape. Tight red dresses, shimmery tank tops, miniskirts, and mutually admired spaghetti-strap gowns emerged from under the *roopoosh*. The women joked and grumbled about the Islamic hijab as they pressed tubes of lipstick to their mouths and smeared eye shadow above their lids. They shared one another's black-market Chanel No. 5, spritzing between their breasts and inside their wrists.

In the foyer, on special hooks Darya had hammered in after the revolution, hung the discarded *roopoosh* in a row. They were lifeless and colorless, even more so without their owners in them.

After greetings and cocktails, after *dolmeh* and pistachios, Baba announced it was time for a little music. He drew the blinds shut and made sure all the doors were locked. Darya pulled curtains over the blinds as an extra precaution, and Mina's uncles piled chairs against the front door. If the Revolutionary Guards decided to break in, the extra buffer would buy them all some time.

"Don't worry, they're not around this neighborhood tonight," Baba reassured the guests. "Big wedding in Yousef Abad. They're all downtown, most of them anyway."

"Well, last weekend they stormed the Honaris' wedding." Aunt Firoozeh sucked an olive off a toothpick. "They heard pop music and broke in, ten Comiteh Revolutionary Guards. Fined the host. Kept the guests in custody. Poor Niloofar said she should've never had a reception."

"Firoozeh Joon, you're being negative again," her husband, Uncle Jafar, said. He sat stuffed in an armchair drinking home-made beer he'd brought with him in yogurt containers. "Don't scare these good people. One shouldn't be paranoid. Maybe think a little before you say things that scare children?"

Aunt Firoozeh glared at him as she sipped her wine. Mina had watched them argue all her life. "May God *release* me from this man and his criticism!" Aunt Firoozeh muttered, then stomped into the kitchen. Uncle Jafar continued talking to no one in partic-ular. "Have you heard of Viktor Frankl? Have you read his books? He knows about the power of positive thinking." He coughed, his eyes burning from the brew. "Also, there's an American woman, by the name of Glooria Gay-Lord who has sung a song with which I'm very pleased. It is called 'I Veel Survive.' Have you heard it?"

A few men nodded politely and feigned interest because he was an elder. Other guests smiled and looked down. Darya then handed Mina a silver tray filled with bowls of different nuts and Mina trotted around the room, balancing the tray in her hands.

"Would you like some nuts?" she asked the old powdered aunts who sat with Mamani on the couch.

"Oh no, thank you, may your hands not ache."

"Please take a nut," Mina insisted.

"No, no," the ladies politely refused.

"In God's name, take a nut, please," Mina said.

"Well, okay then, maybe just one." Mamani extracted a few nuts from the bowl.

"May it nourish your soul," Mina said, bowing her head. Darya always said that before people ate.

"Thank you, my soul is yours," Mamani said.

Mina continued around the room.

AT NINE O'CLOCK, COUSIN LEILA arrived with her father, Professor Agassi, and her mother, Dr. Agassi. Tall and thin, Leila wore dark blue jeans and a white blouse. She was the only Iranian woman Mina knew who didn't dress as if she were attending an opera every time there was a party at someone's house. She didn't wear any makeup, but she still looked better than the others. She had big dark eyes and long black hair that was always moving, fluid around her fair skin. Leila hugged Mina amidst the loud greetings and laughter at her family's arrival.

"*Tavalodet mobarak*, happy birthday." Leila was the only person who remembered what this party was actually for. Presents were piled high in the living room, but few others had uttered "Happy birthday." "How's it going?"

"It's going. Aunt Firoozeh and Uncle Jafar argued already. Baba insists on playing music. My mom cooked my favorites. Mamani wants you to marry Mr. Johnson."

Leila didn't seem surprised at any of it. "Come on." She took her second cousin's hand. "I brought you a book. In English." Leila spoke fluent English and tutored children in their homes. Darya always encouraged Mina to bolster Mrs. Isobel's lessons with English conversation with Leila. "For your future, Mina Joon," she would say. "It will be the language of the world one day." Every Wednesday after school, Mina, Hooman, and Kayvon were dragged to Mrs. Isobel's classes. Darya added an extra Monday session after the war began. She had heard from Baba's brother, now seeking asylum in Chicago, that not knowing English made him feel blind.

Mina and Leila went to the bedroom and thumbed through the paperback: it was a book from the Michelle series. Michelle lived in a place called Portland, Oregon. She had a best friend, Sandy, and was learning how to babysit. Sandy and Michelle both liked a boy called Brett. But Brett only liked the cheerleader Marcia. Marcia smiled on the book's cover, holding pink fluffy balls, her bare legs raised in the air.

"And the English-language bookstore can sell this?" Mina's eyes widened at Marcia's bare legs.

"The booksellers have colored over Marcia's legs with permanent black marker now," Leila said. "But I got this before."

There was no need to say before when. Their world was cleaved into Before and After. Before the revolution. Before the new laws. Before the upside-down.

"You went to trouble, thank you," Mina said.

Leila read out loud about Michelle and Sandy's plan to stop Brett from taking Marcia to prom. Mina sat on her bed and tried to follow their problems, but she couldn't help worrying about the Revolutionary Guards. If they burst in and arrested her parents for the party, it would all be her fault.

"Dinner's ready!" Darya's head popped into the room.

THE GUESTS HEAPED THEIR PLATES with rice and *ghormeh sabzi*, rice and barberries, and poured Darya's walnut and pomegranate sauce on top of their saffron rice. They drank Baba's illegal wine and insisted everything was the best they'd ever had. This time, Mina knew it wasn't just *tarof*. Her mother's cooking truly was superb. Mina broke some fresh *naan* and dipped it into her cucumber and mint yogurt.

"To the chef, the lovely lady at the head of the table." Baba raised his glass.

Darya blushed. "May it nourish your souls," she said.

"To Mrs. Rezayi!"

"Thank you, Khanom Rezayi!"

"May your hands not ache!"

"May you live long!"

Darya beamed, her eyes bright.

"And may God protect us from the Revolutionary Guards, damn them, and from the entire entourage of Secret Police that wrecks the lives of the innocent and tortures people's children! And from British spies!" Aunt Firoozeh said, her face flushed with too much wine, as Uncle Jafar almost spit out a stuffed grape leaf.

SOGHRA ARRANGED THE BAKLAVA into tiny diamonds on Darya's wedding china and made sure the rose-flavored ice cream was topped with threads of saffron. She poured dark chai into small hourglass-shaped glasses. Mina rested her head on her hands at the dining table, inhaling steam from the tea. So far, so good. No Revolutionary Guards, no Saddam. Maybe when dessert was over, they could open the presents.

Aunt Firoozeh chewed her baklava, looking sideways at Mr. Johnson. Earlier in the kitchen, Mina had heard Aunt Firoozeh say to Darya, "It's the work of the Brits. They have a hand in everything behind the scenes, don't you know. Just like when they helped the CIA overthrow our only democratic government in

1953. Wouldn't they love to see this country ruined. So they can have our oil. That's what they *want!*" She had waved a cucumber in Darya's face as she said this. Darya had shooed the cucumber and Aunt Firoozeh's theory away. "What things you say, *Khaleh!* Mr. Johnson is our friend!"

Mr. Johnson was engrossed in a private conversation with Mamani and hadn't noticed Aunt Firoozeh's glares. Mamani pretended to smell something in her arthritic hands and Mina heard her say "foody good" in English. Was Mamani trying to convey cumin? Cardamom? Rose petals? Mr. Johnson nodded and then pretended to smell an invisible spice in his own hand with exaggerated delight, raising his eyebrows at Mamani.

The lovely lesson in mime notwithstanding, Mina felt anxious to get to the presents before it got too late. She tugged on Darya's blouse. Darya and Leila's mother were talking in soft voices now, their heads close together, arms touching.

"The new officials," Leila's mother said, "want to pass a law saying female dentists can't treat men. I can't treat men and look into their mouths. Why? Because they've suddenly deemed it ungodly. Too much closeness between opposite sexes, they say. What, do they think that bleeding gums and teeth turn me on?"

"They're sick," Darya said. "Everything is about sex to these fundamentalists. We have to cover up so *they* aren't tempted. In the Shah's time, just because we wore miniskirts and our heads were free, did everyone go around obsessed with sex?"

"No," Leila's mother said. "Though you have to admit, Darya, our last year in university . . ." She broke off, giggling. "Remember those hikes with Behzad and Bahram?"

Darya and Leila's mom burst out laughing over their bowls

of ice cream, squealing ridiculously. Mina noticed the tiny creases that formed around their eyes as they squeezed them in pleasure. She suddenly felt an inexplicable anger. Darya and Leila's mom had worn miniskirts in college during the Shah's time and hiked in mountains with boys. But for her, all of that was outlawed. Darya's prophecy had been correct. After much discussion within the government and despite protests by women and some men, mandatory hijab was now law. Mina would never feel the sun on her legs again, never sit next to a boy in class the way her mother had. Her hair would not know the feel of wind or sunshine.

Mina excused herself and went to the bathroom. She needed to escape from the political arguments and her mother's squealing laughter. Mina closed the door and climbed onto the edge of the tub to nudge the window open. The cool night air washed over her, smelling of jasmine and dust. Mina could still hear Baba's music. He had put on Googoosh, the most popular female pop singer, now banned as a voice of sin.

Mina mouthed the lyrics, then she heard a noise. At first she thought it was a car crash. But then she realized. An explosion. Of course. From the open window, she saw the night sky. Burning orange-yellow. Saddam.

WHEN MINA WALKED BACK, DARYA was clearing away dessert dishes, still talking to Leila's mom. Aunt Firoozeh sat at the table, picking her teeth with a folded piece of paper. Leila leaned against the wall, talking with Mr. Johnson. He nibbled the tips of his glasses, then said something that made Leila laugh. In the middle of the room, Hooman and Kayvon practiced karate moves. Baba stood in front of the cassette player, arguing with Uncle Jafar, who kept showing him a tape with the English words "I Will Survive" marked on it in big letters. Uncle Jafar said something about its uplifting message.

"No, let's play 'Dancing Queen,'" Baba said holding his own black-market ABBA tape. He pointed to Mina. "See? 'Dancing Queen.'"

Mina's brothers pulled her into a group of people who were beginning to dance in the middle of the room. In a few seconds the emergency alarms would go off all over the city, alerting citizens to the bombs falling outside. They would have to drop everything, get in file, and go to the basement for shelter. The presents would have to be opened later, much later.

But for now, Mina swayed with the guests, dancing to the forbidden music. She threw her head back, pointed a finger in the air, and glided with the group. Uncle Jafar's song had won. A few guests sang along. *I veel survive.* From across the room, Mina caught a glimpse of her mother. She was sashaying, her hands pressed onto her hips. A choo-choo train of dancing guests formed behind her. As the emergency bomb alarm sounded from speakers lining the street and drowned out the music, Mina and her brothers joined the queue. Baba brought up the rear of the line. And they all followed Darya, breathless from their disco dancing, as she carefully guided them down the basement steps.

CHAPTER EIGHTEEN

11:17 A.M.

The next morning, Mamani called to say how glad she was that Mina's party had gone well. No one hurt or killed or arrested. She told Mina to tell Darya that she'd be over at noon to help with the cleaning up. First, though, she was just going to stop by the greengrocer's downtown, the one with the best pomegranates, to get some for her little Mina Joon—wait a minute, make that her big ten-year-old Mina Joon! Mina even remembered to *tarof*, saying things like Oh no, Mamani, don't go down there just for me, you'll tire yourself, it's a long way. But Mamani insisted, and Mina gave in quickly. Okay, thank you, Mamani Joon.

BABA TOLD DARYA THE NEXT day that the body parts were definitely Mamani's—he recognized her clothes. Hooman showed the article in the newspaper that noted the bomb was dropped at

11:17 a.m. Audacious time of day for bombs, even for Saddam. Darya left that day's rice unwashed, uncooked. She didn't soak anything in saffron. Hooman and Kayvon wept for weeks and stopped karate. They all wore black for forty days. Mina looked around and saw that someone, Saddam, had found a way to shut life completely down. Something had brought unbearable grief. She realized that the something was war. She vowed to stop all wars when she grew up. To make sure another war with Iran never began. She'd always known war brought pain and destruction. She just hadn't known how much.

CHAPTER NINETEEN

CUT OFF THEIR TAILS
WITH A CARVING KNIFE

Bread, cheese, herbs spread! Saddam, why are you so scared?
Iran's not going to hurt you bad! It's only messin' to make
you mad!

The sweaty palms of the other girls stuck to Mina's after the seventh time they sang the song and soon it was an exhausting, no longer fun, part of recess. In the late morning, the sun cast an orange-yellow hue. The rays burned into Mina's headdress. Mina wanted to free a hand so she could scratch her eyes, but the other girls gripped her fingers as they walked in a circle singing the song for the eighth time. Mina's vote had been for hopscotch, but Bita, in her usual bossy way, had insisted that they sing the Saddam song today. To hex his evil ways. And how could Mina refuse when only a few short weeks ago he had dropped a bomb on the greengrocer's stall and made her grandmother a statistic. Mina had stepped carefully around the spleens and flattened hearts on the messy road in her dreams a dozen times, trying to identify fragments that belonged to her grandmother. Clearly Saddam had not given one thought to what would happen to her grandmother's body once he'd dropped the bomb. Mina clutched Bita's hand tighter.

After recess was Lessons of Religion. When Mrs. Amiri entered the room, Mina jumped to her feet with the other girls. Just the sight of Mrs. Amiri's acned chin and sucked-in lips made Mina wish she were far away from school and in her mother's kitchen sipping sweetened tea. Mrs. Amiri scribbled words on the blackboard, and Mina tried to copy the words neatly into her notebook, but she found herself instead drawing over and over again the slanted boards of the grocer's stall where her grandmother had shopped. Suddenly Mrs. Amiri was behind her. Mrs. Amiri struck Mina's elbow and the calligraphy ink jar spilled over, splashing across the notebook.

"Next time, before you draw, think a little about the consequences," Mrs. Amiri said.

Deep black blotches penetrated a half year's worth of notes. Mrs. Amiri backed away from Mina's dripping ink. "And don't live so much in the universe of trance. Pay attention to this world."

Mina tried to mop up the spilled ink with her handkerchief, but there weren't enough handkerchiefs to blot the mess. Bita leaned over and gave Mina her hanky. And slowly throughout the class, girls began passing their handkerchiefs under the desks toward Mina, hoping to help her blot out the blackness. Soon there was a pile of scrunched-up embroidered handkerchiefs on Mina's lap, small pieces of cloth that grandmothers had stitched and initialed, tiny sewn-in cherries and roses peeking out from the corners. Mina's own handkerchief, which Mamani had embroidered with two tiny lemons, was now drenched in black ink. She lifted an arm in the air and cleared her throat.

Mrs. Amiri stopped scrawling verses on the blackboard.

"Khanom, excuse me, is there permission to go to the bathroom?"

Without turning from the board, Mrs. Amiri jerked her head toward the door.

Her handkerchief scrunched tightly in her hand, Mina got up, careful not to disturb the pile of the other girls' hankies under her desk. She hadn't used them because she didn't want to stain them. She left as quickly as she could without seeming too vulgar (a few weeks ago Mrs. Amiri had told them that girls who walk fast are loose).

In the bathroom, Mina washed her handkerchief in the sink. She rubbed it hard. Her tears came as they always did these days, almost entirely on their own, as if an infinite supply were stored up inside her. She scrubbed her handkerchief under the faucet, squeezing it and wringing it and rubbing more broken pieces of beige soap onto it. But the handkerchief was still gray. Mina wrung it out, folded it into a triangle and put it in the front pocket of her *roopoosh*. The two lemons peeked out from the top. Mrs. Amiri's voice rang in Mina's head. "A modest girl does nothing to bring attention to herself." She stuffed the rest of the handkerchief inside her pocket and walked back to the classroom.

When she opened the door, Bita looked up with concern, but Mina nodded to let her know she was fine. The song from recess played in Mina's head now and got mixed up with English nursery rhymes she'd learned in Mrs. Isobel's English tutoring class.

"There is in this world, dear girls, evil and then there is good. Your duty is to follow the path of good." Mrs. Amiri sorted through her black bag. She fished out a bottle filled with brownish liquid. Mina recognized the little man in the top hat jaunting happily across the label, walking stick in hand. Johnnie Walker Black. Bottles like this had been passed around at her parents' parties. Just after the revolution, her parents had emptied most of those bottles into the toilet, then buried the bottles under bushes in the yard. But Baba had brought out a bottle just like this one during her birthday party. Uncle Jafar had drunk to a free Iran.

"What am I holding?"

The girls shifted in their seats. Traces of recognition passed across some faces, quickly masked by innocent looks.

"Anyone?"

Silence.

"Khanom, is there permission, that's a bottle of whiskey," Bita blurted out.

Mina's heart fell. Bita was always speaking her mind. Getting into trouble.

"And how would you know that?" Mrs. Amiri asked softly.

Outside the sun burned into the cement where they had just stood a short while ago. It seemed to Mina like ages ago. She tried to think of chopped parsley and the stew her mother would make for dinner; she tried to focus on a tiny bee flying by the windowsill; she tried to remember more English nursery rhymes like "Three Blind Mice." *Cut off their tails with a carving knife.*

"How do you know?" Mrs. Amiri asked again.

"I just know." Bita tilted her head as her mistake dawned on her. "I know . . ." She looked around. "I know from books."

"Books? Don't lie. The liar is the enemy of God. Is there a bottle like this in your home, maybe?"

"Khanom, I know. I just . . . remember." It looked as if Bita were going to explain herself out of this mess. Mina and the other girls got ready to breathe a long sigh of relief. But then, Bita sat up straight and tall. "I drank from one. Just the other day." She stared at Mrs. Amiri, her black eyes shining.

Mrs. Amiri froze. Then a small sneer curled her lips. "You think you're witty? You think this kind of nerve will serve you well? Clearly, your family is familiar with vehicles of sin." She slammed the bottle onto her desk. "To the office. Now!" Mrs. Amiri hissed.

There was the scrape of Bita's chair as she got up to leave. There was the *vheej!* sound of her *roopoosh* cutting through the air as she marched out the room. The other girls sat uncomfortably still.

The next day, Mina heard from a few other girls that the Revolutionary Guards had knocked on Bita's front door at seven o'clock. Bita's dad had been arrested and taken to the Comiteh offices. He'd paid a fine, no one knew how much. His name was entered in the Anti-Revolutionary records. No one answered the phone when Mina called Bita's house. Bita was out of school for the rest of the week but came back after the Friday holiday with dark circles under her eyes. When Mina walked up to her, she noticed a film of pink lip gloss on Bita's lips. She begged Bita to wipe it off before Mrs. Amiri came in.

But Bita just looked at Mina with her shining black eyes. "I'm not scared. The only thing that scares me is God. And guess what,

Mina? God is not a fanatic." Bita took Mina's hand and linked her pinky finger into Mina's. "They can't outlaw happiness, can they, Mina? They can't smother it out of us." She winked. "We're not the type to be suffocated."

Mina thought of Mamani, suffocating under the bomb debris. "No. We're not," she said.

"We will be free. You'll see. Your next birthday party just might be outdoors in the garden. We'll dance. Outside."

Mina dared to think of her eleventh birthday party. In the year 1982. Without Mamani. But maybe, in a free Iran. She squeezed Bita's pinky finger hard. She even tried to wink. They would not crumble. They would not fail.

CHAPTER TWENTY

BARBIE STAYS IN TEHRAN

ina pulled down her chador to cover as much of her face as she could. Her brothers sat next to her, crumpled in the backseat of the taxi. In the darkness, the fleeting streetlamps occasionally lit up the people who were out at midnight. Mina glimpsed a couple, a woman in a dark chador and a young thin man, strolling as they ate ice-cream sandwiches. A few cats roamed the streets, wide-eyed. Mina closed her eyes and prayed.

They hadn't made their beds. They hadn't taken the kettle off the stove, or packed much. They hadn't said good-bye to most of their relatives, trusting the grapevine to spread the news once they were safely out. At the last minute, Mina had thrown into her suitcase her color-pencil case and the markers from last year. Now huddled next to Darya and her brothers in the speeding taxi, she started to remember all the things she hadn't brought.

Underwear. Did they have enough underwear? She could see Baba press on an imaginary gas pedal as he sat next to the taxi driver in the passenger seat. The taxi driver, Ali, kept cracking his gum. The music he played was religious. A good front. If the guards leaned in and asked them questions, maybe Ali could help them.

"We are going to America," Baba had said at breakfast, a few months after Mamani's death. Each week more boys were sent to the front to fight. When he made the announcement, Mina saw in her father's face that the decision had already been solidified between her parents, the details already worked out. When Darya had definitively said that her sons would not die killing their innocent Iraqi neighbors and Baba had said that his daughter would not be brought up silenced and stifled, together they had made their plan. At breakfast over sweetened tea and bread smeared with Mamani's sour-cherry jam from summer, the children had simply been informed of the decision. And every action since then had been one of rushed secrecy, a heightened sense of urgency informing their charade of living as though they weren't leaving.

At the airport, Ali threw their suitcases onto the pavement. It was half past midnight, and their flight left at five in the morning. They needed time to get through all the official checkpoints. Ali shook Baba's hand and bowed his head at Darya. He took a good long look at Hooman and Kayvon. "*Bereen. Bereen zood.* Go. Go quickly," he said. "In a few months, they'll have you killing Iraqis."

Hooman and Kayvon leaned over to pick up the suitcases. Mina looked at her brothers' long arms and legs. She couldn't imagine their bodies crouched in ditches near the border, ready to kill.

Inside the airport, Darya and Mina were separated from Baba and the boys. Darya and Mina made their way to the women's section. Mina kept pulling her chador tighter, she didn't want the authorities to find anything wrong with her hijab, she didn't want to be the reason they were refused permission to get on the plane. They were told to empty their suitcases. Every item was carefully examined and massaged by the three chadored customs officials.

"Nothing valuable can leave this country," one of the women said, looking Darya and Mina up and down with scorn.

Another woman body-searched them from head to toe, squeezing and patting them. Questions were asked about why they were going to America (for medical reasons—Baba had managed to create medical urgency with the help of his colleagues already in New York), how long they were staying (nine months), what, if any, jewelry, money, Persian rugs, pistachios, gold they were taking. A Barbie doll tumbled out of Mina's suitcase.

The customs official lifted up the Barbie and looked at it at arm's length. Her face contorted into a sneer. "Why do you need this?" she asked Mina.

"Remember how you had dolls when you were little?" Darya said quickly, desperately.

The female official smiled wearily at Darya. "No, Khanom, I do not. I never owned a single doll. It is you, the rich, who owned the dolls. It is you the spoiled rich class who owned everything in this country. Now look at you, scurrying away like frightened cockroaches."

Darya stiffened. Mina readied herself for the throbbing fore-head vein and a tirade from her mother. But instead, Darya only looked down at her feet as the customs official shoved their belongings back into the suitcase. A third woman was called over to look at their paperwork. The few minutes she spent leafing through their passports felt like an eternity. Then the woman jerked her head toward the terminal and handed Darya two boarding passes. Mina had expected more resistance, more struggle, expected the officials to even deny them permission to leave.

They walked quickly to reunite with Baba and Hooman and Kayvon. Mina realized she hadn't repacked Barbie. The customs official had insisted on examining Barbie, twisting her arms, cracking her knees. As Mina turned to look back at the search station, where the chadored women were throwing around the belongings of another nervous-looking mother and daughter, she caught a glimpse of her Barbie's dismantled arms and legs in a neat pile next to a picture of the Ayatollah.

ON THE PLANE, BEFORE THEY TOOK OFF, Mina looked out the window at the Tehran tarmac one last time. Baba had promised they would come back very soon, as soon as the "craziness" was over, and their country became normal again. Suddenly Mina's heart tightened as panic washed over her. A dozen faces seemed to press against the tiny oval window of the plane. She could see Cousin Leila and Aunt Nikki and Reza and Maryam. She clearly saw Aunt Firoozeh's nose pressed against the pane, and Uncle Ja-far's big mustache was squashed against the glass too. There was Soghra, dabbing her head with a hanky. And in her mind's eye, Mina saw Agha Jan. She saw him sitting alone at his kitchen table, the newspaper limp in his hand, bent over an empty bowl. At that moment, Mina even saw Mrs. Amiri, looking at her with something like envy as she sat behind her teacher's desk. Lastly, Mina saw Bita marching off to detention, turning around to look one last time at Mina. Lip-glossed, shining-black-eyed defiant Bita. The relief that Mina had expected once they were safely on the plane was not there. There was instead only a strange sensation: a suffocating feeling of guilt.

"We never said good-bye," Mina said as they got ready to take off.

"We'll be back," Darya promised. "This is all just temporary."

Mina closed her eyes and saw their house, its doors wide open, the windows unshuttered with the wind blowing through. The lemon trees that Darya had planted in the garden, the roses in the yard, the jars of tea leaves and baskets of fruit on the kitchen shelves.

She turned to look at her mother. Darya's eyes were half-closed and her mouth was barely moving. But Mina recognized the words her mother whispered. She was stunned to see her mother praying. She had never heard her mother recite prayers, the Koran verses from which she had always distanced herself. When she prayed, Mina thought, Darya looked more like Mamani. Across the aisle, her father sat glassy-eyed. Hooman kept pulling nervously at his upper lip. For a minute, Kayvon's head was covered in his hands. Then he looked up and saw Mina watching him. He managed a smile. "Freedom." He mouthed the word as the plane lifted into the air. He held his trembling fingers in a "V" for Victory.

The plane went up higher and higher. Mina leaned her head back and listened to the buzz of voices and white noise. The pilot's nasal muffled voice came through the speakers. She could smell a stranger's cologne. She held on to Darya's hand as they flew into the blackness.

CHAPTER TWENTY-ONE

LANDING IN LIGHTS

Somewhere between Iran and America the women on the plane had slid their headscarves off and unbuttoned their *roopoosh*. Just before they landed in New York City, compact cases emerged from handbags and powder puffs were pressed against tired skin, mascara was dragged across already-black lashes, and gobs of goo in small round tubs were pressed to lips.

Darya had spent most of the plane ride thinking. She marveled at how Mina slept so soundly next to her. She felt again the overwhelming sense of responsibility that she'd gotten accustomed to ever since the birth of her first child: the stunning knowledge that where her kids were going was due in large part to where she, as mother, led them. This duty felt at times as if it could drown her.

Parviz had told her early in the morning, before the kids came into the kitchen for breakfast. Darya had been pouring boiling water into the teapot, thinking how much her mother had taught her about brewing things correctly, when she saw the look on Parviz's face. She wanted to stop pouring but couldn't. Even before he said it, she knew he had big news. He'd been talking about leaving for some time.

"America . . ." he started.

"We can try," she said finally. She felt herself sink. In order to live in a normal way, they had to leave their home. She wanted to scream at the top of her lungs.

Parviz talked about schools and education in America. All Darya could do was stare at the bottle of dishwashing liquid on the kitchen sink. The green liquid glinted in the sunshine streaming through the window. The bottle was half full. Parviz discussed Hooman's future, the possibility of his becoming a doctor. Darya noticed a few bubbles floating inside the bottle of the dishwashing liquid, at the very top. Parviz moved on to Kayvon, discussing his talent with people. When would it end? Darya thought. Parviz talked about how such a talent should not go to waste. Would the dishwashing liquid be used up before they left? How many more sinkfuls of dishes would she wash with the remaining detergent? How many weeks did they have left?

"And Mina," Parviz continued. "Think of her spirit, her *shadi*, her joy. She lives in color. Here, she's been drained to black and white . . ."

The dishwashing liquid would outlast their stay in Iran, Darya realized. She had mentally calculated how many sinkfuls of dishes the remaining liquid would wash, and it was more than the number of sinkfuls that she estimated they'd dirty before they took off. She had solved the math problem. It was strangely fascinating to think that the leftover dishwashing liquid would stay in Iran longer than she would.

Now the plane soared in the night air. Who knew if it was right or wrong? They had uprooted their lives. The children. She knew by heart Parviz's speech about freedom and possibility and the future. But she was taking them away from the safety of the extended family. Plucking them out of the life and the world they knew and dropping them somewhere else. Even if their country had turned crazy, it was still their country. But this new place, the Land of the Teacups as Mina liked to call it, what on earth did they really know about it? Darya saw teacups spinning before her eyes and rested her head on the tiny airplane pillow and tried to sleep. She wished she could line up all her relatives, line them up one by one and stand in front of each one, just for a few minutes. Tell them that she didn't want to go, that it wasn't right that she should go and they should stay, how if she could she would jump into the sky and catch each and every bomb Saddam was dropping on them, leap into the air and catch it and stop it— THUNK—the bomb would land in her hand and go nowhere and they, those loved ones with whom she shared her days, would not have to die.

In her head, she mentally said good-bye to each of the relatives. To Soghra too, and the greengrocer Hassan. But when she opened her eyes, the gaping truth remained. There was no mother. Even in make-believe, she could not envision standing in front of her mother's frame and saying good-bye. Darya reached for Mina's hand as Mina slept. To a mother, there was never a good-bye. Eleven seventeen a.m. Greengrocer's. Pomegranates. A bomb. She sighed and turned her attention to her daughter and her peaceful face. Mothers did not die.

"WELCOME TO AMERICA," DARYA WHISPERED.

Mina put her hand on her head, dazed. She looked over at her father. He was writing on the customs and immigration forms. He held on to the forms tightly, careful not to crease or bend the paper, treating with great care the tiny manifestos that held a key to their future.

"Look, Mina," Darya said, pointing out the window as the plane began to land. "Look at all the lights."

Outside the window, Mina saw what looked like a velvet cloth with gems of silver and gold crushed deep within its folds. The new city. She thought she saw a structure that might be the Statue of Liberty that Kayvon had showed her in books, she wasn't sure. But what she knew for sure was that she could see countless lights everywhere, endless lights, even the tiniest ones made more visible the closer they got to American soil. "They can keep their lights on at night here," she muttered in wonder.

"They can keep their lights on whenever they want," Darya said.

As the plane descended, Mina was filled with an inexplicable rush, a dizziness even, and as she pressed her forehead against the pane of the window and gazed down at the lights below, she felt as if she could reach down and swallow that world up. For one brief moment, she felt as if anything could be hers if she wanted it, anything at all. She wanted to jump out of the seat and run, run anywhere fast, it didn't matter where, but she wanted to move, to shout, to announce to everyone that she loved those lights. She wanted to pick them up one by one and put them in her free hair, press them over her body, lightly place them on her tongue and then slowly have them melt inside her, until all of New York was there, giving her warmth and light and actually becoming a part of her, until the lights of that city were stored so safely inside that no one could ever take them away. To have that freedom inside her and have it shine from her eyes for the rest of her life. Forever.

They moved their bags down and waited in line to exit the plane. People coughed. The murmurs, the hiccups, the sneezes— would they all begin to sound different now? Mina pushed a strand of hair back from her face and looked ahead. Darya was right in front of her, her back concealing Mina's view. Mina tightened her grip on her carry-on bag and felt her heart pounding. They were about to enter the lights. If she could draw those lights, she would. If she could draw them for the rest of her life, she would.

CHAPTER TWENTY-TWO

A BOX OF CRIMSON RED

It takes four seasons. To feel at home in a new country," Baba said. "That is the rule. Once you pass four seasons, then you're home free."

They had arrived in snow. They rented a room in a tiny hotel in Manhattan, using savings from the old country. Darya leaned against the iron bars of the clunky gated elevator as Mina and Kayvon tap-danced their way up and down, pretending to be characters in an old Julie Andrews movie they'd seen in Tehran. In their hotel room, the buttons on the TV remote commanded seemingly endless channels. Thirteen TV stations in all! Mina never knew there could be so many.

On the street outside their hotel, small kiosks spilled over with newspapers and magazines and row after row of pink, green, and orange candies. They walked in the snow and bought the newspaper and tried to keep pace with the brisk energy of the city. Baba circled ads in the paper, got on the phone, and contacted the few Iranian expats he knew. He spoke to former colleagues, professors, scholars—the ones who'd left before them. One of Baba and Darya's old university friends, now a chemistry professor at New York University, gave them the most important piece of information: the top ten school districts.

Number one goal—good school. A good enough school, in an affordable neighborhood. "What matters is the *school*. Once we have the school, we have our neighborhood," Baba kept saying. Mina nodded. She knew that school was the key to her and her brothers' future in freedom. There was a growing, gnawing feeling in Mina's gut that they would be in America for more than just a year or two. Despite what Baba said. Mina and her brothers were now grateful that Darya had dragged them to Mrs. Isobel's English lessons in Tehran.

In their first few weeks in New York, there were no sunny days. But then one morning, Mina was awakened by a warmth on her face. Apricot rays shone through the hotel window, straight into her eyes. She sat up, got out of bed, and rushed to the window. Sunshine lit up the slush on the street. Up until now, they'd had to wear hats outside—woolen beanies bought from the Pakistani man who sold hats, gloves, and small black umbrellas from his wooden table on Lexington Avenue. But today was bright, clearly warmer. While Hooman and Kayvon snored and Baba dreamed his Farsi dreams, Mina tapped Darya awake. She pointed to the sun and Darya understood. It was warm enough to go outside without anything on their heads. They were dressed in minutes.

Inside the clunky elevator, Mina tapped her feet. She practically ran out of the hotel, with Darya right behind her. Feeling their scalps warmed by the sun was new again. They laughed as the rays soaked into their hair. Mina's thick mane swung down her back, black and lush, as she held Darya's hand and they walked down Lexington Avenue. Mina noticed that Darya's dark hair looked tea-colored in the light. How ordinary they must have seemed to others, mother and daughter strolling down the street. But no one knew their private joy. Was freedom just tiny moments like this? Simply knowing that no one cared if the sun shone on your hair?

Loud buses drove past, splashing slush onto their legs. No matter. The smell of burnt nuts and smoke was in the air; a man who looked as if he could be from central Tehran sold peanuts by the bag at a kiosk. The wisps of women's hair blew in the wind. A grumpy young woman in a gray suit and sneakers held a briefcase in one hand and a paper cup of coffee in the other. She looked impatient and stressed, waiting to cross the street. Mina almost tugged at the young woman's suit. *Hey listen, it's not that bad. Don't look so upset. You can do whatever you want, wear whatever you want! Do you know how incredible that is?*

The sign changed from "DON'T WALK" to "WALK" and the woman ran. Coffee spilled out of her paper cup. She cursed. Mina watched the woman sprint down the blocks in her sneakered feet. Of course she had work to do. Places to be. Everyone was so busy here.

The sun cast black shapes onto the pavement, covering forgotten pieces of flattened gum. Cars sputtered and coughed in the street, stopping more than they moved. Darya and Mina took in a lungful of the exhaust fumes as litter swirled around their feet.

"Do you think they're happy here?" Mina asked Darya suddenly. She wanted to hear yes. It would be wonderful if they'd landed in the Land of the Happy.

"Happy?" Darya repeated the word as though it was completely irrelevant. "Well, nobody's happy everywhere. I mean, not everybody's happy in any country. It doesn't work like that."

"Oh." Mina was disappointed.

"Then again, maybe they're happy and don't even realize it. It's like that sometimes."

"Maybe that's why you're happy. Because you're not even thinking about it?"

"Something like that," Darya mumbled. "Though in my opinion, happiness isn't the goal of life. Happy, happy, happy! Who needs happy? They're too concerned with being happy in your America."

From the very first day of their arrival in New York, Darya referred to the U.S. as "your America" when she talked to Mina, Hooman, Kayvon, and even Baba. As though it already belonged to them but not to her.

Darya slipped into a place called Woolworth's. Mina followed. Darya hovered in the hair-care aisle for a moment, then scooped up a box of crimson red dye. When they got back to the hotel room, Darya locked herself in the hotel bathroom and did not come out for thirty-five minutes. When she finally emerged, her hair was wet and red. Hooman, Kayvon, and Mina were confused. But Darya shook her newly red hair, and Baba clapped and cheered. Then Baba went in and scrubbed the bathroom walls clean. The colors that always remained of that first winter were the white of the snow in the early morning, the gray slush it soon transformed into, the red on the walls in the bathroom, and—an eternal memory—the dark crimson of those pomegranates dancing in Mina's head, the ones her grandmother had gone to buy for her when the bomb came down. But dominating all the new colors was the jarring red of Darya's hair, an unfamiliar defiance that screamed silently at the start of their American life.

CHAPTER TWENTY-THREE

PIZZA WITH DAVE

ood morning, Mina!"

That's how they sang it out. The words were dictated by Mrs. Krupnick and repeated by her new classmates in the fifth grade classroom. Mina stood in the front of the room on her first day, feeling strangely naked in her jeans and Mamani-knitted sweater. Mrs. Krupnick was tall and thin with a tanned and wrinkled face. Her blue eyes were outlined by waxy green eyeliner. For a minute Mina thought Mrs. Krupnick had crayon on her face. Black mascara clumped her eyelashes together and crayon-red pencil defined her lips. The whole classroom smelled of Mrs. Krupnick's citrusy perfume.

"All righty—grab a seat, sweetie," Mrs. Krupnick said.

Mina looked up. Close to thirty pairs of eyes were watching her. Girls and boys sat behind stand-alone wooden desks. They were dressed in jeans and sneakers and T-shirts and sweatshirts. Their hair was brown, black, blond, red. Posters of apple trees and zoo animals covered the walls. Mina turned to look at Mrs. Krupnick and saw behind her, hanging from the top wall, a huge American flag.

"Over there, sweetie, next to Michelle." Mrs. Krupnick pointed to the one empty desk. Mina walked as if in slow motion, sweating, heart beating, under the eyes of the other children. She slid into the chair, brittle and perspiring while attempting to look confident and casual.

Tinny musical notes rang out. A voice came from a speaker somewhere. Then, as though lifted by an irresistible wave, the girls and boys rose to their feet. Mina sat still for a second, then got up too. Her classmates placed their right hands on their chests and faced the flag. Then Mina heard, "*I pledge allegiance to the flag of the United States of America. And to the Republic for which it stands, one nation, under God, with liberty and justice for all.*"

When the chant ended, everyone burst into song. They sang about a star-spangled banner and the flag being still there. There were bored faces, passionate faces, faces proud and faces still. The last notes of the song were long and high. A girl in blond pigtails sang the loudest, not stopping her high note till everyone else had sat down. Just a few weeks ago in assembly, the chant the head-mistress had Mina and her classmates recite was called "Death to America."

"Hey, want some gum?" The girl next to her, the one the teacher had called Michelle, held up a tiny rectangle wrapped in pink paper. The glittering horn of a smiling unicorn shone on her sweatshirt. Mina noticed the elastic rainbow belt around her waist, and the rainbow-patterned cloth that covered her jeans from the knees down.

"Leg warmers," Michelle said, caressing the wool on her calves. "My mom got them for me at Macy's."

"Thank you very much," Mina said in her best, most articulate English, as Michelle handed her the gum, making a mental note to look up "leg warmers" and "Macy's" in Darya's dictionary. Mina looked at the gum uneasily. Was gum allowed here? Was chewing it in front of the teacher okay? And the bright glitter of Michelle's sweatshirt and the careless way a boy behind them had propped his feet up on the back of Michelle's chair. So relaxed! Mrs. Krupnick didn't mind any of it. The huge purple earrings on a girl in front, the piercing tangerine headband of the girl two rows up. Enough colors to make Mina's head reel, more colors than in the paint set, the colored pencil set, and the crayon set put together.

Mina unwrapped the gum, stuffed it into her mouth, and bit into a gush of flavor. An unfamiliar sweetness. A newfangled brand-new taste.

THE LIGHTS IN THE PIZZA SHOP were blinding. Mina held her hand to her forehead to shield her eyes from the bright fluorescent lights. She squinted up at the blackboard to read the scribbled pizza choices and their prices.

"Regular Cheese slice—75 cents. Sicilian—85 cents." Regular was the thin slice, the chewy, stringy one. She knew that now. Sicilian was thicker, richer. Hooman usually liked Sicilian sprinkled with oregano. Kayvon always added lots of red pepper flakes. Mina preferred regular cheese. When Darya joined them, she didn't order any pizza. Just tea: a Styrofoam cup filled with luke-warm water and a stapled tea bag floating inside.

"May I please have a slice of cheese," Mina said quietly. She often went to the pizza shop alone now, to do homework after school.

The man behind the counter ignored her. It was Thursday af-ternoon, and all the kids from the local schools seemed to have descended on this very pizza shop. Girls cackled as boys teased them. The pizza man behind the counter drummed his fingers im-patiently. "You gotta speak up!" he shouted.

"May I have a slice of cheese, please," Mina said louder. Did she have an accent? She thought she had managed to iron out most of the Iranian-ness from her speech over the past few months. She had almost mastered slurring her "r"s in that luxuriant American way.

The man behind the counter slid her a slice, its grease oozing onto a paper plate. Mina gave him three quarters in exchange and a smile. This man was probably new, she thought, he didn't know that she was "Dave" Rezayi's daughter. Her father worked here, after all. He was the one who made the pizza. When he had first applied for the job, after they'd moved from their Manhattan hotel to their Queens rental, he'd told the owner his name was Parviz. "How about I just call you Dave?" the owner had said. Baba always told the kids this story with a mixture of disbelief and wonder. "He wants me to be a Dave!"

After Mina organized her textbooks and notebooks at a table by the door, she flipped open her American history book and took a bite. The tip of her tongue burned from the hot pizza. The teenagers around her joked and squealed. Someone from the kitchen shouted to the man behind the counter to "dump anotha bucket intha sink." It was almost six o'clock, that blurry time between day and night. For a minute it seemed as though the sun would last and the sky would remain blue, but in the next minute, everything was gray and violet. Soon night took over. Mina felt a draft each time the door to the pizza shop swung open. She read under her breath, sounding out the increasingly easy English words. The hot cheese and tomato sauce filled her cheeks. Baba sure knew how to add just the right amount of tomato sauce.

"Yes, please?" She heard Baba's voice. He was behind the pizza counter now. She watched Baba from behind her pile of textbooks. He looked smaller here than he used to back home. He'd lost more hair. When he spoke English, he sounded uncharacteristically unsure. In Farsi, his voice came out strong and authoritative. But in English, he faltered and paused, as if trying to catch the right words as they randomly passed through his brain. His hands were always caked with flour now, or stained with tomato sauce, or smelled of onions. The colors were similar to the colors he'd worked with before. Dough like skin, tomato sauce like blood. Skin and blood—a doctor's everyday colors.

"Can ya hurry up?" A teenager in a Yankees baseball cap yelled at Baba. "*Por favor?*" He grinned through his braces.

"Please . . . yes," Baba said and shuffled back and forth.

Mina concentrated on her textbook.

The chapter described how Americans had staged a revolution in the eighteenth century. Mina wondered if all the American girls back then had felt the same gnawing uncertainty she'd felt during her revolution. But the American Revolution seemed different. Mina studied the black-and-white sketches of stocking-clad, long-haired men galloping on horses and women in long billowing skirts and bonnets marching with banners.

Amidst the buzz of the fluorescent lights, the shouts from customers, the tinkle of change, and the whir of the soda machine—Mina studied. Hooman and Kayvon were probably at the library, crunching through algebra and *The Catcher in the Rye*. Hooman was acing his algebra exams these days. Kayvon kept telling Mina that Holden Caulfield was one of his favorite book characters ever. She and her brothers had gotten used to keeping one another up to date on their schoolwork. Academics were their solace and purpose, the one thing in which they had to excel. Mina preferred studying in the pizza shop to studying in the library. Even though it was overly bright and loud, there was something comforting about knowing Baba was right there. And he really did make good pizza.

Mina played with a brass key on a green piece of yarn that hung around her neck as she read. The key to the front door of their two-bedroom apartment. Darya had said that their new home was the size of Soghra the housekeeper's lounge room in Tehran. When Mrs. Krupnick had seen the key around Mina's neck, she'd murmured, "Another latchkey kid!" as if it were an amusing yet sad thing. Half the kids in her new fifth grade class had keys around their necks so they could open their front doors in the evening while their parents worked. Mina didn't necessarily miss the red sliced apples placed neatly on china plates, the slices of banana and oranges that Darya used to prepare for them after school back in that other country. Spoiled is what they were. Spoiled with a perfumed mother cutting up fruit for them in the afternoons and a father marching down hospital corridors in his white coat and stethoscope, listening to heartbeats and reading medical charts.

Her mother was busy now. Her father too. America was a busy place, with people working hard all the time, extending themselves with all their energy, drinking coffee in paper cups as they ran to the bus instead of sipping tea by a samovar while relaxing on carpeted cushions. Now that she was here, she realized there were no huge teacups in which people sat and laughed, but the people still spun endlessly. Her other country now seemed slow and lazy, with days that must have contained more hours than the days here. She couldn't imagine having all that time back.

Mina's mind wandered to Darya, who was at work at the dry cleaner's. It was only a few blocks down from the pizza shop. Mina could just as easily sit at the back of the dry cleaner's and do her homework. The owner's own kids often did their schoolwork back there. But the smell. That pressed steamy smell of water hanging in the air. And the clang of presses and the sound of the owner and her husband yelling at each other and the whir of the racks starting and stopping all the time. And the lights. The lone lightbulb over Darya's sewing machine and the white-hot electric beams hanging from the ceiling. Mina's eyes hurt just thinking about it. She preferred the smells and sounds and lights of the pizza shop because, hard as it was to see Baba pushed around by teenagers, the sight of her mother bent over that sewing machine was harder for Mina to see. Darya wasn't supposed to bend. Her perfect-postured mother, who always used to hold her head high, the one who seemed to be connected by an invisible string to the sky, the no-nonsense, couture-wearing, chic mother from the northern hills, the "lady doctor," as doctors' wives were called back in the old country. Now sewing clothes for fat, blue-haired ladies of Queens, squatting near the old ladies' ankles, pins between her lips, as she balanced on her haunches, measuring the rims of their pants.

Mina bit into her father's pizza and began to commit to memory the accomplishments of the founding fathers.

WHEN SHE WALKED OUT OF THE PIZZA shop an hour later, a cool breeze lifted Mina's hair and whirled the strands around her face like a fan. A delicious, exhilarating sensation. To think that only a few months ago, she'd thought the wind might never lift her hair again.

Mina walked quickly down the street. She had to get home. At the pizza place, Baba had nodded at her and raised his eyebrows toward the door as he took a customer's order: his signal that she needed to get back before it got too late. Mina pressed onto the sidewalk in her new American sneakers. In twenty minutes she'd be home, just in time to set the table. Kayvon most likely was already at home, washing rice, and Hooman was probably browning the meat. The basic steps of the *khoresh* would be done so all Darya needed to do when she got there was finish the vegetables and add the spices. Mina pulled the collar of her jacket up around her mouth and kept a good pace. Some shops had already closed, but their lights were still on, glaring indulgently into the night. Mina passed lit-up mannequins, their oversize nipples sticking out under striped T-shirts and sailor tops. What details the Americans created! The scent of sausages and pastrami wafted from the European-style delicatessen as she passed by. Near the deli was Wang Dry Cleaning. Mina buried her face deeper into her upturned collar and kept on walking. Mina didn't want to look as she passed by, but at the last minute, her eyes shot up.

And there was her mother lit up behind the glass, bent over at the sewing machine, the neon blue "Wa-g Dry Cleaning" sign flashing above her head. Darya guided a pair of brown pants under the needle of her machine, supersize scissors by her side, her hair bound in a neat bun, her eyes focused and steady. She cut meticulously, measured exactly. She looked like the kind of woman to whom one could entrust a prom dress or the elaborate stitches on a wedding gown.

As Mina crossed Queens Boulevard, she wondered for a moment if a new girl, from another traumatized country, hovering in a plane above the U.S. for the first time, would see those millions of lights that had stunned Mina when they first landed in America. And if that new girl could see from her plane, amidst the many shining bright lights, the flicker from B&K's Pizza where Baba dashed back and forth, the flashing sign from Wa-g Dry Cleaning where Darya sat stitching, and the light of the streetlamps under which Mina hurried home.

CHAPTER TWENTY-FOUR

YELLOW BLOSSOMS
AND TV NEWS

Spring in Queens brought bursting purple flowers, tinges of pink and white on previously bare trees and tiny yellow blossoms that carpeted car hoods, wedged themselves into the crevices of baby carriages, and nestled into Mina's black hair.

Mina walked to school, her stomach full from Darya's food. Darya had mastered the art of food shopping in Queens. Israeli pickles from the kosher deli, melon from the Korean grocer's, ground walnuts from the Ukrainian lady, and baklava and turmeric and tea from the Iranian shop.

The Iranian shop in Rego Park was small and smelled like home. The owners were the Hakimians, Iranian Jews who had moved to America right after the revolution. The sign outside said "Persian Gourmet Foods" in English, but a smaller Farsi sign read "Maghazeye Irooni"—Iranian Shop. Mina and her brothers quickly learned that in America, "Iran" was a bad word associated with terrorists, mullahs, and hostage-taking.

"Just say 'Persian' and make it easy for yourself," Kayvon advised. "People associate 'Persian' with good stuff—like fancy rugs and fat cats."

"Fat, really cute cats," Hooman said.

"Cats?" Baba looked up from practicing chopping tomatoes, looking as if he might explode. "Kittens? 'Persian' should remind people of the empire that stretched from one side of the East to the other. The empire that set a new global standard, contributed mountainfuls to astronomy, science, mathematics, and literature, and had a leader, Cyrus the Great, who had the gumption to free the Jewish people and declare human rights! *That* empire! You can't be shortsighted when you look at history. History is long!" Baba was shouting now. He continued to slice tomatoes. "Cats! What have we been reduced to?"

THAT WEEK IN CLASS, MRS. KRUPNICK assigned each student a state to research in detail. Mina got New Mexico. She memorized New Mexico's official state flower, the colors of its flag, and details about its geography. She learned where all the states were on the class map. There was no world map in class, only one of the U.S. Most of her classmates gave blank stares when Mina mentioned where she was from.

Only one boy knew.

"You from that place that took the hostages." Julian Krapper's speckled blue eyes grew wide. "I know about that." He flicked his pencil.

Mina burned with shame and anger when Julian brought up

the hostage crisis. It was a story she wished would go away. But Julian went on and on unless Mina gave him what he wanted.

"Hey, Mina! Did you feed your camel this morning?" Julian asked. "Has your dad washed his head rag?"

Most of Darya's homemade meals from Mina's lunch box were handed over to Julian, and Mina obliged only to stop his yacking.

One yellow-blossom spring day, Mrs. Krupnick allowed the class to eat lunch at the playground because it was so nice outside. Mina sat on a bench under a huge tree and took out her enameled tin lunch box. Before she could take a bite out of her *kotelet* sandwich, a shadow appeared on the ground near her. She knew it was Julian Krapper without even looking up.

"What did Mama make today? Give it up." He waved his hand near Mina's face.

Mina tried to ignore him.

"I said give me it!"

Darya had stood in the kitchen the night before, frying the *kotelet* after her shift at the dry cleaner's. Mina remembered how Darya had leaned against the counter after she was done, her face sallow and exhausted.

"They're not for you," she said in her best unaccented English.

"Excuse me? Hostage taker, did I hear you correctly?"

"I said, it's not for you."

"Listen, I-RAIN-ian. Do you want me to remind everyone about your mullah country again?" Julian's hand remained in Mina's face. "Because you know I will. Half these kids are so dumb they don't even know we have a terrorist in our class now. I'll tell them all about your backward-ass country and how it took Americans hostage for 444 days."

"Go ahead," she said. "Tell them." Her body felt limp but her heart was beating faster and faster.

Julian lowered his hand. He walked toward the rest of the kids, ready to unleash a tirade of Mina-insults so that everyone would hear.

But before Julian could say a word, Mina stood up, *kotelet* sandwich in one hand, and the yogurt-seltzer drink *dough* that Darya had made in the other.

"I DIDN'T TAKE THEM!" Adrenaline pumped through Mina. "Got it? It wasn't me. It wasn't every Iranian. So shut the hell up and learn some history!"

Silence filled the playground. Julian Krapper froze. Mina could feel the stares drilling through her body like the sewing needle piercing through the clothes that Darya tailored.

Julian Krapper grew red and marched toward her. He came so close to her she could see every single speck in his bright blue eyes. His breath smelled of milk and soda. He held her chin with grubby, warm fingers.

"You'll be sorry," he whispered.

Mina thought of Bita, how she always stood up for herself no matter what, how she didn't let Mrs. Amiri or anyone get the better of her. She thought of when Bita had linked her pinky finger with Mina's and said that their happiness couldn't be smothered.

"You know nothing." Mina stared at Julian.

He let go and backed away, squashing yellow blossoms under his sneakers as he walked back to join his cronies. Mina couldn't believe how quiet the playground had become.

She sank back onto the bench, drained. Her fingers had stayed curled around Darya's *kotelet* sandwich during their exchange.

Mina reached into her lunch box for a napkin, and found instead that Darya had packed the handkerchief embroidered with two yellow lemons that Mamani had made in that other world. The sight of that handkerchief and its old ink stains made Mina's heart tighten. Her arms felt limp. She remembered washing that hanky under the faucet in the school bathroom in Tehran. Walking back into the classroom, Bita looking up to check if she was okay, and later, Bita being sent to detention for identifying the whiskey bottle. What Mina would give to have Bita appear next to her right now and sit under that yellow-blossom tree with her. What she would give to talk to her old friend again.

Mina watched the other kids from a distance. Some boys took Michelle's jacket from another bench and stuffed it with leaves. Michelle and her friends squealed and tried to grab her jacket back, fake-screaming in that delighted we're-getting-attention-from-the-boys way. After a short chase, Michelle finally caught up to the boys, and she and Chad half-wrestled, half-just-got-mangled-and-touched. The chorus of girls soared in their squealing.

Mina leaned back. Blossoms fell around her forming a thick carpet of yellow on the ground. The bell rang. Lunch was over.

Mina did her best to create that yellow-blossom carpet in art class later that afternoon. She worked hard on her painting.

LATER THAT NIGHT, MINA TOLD DARYA about Julian Krapper. Instead of suggesting that Mina show him a miniature Persian painting, recite a Rumi poem, or have him over for Persian food to discuss Cyrus the Great (all of which Baba would have recommended in order to introduce Julian to the greatness of the culture he was missing), Darya just shrugged.

"*Velesh kon.* Let him go. He doesn't understand. He's confused Iranian people with their government. It's not his fault. It's that TV."

Then Darya sighed as though the TV were a ranting abusive uncle torturing poor Julian Krapper.

Mina dreamed that night that she had punched a hole in the TV screen and toppled it over. She jumped up and down on the broken TV as miniature news anchors ran away. Mina lined up the network anchor figurines in a row and told them they had to start showing her country in a fairer way. Show the normal people, not just the crazy leaders. The TV anchors nodded and obeyed, promising it would be so. At the end of the dream, Mina shook hands with all three news anchors, holding in her fingers their tiny hands.

BABA AND DARYA LIVED FOR the network evening news. When it was on, they hushed the whole family into silence and sat transfixed, waiting for a vision, any glimpse of that other country. Baba switched between CBS, NBC, and ABC—the three major networks. There was a sense of anticipation, hunger, mostly hope. But the news about Iran only contained clips of chadored women and bearded fanatical men. Sometimes there was footage of the Iran-Iraq War: pubescent soldiers with bandanas jumping out of army vehicles in the desert. The camera always cut back to the news anchors: Dan or Tom or Peter, where they sat in their perfect studios, cleanly shaven and calm, the picture of civilized men. Mina could practically smell their cologne and their minty breath. In perfectly modulated voices, Dan/Tom/Peter elaborated on the footage. So measured and controlled compared with that excitable riffraff in the Middle East.

Mina hated the news. It only gave Julian Krapper fresh fodder.

One evening after Dan showed a chaotic street in Tehran, Baba looked around, giddy. He put down his bowl of pistachios.

"Did you see," he asked in an excited voice. "The beet seller's wagon? Did you see the beet seller?"

Hooman, Kayvon, and Mina stayed silent. Mina had seen bearded angry men in a mob, but she'd neglected to notice a beet seller's wagon.

"I did!" Darya piped up, like a child answering a question in class. "I did!"

"I could almost smell the beets!" Baba's face glowed.

Darya straightened the pleats on her skirt. "You don't suppose"—she looked up at all of them—"that there was a *balal* seller too?"

Balal. Corn barbecued on a grill, then dipped in salt water. Suddenly Mina could smell the *balal* and feel the breeze from the peddlers' bamboo fans waving over the grill. The sweet and salty taste of barbecued corn filled her mouth.

"Perhaps," Baba said. "There very well could've been a *balal* seller."

"Nice to know the regime's not falling apart this week," Hooman said. "Hasn't toppled yet, has it? And the war. Doesn't look like they'll be signing a peace pact anytime soon. Guess I can stop holding my breath. Cuz we're going back, ANY DAY NOW, right, Baba?"

Kayvon raised his eyebrows the way he did anytime Hooman

made one of his this-will-get-under-Baba's-skin comments.

"Is this"—Hooman pointed to the TV—"the culture you want us to be proud of? Because it doesn't seem like I should be proud of that. And I'm not."

Baba's arm stopped in midair on its way to the pistachio bowl.

Darya froze, her head cocked to the side, arms bent at the elbows, like one of the mannequins she now tailored on.

Mina sucked in her breath.

Kayvon shook his head again.

Like a soldier jumping into action, Baba dove toward the coffee table. With a sweep of his arm, he collected five or six thick books. Mina saw him flutter desperately through the pages. She knew he was searching for the most poignant accomplishments of the Persian Empire. Kayvon leaned in and tried to help his father. Hooman rubbed his face with his hand, resigned. They all knew that Baba would soon be telling them about their thousands of years of history and the many reasons they should be proud of their heritage.

Darya left the room then but came back and stood in the doorway after only a few minutes. She held a book, casually, as though she'd just come back from the bedroom where she happened to be reading on a nice spring evening.

It was the blue leather cover that made Mina's heart skip a beat. It was the golden lettering. It was the memory of the last time she'd seen that book, nestled into her grandmother's arms, lying next to her on burgundy carpeted cushions, hearing Mamani's voice read aloud from her book of poems.

Mina's knees weakened and she found herself sinking to the floor. She could feel the softness of the upper part of Mamani's arm against her head. She could smell the tea brewing on the samovar, the sound of her grandfather's voice. The living room in Queens with its TV set and coffee-table books melted away. She was there again, next to her grandmother, the big carpeted cushion scratching her elbow, the song of the evening prayer coming in from the loudspeakers outside. Mamani recited the poems loudly, confidently, proudly. Their stomachs were full from Mamani's thick *aush* soup. They had sat like that together, read like that. They had been like that.

Mina sat on the floor now, on her knees. To stop her body from shaking, she rested her forehead on the ground. She was crouched in a child's pose.

Hooman, Kayvon, and Baba were still studying the coffee-table books. "All of this was Persia," Baba said as his fingers tapped across what must have been a map page. "All of this!"

Hooman was quiet now.

"The post office! Who doesn't use a post office? Who invented the postal system? The Persians, that's who!!" Baba banged on the book. "*This* is who you are!" Mina heard the pages turn. "Who discovered the properties of alcohol? Who outlined the stars? The Persians! THIS is who you are!! Not that!" He turned to the TV, pointing as though at a heap of stinking garbage. "Not that!"

Mina heard the sound of a commercial from the TV. She knew it well: an ad that showed young women sashaying in miniskirts singing that they could now wear short shorts because they had successfully removed hair from their legs. Baba was quiet as he took in the image. "Not that! I mean what they say in the news! They *cannot* erase our accomplishments. They can't undo the truth of our history. All they do is demonize us, show the hardliners.

Why don't they ever talk about the rest of the people? Why don't they show the . . ."

Mina remained slumped on the floor. If anything could bring back the essence and memory of Mamani, it was that book. If only she hadn't asked for the pomegranates. Her forehead still on the living room carpet, Mina felt her face grow hot. Silently, slowly, the tears began again. The tears felt hot on her cheeks. She could taste their salty sweetness. Baba's voice continued over her head— his lectures, his pleadings. Mina cried for the way it happened. She cried for the loss. Still kneeling, her rear end on her heels, her hands by her face, her forehead to the ground, she realized she was in Mamani's prayer position. The tears blurred her vision. The grief that she thought she'd suspended when she slipped her feet into those American sneakers, when she bit on Michelle's pink wad of gum, when she walked under that rain of yellow blossoms, was back. It would, she knew, never really go away. She'd had a grandmother, she'd had a family and friends and a life and a place and a home and all of it was up and away. Gone. From what felt like far away, loud rock music came on. The TV with its endless noise. She knew her father's socked feet and her brother's feet were close together where they stood, discussing lost empires and TV news. They would never go back. She knew that now. They would never live there again. That place, that country that Dan and Tom and Peter talked about with such remarkable ease and polite distance, was over for her. Her forehead felt attached to the floor. The tears continued their relentless stream.

And then, a hand on her back. She sensed Darya's face next to hers. The forehead was on the ground right next to hers. The rear end on the heels, the hands by the face. Mamani's prayer position.

They stayed that way for a while, kneeling, in a position they had never before been in together. The blue book of poems lay between them. Then, as Baba continued to discuss the effects of history, Mina moved her hand across the book and held her mother's hand in hers.

CHAPTER TWENTY-FIVE

FEAR AND FIREWORKS

mina had to stop Darya from marinating the hot dogs.
"But it's absurd to grill meat without marinating it
first!"

"I don't think that's how it's done here." Mina held her mother's hand back.

"Olive oil, lime juice, salt, pepper, sliced onions, and dissolved
saffron. For about six hours. It would taste so much better."

"No, Maman." Mina hid the saffron. Darya tended to overuse
it lately. And this was, after all, a Fourth of July barbecue.

The Hakimians, the owners of the Iranian shop in Rego Park,
had written a list for them. Hot dogs. Chicken. Hamburgers.
Corn on the cob. Darya had marinated all the other meats. In her
special combination from that other country. The corn would be
grilled till its kernels went practically black, then dipped in salt

water—rightful *balal*! This was a special barbecue. Their very first Fourth of July. Celebrating independence. They were all healthy. They had their freedom now. What more could they ask for?

"Fireworks!" Mr. Hakimian had said. "Wait till you see the fireworks."

Mina had been especially looking forward to the fireworks.

Fireworks comprised the colors of summer. Kaleidoscopic colors, magical colors, colors that literally burst and splattered, then vanished, leaving Mina to scratch her head and wonder if they were ever really there. Summer was season three. Baba said it took four to feel at home in a new place, and here they were 75 percent of the way there, three-quarters of the journey done.

The hot air hung heavy and humid all day long and curled the edges of leaves on hedges, dampened the paper on Mina's sketch pad, and stunned the spiders into slow demise. New York baked that summer. Baked and sizzled and roasted as its cement sidewalks seemed to melt. Mina and her brothers mopped their foreheads and fanned their faces and reapplied glossy shiny deodorants from American drugstores to their underarms as though that could prevent them from being cooked right through. Like the naked, unmarinated sausages sizzling on their Fourth of July barbecue, Mina and her brothers swiveled and turned and hissed as their skin grew darker and thicker in the heat. All of winter and spring (season one and season two), Mina had tried to avoid going to the dry cleaner's where Darya worked, and now here, in season three in the midst of New York's summer, the dry cleaner's had come to her. The hot stifling air, the suffocating heat, the feeling that she could barely breathe; it was everywhere now. Stepping out of the front door was like stepping into Darya's dry-cleaning shop. And how was it for Darya? Mina wondered. To walk from the steamy dry cleaner's into a steamy world, to never really escape the all-encompassing invisible blanket of heat.

The promise of an air conditioner kept them hopeful. Baba hinted that they'd get one soon. That's how it was now. You waited. Money wasn't like before. You waited and worked and saved your dollars. And then maybe, you went and bought the desired item, most likely secondhand. "Get with it, Mina," Hooman said. He was quick to pick up American slang. "Get with the program." Air conditioners did not grow on trees in Queens. Mina slept in her white nightgown, the bedsheets sticky against her skin, nightmares free to roam and lodge in her newly American brain.

Mina's top-ranking nightmare of season three: NYPD chases eleven-year-old girl for lack of proper Islamic hijab.

Scene one: Mina is standing outside, leaning against the brick wall of their apartment. She's bouncing a small blue rubber ball or holding on to a crocheted orange bag or snapping pink bubble gum. Minding her own business. Footsteps. Mina turns around. Heavy footsteps. Approaching her. Clean-shaven, muscular, red-cheeked NYPD policeman approaches from behind. The faintest glimmer of panic begins its travel from the tips of her toes through her calves, up her thighs, to her wibbly-wobbly stomach. BAM BAM her heart starts to beat louder and louder. Panic, panic rising from fear. Mr. NYPD walks closer and closer to Mina. And then within seconds the metamorphosis occurs, the clean-shaven, rosy-cheeked NYPD man morphs into a dark-bearded, sallow-eyed, scowling Islamic Revolutionary Guard. Mr. NYPD is gone, and in his place stands the judgmental, scornful man in his heavy black boots who hated every strand of hair on her head, who

deemed illegal and immoral the bumps forming on her chest, who
thought sinful the curve of her lower back (too seductive), and who
would get her for not covering her schoolgirl thighs. The thought
that somehow her lack of proper covering would have a ripple effect and get her family into trouble engulfs her. Because the Revolutionary Guards work like spiders in a web, all they have to do
is pull at one strand, and soon the family is found: mothers and
fathers implicated, questioned, arrested, tortured, raped, killed.

Mina's lungs fill with dark, thick black oil. She wants to
breathe, wants to find the energy to run, to escape, but her lungs
are clogged. If only she could cover herself. If only she had the
hijab now, the long baggy billowing *roopoosh* to cover her legs, the
coarse thick headscarf to cover her naked head. She looks for cloth
to cover herself. She grabs at her T-shirt, wants to tear off a piece,
find something, anything, with which to cover her head and lessen
her crime. When she finally does manage to rip the T-shirt, the
piece isn't big enough. She breathes faster, and suddenly her lungs
are free of the thick black oil and she can run. She runs and runs
and runs, looking over her shoulder. The Islamic fundamentalist
is right behind her, running in his heavy black boots, catching up
with her, his rifle by his side, his face filled with disgust. Mina's
heart pounds against her chest, her hair flies everywhere as she
runs. He mustn't catch her, he can't get her, can't corner her. But
when he does, when the thick-bearded, sallow-faced, black-eyed
guard finally catches up with her and grabs her arm, she turns to
see her grandmother's face, scattered with bloodred pomegranate
seeds.

Mina woke up screaming. She clutched at her hair, wished
she'd never exposed herself, never taken her headscarf off, never

ventured to endanger everything and everyone she loved. She sat shaking in her bed, sweating from the nightmare and the New York summer night.

Darya ran into Mina's room. She sat by her bed, holding Mina tight. Over and over and over again she whispered, "You don't have to be afraid. It's okay. *They* are not here. We left. You don't have to be afraid of *them* anymore."

CHAPTER TWENTY-SIX

SPIDERCOBWEBGHOSTS- ANDGOBLINS

They spent a lot of time smearing blood on the walls, these people. Darya had volunteered to help decorate Mina's classroom for the Halloween party. One afternoon is all they asked of her and the other mothers. One afternoon, two and a half hours, the missed pay would hurt, but Darya wanted to contribute, wanted Mina to know that even in this new country she was engaged with her child's activities. Darya's assigned job was to take the red paint and make it look like blood. She managed to do that without actually vomiting. It was too close to the description Parviz had given her of the puddles near her mother's and all the other people's dead bodies. Blood was not a game.

Mrs. Beck, Mina's sixth grade teacher, smiled and patted Darya on the back. "You're doing real good," Mrs. Beck said extra loudly. In this country everybody talked loudly to her, sounding out the words as though they were speaking to a toddler, assuming her English was sketchy.

Darya smiled and nodded. For the sake of her daughter she resisted the urge to slap this painted woman across the face. "Thank you," Darya mumbled.

"AND YOU SEE, WE TAKE THE COTTON AND SPREAD IT OUT LIKE THIS SO IT LOOKS LIKE A COBWEB!" Mrs. Beck shouted to Darya and another foreign mother, Mrs. Kim. Yung-Ja Kim and her daughter Yooni had arrived from Korea just a few weeks ago.

"FOR A SPIDER! FOR HALLOWEEN WE DO SPIDERS!" Mrs. Beck joined her thumbs together and alternately twisted them and her forefingers together as she mimed the movements of a spider. "YEAH?" She raised her eyebrows.

"Yes," Darya said. She and Yung-Ja Kim held opposite ends of a large cotton pad and pulled to separate the soft fibers.

"WE STICK IT WITH GLUE!" Mrs. Krupnick handed Darya a white plastic bottle with an orange cap. "MAKE SCARY!!!"

Why is she using incorrect grammar? Darya thought as she glued cobwebs onto Mina's sixth grade classroom wall. She thought of the costumes she had to finish for the kids. Mina wanted to go as a fairy. Hooman wanted to be an Adam Ant, whatever that was, and Kayvon insisted on going as Ronald Reagan.

Mrs. Beck talked about their classroom-decorating goals and made the noise of ghosts howling. The sound effects were for the benefit of Darya and Yung-Ja. She showed them cutouts of skeletons and graveyards, as though such things were fun. For the life of her, Darya couldn't understand why so much effort was spent in scaring the children. She shuddered at the skull and bones pasted on the classroom door. She dipped her hands in pretend blood with the other mothers.

Some of the parent volunteers prepared a huge bowl of blood-colored Kool-Aid, pouring red crystals into a punch bowl and stirring with a wooden spoon. "How about we scatter drops of paint, washable of course, from the classroom door to the Kool-Aid bowl, and the kids can follow the blood and get their ghost cookies?" one of the other mothers said.

Yung-Ja Kim and Darya looked at each other, horrified.

"My apologies, but I must pipe in here and assert that I do believe that is a dreadful, albeit creative, proposition!"

Darya turned to see who had spoken up. One of the mothers emerged from the group standing by the Kool-Aid bowl. Her dark hair hung in a braid down her back, and she wore a beautiful sari. Other than Yung-Ja Kim and Darya herself, she was the only mother who had taken care with her makeup and dressed well for the occasion.

"Allow me to introduce myself." The woman in the sari walked past Mrs. Beck and extended one hand out to Darya and another to Yung-Ja. "Kavita is the name. Kavita Das. Mother of Pria."

"I am very pleased to meet you." Yung-Ja bowed her head. "I am Yooni's mother."

"And my daughter is Mina," Darya said. "Nice to meet you."

"So glad you guys met!" Mrs. Beck said. "Now, let's get back to work, ladies! We can ditch the blood drops, okay? We don't need to go overboard."

The mothers got back to work. As they picked up scissors and glue and decorations, Kavita lowered her voice and said to Darya and Yung-Ja, "Don't worry. Halloween is actually quite good fun. You'll get used to it."

Darya and Yung-Ja must have looked skeptical because Kavita then said, "You know what? I would like to invite you to my humble abode for a proper welcome to our coterie. Would you like to join me for tea after this?"

Yung-Ja nodded and said thank you. Darya looked at Yung-Ja and then at Kavita and felt a little better about the whole scary ghost/skeleton holiday. "Yes," she said. "I would like that."

ON HALLOWEEN NIGHT, MINA WORE Darya's home-sewn glittery pink fairy costume and purple wings. Hooman pranced around the living room in tight pants, playing air guitar.

"You are an ant?" Parviz asked. "You don't look like an insect."

"Oh, Baba, I'm Adam Ant! A rock star! Come on, everyone knows him!"

Kayvon tightened his tie and practiced his politician handshake on Darya and Baba. When he put the Reagan mask on, Darya squealed in fear.

She glanced at Parviz. He shrugged back at her. Something was slipping away from them. Something new was taking shape. It was a familiar feeling; they'd experienced it many times before as parents. Children changed all the time, phases came and went. It was impossible to keep up with all their tastes and interests. But this time, the very territory was an alien one. Autumn, Darya thought, meant pomegranates. Pomegranates seeded by your mother, eaten with a teaspoon with some echinacea powder. Autumn meant getting ready for the korsi. Heating up the stove as the nights grew longer and taking out the heavy quilt and throwing it over the heater and sticking your legs inside. None of this dressing up, sugar-eating, blood-smearing, spidercobweb-ghostsandgoblins stuff. So much time and effort and money spent on making things frightening. Why would they want to feel horror? Why would they look for it, make it up, create blood where there was none, play with graves as though they were toys? Darya watched her children get revved up for a night of fear and sugar. *Who are these people?*

THE FIRST AUTUMN FELT STRANGE. And then, year after year, the autumns came and went. From their very first one that arrival year when Mina dressed as a fairy to the ones in junior high, high school, and later in college when she dressed as a cat, Madonna, and Frida Kahlo among other characters. The autumns came and went.

Mina, age sixteen, her Halloween costume that year a polka-dot black and white dress, which, she explained to Darya, symbolized a Zen zebra.

"A Zen what?"

"Oh, Maman!" was all Mina said.

Mina the teenager. Her closest friends: Michelle, Heather, Pria, and Yooni were often at their house during those years.

"Hi, Mrs. R.," the girls would say and plop sleeping bags on the floor.

"We brought *The Breakfast Club*," Michelle said.

"Emilio Estevez is so cute!" Mina ran her fingers through her hair. Darya wondered why she kept doing that. It was a new habit of Mina's that she found annoying.

For the fall formal her senior year, Mina went with a certain

Julian Krapper. Darya and Baba waited outside the building where the dance was held, ready to drive Mina home as soon as the party was over. It was bad enough that Mina had a date. That much they tolerated. But there'd be no "after-party" or whatever it was these American kids called it. Julian walked Mina to the car after the dance and shook Baba's hand. He waited on the curb and watched as Mina and her parents drove away. Darya saw him standing there under the streetlamp in his tuxedo, waving to Mina. Mina waved from the backseat of the car for as long as he was in sight, then turned around and sulked the rest of the way home. Persian rules in New York City were "so not fair," she whined.

The autumns came and went. Darya learned that autumn meant wearing costumes, eating candy, and carving pumpkins. Parviz mastered the art of cutting the best jack-o'-lanterns. Darya strolled through the huge supermarkets, looking for a pomegranate. They gave up on having a *korsi* to warm their legs. They didn't need to sit in a circle, their legs under a quilt thrown over a heater. They blasted the central heat instead.

With each coming winter Darya felt a part of herself die. It took four seasons to feel at home. That's what Parviz always said. But for her it would take four hundred. The years rushed at them. And this country—the one they were supposed to stay in until things got back to normal back home—became the one in which her children grew up. Darya sucked in her stomach and fingered her thinning hair. She was growing old in the Land of the Tea-cups. Parviz excelled at his work, the pizza shop was left for the corridors of a hospital after he passed his medical exams and got his American license. He was back at the work he loved again. Darya no longer had to bend over the sewing machine at Wang

Dry Cleaning. She became a rightful stay-at-home mom for several years. Then Parviz's rousing speech, his support and enthusiasm, propelled her to math camp, and she even had the guts to apply for the job at the bank. She got promoted. Progress.

Their children were at the top of their classes. Michelle, Heather, Pria, and Yooni giggled in Mina's bedroom. Hooman made out with his blond girlfriend in the back of Parviz's car—Darya pretended she didn't know, but oh, she knew. Kayvon ran for Student Union president and got elected. Certificates of achievement filled their kitchen walls, the family room shelves were crowded with the boys' sports trophies. After college, Mina agreed to business school. Progress.

One day, Darya woke up and looked at her children as they slapped on sunscreen for their fifteenth Fourth of July barbecue and realized they were Americans.

But I will never be one. The children, maybe, with their slurry accents and soft-soled sneakers and the way they slurped creamy American milk shakes through straws. And Sam in her spreadsheet class, the man she felt pulled toward. *But I will never be.* The math notebooks from her university days, she hadn't even brought them over. They were still stuffed in a box under a bed in Agha Jan's house. What happened to the bed? Did Agha Jan sell it? Was he able to take care of himself? Was he lonely?

She'd watched July freedom fireworks on TV. Every year, she'd seen the colors explode, and every year it felt as if the fireworks and celebration weren't for her. She'd seen the lights reflected on her children's faces as they looked up with wonder at the night sky in those early years. She never had the heart to tell them that every burst, every loud explosion still filled her with heart-stopping fear. She instinctively felt the need to crouch, to fall on her knees with her hands on her head.

Now, in 1996, as she sat on the sofa after Mina had announced her desire to go back and visit Iran, she looked sideways at Parviz. He was reading the paper, a bowl of pistachios in his lap. Was he still upset about Sam? Was he hurt by that coffee/tea that was nothing? Darya sighed. It was just the two of them now. Hooman was with his wife in their Upper West Side apartment. Kayvon was probably still working at this late hour in his law offices in Midtown Manhattan. Mina was, hopefully, studying for her business school exams. Darya watched Parviz place pistachios in his mouth.

Had they made it? Were they almost there? Would they ever be?

She thought of Mr. Dashti and all the charts and graphs she'd ever made. She thought of the hours spent (wasted) on those men. Something about how her heart tightened when Sam was near her. It made her doubt all the graphs and charts she'd made for men. Maybe it wasn't so clear-cut. So black-and-white. She loved Parviz. She liked that Sam. It wasn't as simple as sheet rows and columns. It didn't add up that way. Now she knew.

PART III

1996

CHAPTER TWENTY-SEVEN

YOU'VE COME HOME TO US

People crept and muttered quietly as they inched their way through the passport check line. Small women swathed in chadors appeared out of nowhere. Bearded men in army fatigues stood in doorways. Darya and Mina had exited the plane, going down the metal stairs that had arrived on wheels, and they smelled the dusty night of Tehran once again. They hit the ground, and fifteen years evaporated. People spoke Farsi, the night air caressed their faces, the hustle and bustle and busy sounds seemed the same. Darya smiled her high school smile, the broad, chubby-cheeked version Mina had only seen in black-and-white photos from long ago. In those initial moments, it felt like coming back to something they knew. *Maybe you could go home again.*

It was the posters that jolted them out of their giddy feeling.

Immense pieces of fabric and huge rugs draped over the airport walls, cascading from staircase rails. Faces of the regime leaders, larger than life, looked down at everyone. Everywhere she looked, Mina saw them. The deep lines on their foreheads, the painted eyes and scowling expressions were far more jarring than the sight of real young men who peppered the airport in army fatigues, holding rifles. Mina didn't dare look directly at the faces of the guards, but it was clear from a stolen glance that these guards whom she'd dreaded years ago and who had featured in her nightmares for so long, were now younger than she. A few looked like teenagers. Mina recognized the uncomfortable stance of adolescence. She noticed acne sprinkled across one of the guard's faces, peach fuzz above his lips. The guard looked back at her, then looked quickly away, as if embarrassed. Mina almost felt sorry for him. But then she remembered that with a simple nudge of his rifle and a word to one of the airport bureaucrats, he could prevent her from entering Iran or keep her stuck there indefinitely. And then her pity returned to fear.

"Don't be afraid," Darya whispered as a few women shoved them and cut ahead in line. "Just stay calm. They can't do anything to us. All of our papers are in order."

How fearfully they'd left Iran, inching their way toward the passport officials, praying that nothing would go wrong. Now, here they were again, trying to reenter the country with that same sense of powerlessness and the knowledge that their fate depended on the whim of a bureaucrat. Mina prayed for the passport check man to be in a good mood. The barrage of horrifying images from the news had prepared her for half-beasts behind the airport counters, waiting with handcuffs and ropes to shackle returning exiles so they could transfer them to isolated torture cells simply for having the wrong stamp in their passport or for having a strand of hair sliding down their forehead. Mina tied her headscarf as tightly as possible for the umpteenth time. She knew it looked awkward, but she was unschooled now in the fine nuances that those who never left had surely mastered. She no longer knew how to walk with the correct mixture of modesty and confidence to show a Revolutionary Guard that she was not in the wrong.

She cleared her throat and rehearsed in her mind the short answers Darya had told her to give the bearded bureaucrat. Mina shook off the image of torture photos passed around by Amnesty International on the Columbia campus last month.

Darya nudged Mina. It was her turn at the window.

Behind the counter sat a girl, young and petite. Mina searched behind the girl for the airport bureaucrat. The girl tapped the counter and slid her skinny hand across. In her nervousness, Mina placed her own hand against the girl's, giving it, in effect, a mini high five. Realizing what she'd just done, Mina withdrew her hand, melting in embarrassment.

"Passport, please." The girl's voice was matter-of-fact, louder and more confident than Mina would've expected. Her whole demeanor was calm and composed, as though she were accustomed to dazed former exiles behaving strangely in front of her window.

Mina slid her passport across the counter. Darya had renewed Mina's Iranian passport especially for this trip; her exit permit was clearly printed. Mina knew because she'd checked it five dozen times. *You are not going back there until you are sure you can leave. Curiosity has its limits*, Baba had said as he nursed his biggest migraine yet since her decision to make this trip.

The girl flipped through Mina's passport. "When did you leave?"

"Fifteen years ago. With my parents and two brothers, we went to America, to New York. It was winter actually . . ." Darya had told her to keep her answers brief and to the point. But she couldn't stop rambling.

"Do you also have an American passport?" The girl interrupted Mina's monologue.

Mina stopped in midsentence. "*Baleh*. Yes." As soon as she said this, Mina felt she shouldn't have. Dual citizenship was not recognized by Iran.

"Can I see it?"

With shaking hands, Mina fumbled through her handbag and plopped the telltale navy blue American passport on the counter. What had she done? Would she get into trouble now? Her university's chapter of Amnesty International wouldn't even know to post her photo during their next campus demonstration for political prisoners. Did the girl have any idea that this passport was the result of years of hard work, endless visits to the Immigration and Naturalization Service office, loops of forms filled out at her parents' dining room table, and years of waiting? It was only with this passport that they weren't harassed at airports and no longer needed special visas to visit other countries. Did the girl know what she cupped in her hands?

Mina sweated under her headscarf. Her poor mother. From her peripheral vision, Mina saw Darya rock back and forth impatiently on her heels as she waited behind the yellow line a few feet away. Was she imagining it, or was Darya's forehead vein throbbing at diesel speed? Of course it would be.

The girl stroked the passport cover with her tiny thumb. Then she slid it back across the counter to Mina.

"Thank you," she said.

Mina stood across from the girl, dizzy.

"Go on. Next!" the girl called out to the queue.

Quickly, Mina shoved both passports back into her handbag and almost tripped as she stumbled away from the airport counter. She power walked toward a staircase a few feet over and leaned against the rail to catch her breath. The bottom of a heavy fabric poster depicting a scowling leader caught on her headscarf and almost yanked it off. Mina tried to remain nonchalant under the watchful eyes of the guards.

She looked in the direction of the girl's counter and saw that it was now Darya's turn. Mina's heart pounded as she absorbed the reality of how much power that girl had over them. Darya said something, laughed, then made a face as if imitating a crazy person. Mina couldn't see the girl's face from where she stood, but she guessed that Darya had expertly switched into that quick intimate manner she had with other Iranians, joking and acting as if she and the girl were the best of friends.

WHEN DARYA WAS CLEARED, THEY went to the baggage claim and then to the arrival gate. There Mina saw a group of people holding yellow and white flowers, some red carnations, a bouquet of pink roses. They drank from Styrofoam cups. A stainless steel thermos was being passed around. It was four in the morning and there they were, craning their heads, searching the faces of the arriving passengers. Then a few of their hands rose up in the air, waving.

"Darya Joon!"

"Mina?"

"*Een Mina-e?* Is this Mina?"

When Darya and Mina approached the group, they were engulfed in hugs. Mina was kissed, her cheeks pinched, her body squeezed in excited delight.

"*Mashallah! Mashallah!*"

"Would you look at her? That's our little Mina!

"Darya Joon! Mina Joon! May I die for you!" In her jet-lagged daze, Mina recognized Aunt Nikki's voice. It came out of the mouth of a woman whose headscarf was slipping, showing gray hair beneath. A woman whose face was lined, whose slender figure was now round and wide. Darya squeezed her sister tight.

A team of small children tumbled around exuberantly. Darya held her hand to her heart and exclaimed. "And you must be Arianna!" she said. "And you are Mehdi, right? Look at your cousins, Mina! Look at them!"

Mina looked at the row of small round faces, some of them missing teeth, a few of them shy, all of them strangers. These were the cousins she'd never seen. "How big you've gotten!" Darya said as she hugged each of them. And Mina thought, *But we never saw them when they were smaller.*

Fingers touched Mina's face, she was embraced by Uncle Jafar. Small black dots danced in front of her eyes. Maybe it had to do with the plane ride, the exhaustion, but her vision was blurred. Aunt Firoozeh was near her, her hair clearly dyed light brown, her gray roots showing from the front of the headscarf, her cheeks sagging below her chin now. She wept into a handkerchief.

A tall woman wearing a white headscarf smiled at Mina.

"Leila Joon! Leila-ye Aziz!" Darya hugged Leila.

Mina suddenly remembered Mr. Johnson standing across from Leila at her tenth birthday party, nibbling the tips of his glasses, his arm pushing against the wall near her shoulder. Mamani's wish to get Leila out of Iran.

Leila pushed forward two fair-skinned, hazel-eyed children, a boy and a girl around eight and five. "See?" she said as she bent near them. "It's Mina Joon. Here all the way from America!" Mina hadn't heard Leila's voice in fifteen years. Where was Mr. Johnson?

Then she saw her grandfather. He stood at the front of the crowd. How had she missed him? He wore his khaki suit, his pants were crisply ironed, his white shirt starched. He held a pink rose. He held Darya for a very long time, then turned to Mina.

"You've come home. *Omadi peesheh ma.* You've come to us."

It was the same voice that used to tease Mamani as they bantered in the kitchen, the one that called out Mamani's name in the middle of the night, in his sleep, unabashedly romantic, on the nights Mina had slept over at their place. He looked at her now with rheumy eyes. She walked over and kissed both his cheeks. Agha Jan took Mina's face in both his hands. She could see the hazel eyes so much like her own mother's.

"We have missed you," her grandfather's voice from long ago said. Only she heard it now, in the present. He was in front of her. "We have missed you so very much. Did you know that?" A few of the adults in the group stayed silent as they watched Agha Jan put one arm around Darya and one around Mina. Aunt Firoozeh started it. With the wet hanky in one hand, she started to clap, and the rest of the group—Leila and her two children, Aunt

Nikki and Uncle Jafar, the small collection of young cousins, and all the rest who had come there to greet them—broke out into applause even if a few of them had to clap against their thigh, due to their other hand being occupied, resolutely and expertly, with that perfect cup of tea.

CHAPTER TWENTY-EIGHT

RED LAMPS

*L*aboo! Laboo!"

A voice came from outside the window. Mina sat up in bed, not remembering where she was. Mamani's handmade quilt was over her, a black-and-white photo of her parents' wedding rested on the bureau, burgundy silk cushions were scattered across the bed and on the floor. Slowly, reality set in. She was in Mamani and Agha Jan's house. The voice from outside continued—it was both familiar and strange. Mina went to the window and saw a hunched man in a gray shirt and dark pants pushing a cart down the street. The beet seller. With his cart filled with hot cooked beets: *Laboo! Laboo!* Could it be the same bent-shouldered beet seller from years before?

"*Pasho*, wake up." Darya walked in wearing a lemon blouse

and white skirt, her hair freshly washed and blow-dried. "Come and have tea."

Breakfast was hot fresh *barbari* bread, feta cheese, homemade sour-cherry jam. (For a minute Mina wondered if it was Mamani's jam, but of course it couldn't be. Aunt Nikki must have made it at the end of summer, and saved it in jars for Agha Jan.) Steaming black tea. Agha Jan was listening to the radio. The announcer had that booming, melodramatic voice that had been a hallmark of Persian radio for as long as Mina could remember. It was easy to believe that the announcer was the same broadcaster from her childhood. And Mina wanted it to be the same person. But most of the media figures had been replaced, sometimes imprisoned, occasionally executed, at the time of the revolution. So it probably wasn't the same guy.

The clock in Agha Jan's kitchen was the same, the red-and-white chairs were the same. The wooden box the pigeons ate from outside the window still bore the traces of the flowers and fish shapes that Mina had painted years ago, in that other life. The cushions and the tables and the plastic roses in the vase were the same. But Mamani was missing. It seemed as if someone had set up all the props on a stage, but the lead actress had forgotten to show up. Darya whizzed around the kitchen, opening and closing cabinets, bringing out saucers and bowls and spoons for breakfast. Agha Jan spooned jam on his bread and chewed, listening to the news. The pigeons pecked at the bread in their box, and Mina sipped on her tea, which in this kitchen, in this home, at this time, tasted remarkably as though Mamani had brewed it.

"Leila called," Darya said. "She's coming tonight, to our welcoming party."

When Mina had left, she'd been ten years old and Leila had been nineteen. And now, she was twenty-five and Leila was thirty-four, married with two children, working as an engineer.

"I can't believe she married Mr. Johnson," Mina said.

"It's been a good match," Agha Jan said.

Mina remembered Mamani whispering into the phone, "I've found someone for Leila. If all goes well, she can leave Iran before she's twenty. She can study in England . . ."

"But they stayed in Iran," Mina said.

"Why wouldn't they?" Agha Jan said.

"Come on," Darya said to Mina. "Let's go for a walk. Go put on your *roopoosh*."

MINA WALKED BEHIND HER GRANDFATHER and Darya, who were huddled close together and chatting quietly, catching up on family gossip and changes in the neighborhood. Darya held on to the tweed of her father's jacket elbow, at once protective and dependent, helping him climb the curb, yet also hanging on to him. Mina wondered if Darya had dreamed of this walk. Even though the sun was weak, Mina began to see shadowy black spots floating in front of her eyes again. Was this still part of the jet lag? She wanted to swat at the spots like flies.

They walked past stores Mina had forgotten about. The dry cleaner's and the *noonvayi* bread shop. Still there. At the corner of the main street, Mina saw the greengrocer's shop. The one she always passed on her way to her grandparents' house. They had good pomegranates, but not as good as the ones at the store Mamani had gone to on the day she was killed. Mina followed Agha Jan and Darya into the shop.

The store was a small square room. In Mina's memory this place had been huge. There was dust everywhere. An unshaven man with red plastic slippers on his feet stood in one corner, smoking a cigarette. Bruised oranges and withered apples were stacked in carts around him. Carrots and lettuce lay in bins. Agha Jan bent over a cartful of cucumbers.

"Agha, let me help you," the grocer said.

"I can select my own cucumbers, may your hands not ache," Agha Jan said.

"As you wish," the grocer answered. Mina sensed that her grandfather and the grocer had had this conversation many times, had argued over cucumbers and carrots, maybe celery too. Agha Jan straightened himself, as if fighting for a sense of dignity, then handed the grocer his purchase.

"Two kilos." The grocer weighed the cucumbers on a scale.

"Check again," Agha Jan said.

"My mistake. One and a half. But I am not worthy of your payment."

Mina couldn't believe they were *tarof*-ing over payment. The grocer mumbled something about being a humble servant and about *farangi* guests. *Farangi*. Foreigners. Mina looked behind her for European tourists. But there were only her grandfather, tall as the Persepolis pillars, and Darya, standing by her father as any respectful Iranian daughter would. Mina looked down at her mud-caked, thick-soled, made-for-adventure hiking boots. It was she. The *farangi*. The foreigner.

Agha Jan added oranges to the scale, and the grocer summed up the total with a stubby pencil on a tiny pad of paper, then counted the *toman* bills Agha Jan gave him.

"May your eyes be brightened at the arrival of your guests."
He dropped Agha Jan's cucumbers and oranges into crinkly plastic bags and twirled the tops. He handed the bags to Agha Jan. Then he turned to Darya and bowed. "It's nice to see you again, Darya Khanom."

"And it's nice to see you again, Hussein Agha," Darya said.

Hussein Agha pulled out a chocolate egg from near the scale and gave it to Mina. "For you."

"Oh no, I can't," Mina started.

"It's yours. You must excuse my conditions. I am embarrassed. My shop needs repair. My fruit is not worthy. But if you break that chocolate egg in half, there is a little toy inside."

"Thank you," Mina said.

The sun was blindingly bright when they stepped out from the dark interior of the shop.

"He was just a kid when we left," Darya said. "He hung around and helped his dad with the store. Mamani used to give him extra change."

Mina turned around. Hussein Agha stood in the door frame of his shop, smoking next to his boxes of onions. When he saw her, he put his hand on his chest and bowed his head.

BACK ON THE STREET, MINA NOTICED that the cars were exactly the same. Even though it was 1996, most of the cars were still from the seventies, before the revolution.

"We're the pariah of the world now," Agha Jan said with a nervous laugh. "Other countries can't do business with us. These leaders have taken our country, hijacked it, and held us at the throat for years."

Three large metal stands with red lamps flanked the middle of the sidewalk. They seemed out of place. Mina looked up ahead and saw that there were at least two dozen lamps on this block alone.

"What are those?" Mina asked.

"For the soldiers that died," Agha Jan said. "In the war. You remember, don't you? The war with Iraq."

"Of course. I know. I was here."

"The war lasted eight years. You were here for one year." Agha Jan stopped walking. "Why does your government over there hate us so much?"

Mina froze in the middle of the street.

"Tell me, are we even humans to them? Do they know we also mourn every life lost?"

The sun blinded Mina, the black spots multiplied in front of her eyes. The American hiking boots suddenly felt as if they were filled with lead. Every one of Agha Jan's remarks pierced like a needle jabbing at her chest. The grandfather she had left was calm and wise. Not bitter. Mina wasn't responsible for America's actions, just as she wasn't responsible for Iran's. But always, the questions came. No matter which country she was in. People wanted an explanation.

"America sold arms to Saddam Hussein," Agha Jan went on. "Sold him weapons. To *kill* us with."

"Baba, enough." Darya pulled at her father's tweed sleeve.

"All I'm saying, Darya Joon, is why sell weapons to a madman who wants to kill us? I thought your country was a good power!" His breathing was labored now, heavy. He bent over and coughed fitfully. Darya patted her father's back, worry darkening her face.

When the coughing stopped, Agha Jan stood up again. Beads of sweat covered his forehead. He wiped his face on a handkerchief embroidered with two tiny lemons. Mamani must have made that one too. Mina stood glued to the ground in her hiking shoes, her head spinning.

"I am sorry, Mina Joon," Agha Jan finally said. "The war." He paused. "It has broken us." Then, as easily as if he were blowing his nose, he covered his face with the lemon-embroidered handkerchief and started to weep. Tears soaked Mamani's handiwork.

Rusty cars drove by. Cloaked women walked. Somewhere a child yelled. Darya held her father's hand as he wept. They just stood like that under the metal stands. Mina had not expected this. She had not known what she was coming back to.

Slowly, Agha Jan dried his eyes. The awkward way he dabbed his face made him seem like a small boy. He wheezed, then glanced around the dusty street helplessly, looking as if he might sway and fall. Then he said to the street, to Mina, to Darya, to no one in particular: "We are not ourselves anymore. We are damaged souls. Everyone you see in this country has been pushed to the limit. Those years of bombs. The needless deaths. This surreal life. We have become that which we were always proud not to be before. *Badbakht*. Destitute." He folded his handkerchief, then mumbled, "Forgive me, Mina Joon."

The red lamps on the metal stands swung above them. Mina saw all the streets of Iran in her mind's eye, hundreds and hundreds of red lamps for the boys who died, thousands and thousands for the dead in that war, so many lives cut short. She wanted to tell her grandfather that her new country wasn't what he accused it of being. But here she was again, in one country wanting to describe the truth of the other country—knowing she never really could.

"It doesn't matter," Mina said as Darya steadied Agha Jan and they started walking back. Darya's face was hollow. "It doesn't matter," Mina said again loudly.

Darya led the way home, and Mina staggered behind in her big hiking boots, clutching the chocolate egg. Slippered, chadored women scuffled by with bunches of radishes and scallions sticking out of their baskets. There was no red lamp hanging from a metal stand for Mamani. They all knew that. *It doesn't matter*, Mina had said. But as she stomped ahead, she knew the truth in her heart. Of course it mattered. It always would.

CHAPTER TWENTY-NINE

HOMECOMING QUEEN

The guests arrived at Agha Jan's house later that evening. Aunts, uncles, cousins, neighbors, friends came carrying bouquets of flowers and cardboard boxes full of sweet pastries. Some faces Mina recognized and others were like strangers. Everyone remembered her, though. And everyone was delighted to see the guest of honor: Darya. They were happy to see Mina too, but Darya was the real star. Mina had underestimated the love held for her mother by all the people back here. In Queens, when Darya had been bent over the sewing machine at the dry cleaner's, or struggling to chat with other mothers at Students' & Parents' Picnic Night, or even when she was punching a calculator at the bank, she had seemed awkward, unversed, clunkily foreign. But here she was confident, appreciated.

Mina heard her mother burst into peals of what sounded like a young girl's laughter. Darya marveled at her young nieces and nephews. She politely bowed her head to the older men who were Agha Jan's friends and former colleagues. She knelt down to better see the child who came in with flowers for her. "You gorgeous little lady!" she said, holding a dark tiny girl. She helped the server hired for the party—darting back and forth between the kitchen and living room, arranging pastries on platters, making sure there was always a constant supply of tea. She was both the guest of honor and the hostess.

Mina walked through the groups of people as she carried a tray of tea, smiling and saying thank you when the guests told her she looked like Darya, knowing that they were paying her their biggest compliment by saying that. Darya chatted with old university classmates. Mina noticed one particular ex-classmate whose face was red and excited. He couldn't take his eyes off Darya. How many of these classmates and friends were Darya's former suitors? Mina wondered. How many came and went and didn't make the cut? Why had Mamani picked Baba for Darya and vetoed the others? Were there others Darya would have preferred? Then Mina remembered that Darya had wanted math over marriage, at least at the time. She had other plans until it became clear that Mamani had marriage plans. Mina scoured the room as she passed out the tea. Was there a Mr. Dashti from Darya's past somewhere here?

A tall, blond man walked up to Mina then and held out his hand. "Pleasure. Absolute pleasure," he said in English.

Mina realized she was looking at an older version of Mr. Johnson, Baba's friend who had worked at the BBC, whom Aunt

Firoozeh had suspected was a British spy and who Mamani had hoped would whisk Leila away from Iran.

"Mina Joon! You remember William?" Leila came up behind him, a small girl clinging to her side and a boy holding on to her hand. "How's the jet lag?"

Mina put down the tea tray and shook Mr. Johnson's hand and hugged Leila. "Just fine," Mina said. "And you. How are you . . . two?"

"Oh, we're doing all right," Mr. Johnson said. "It's not all pansies and roses, is it? But we manage! Your engineer cousin here is working very hard on the postwar effort."

Leila smiled shyly. "Engineering's pretty big now. We're still rebuilding. They keep me pretty busy at the firm."

"That's so . . . wonderful," Mina said. And then, she couldn't help but ask the question on her mind. "I thought that maybe you two would have moved to England together?"

"Oh, I have everything I need right here." Mr. Johnson put his arm protectively around Leila. "The whole lot of you left! Best and the brightest and all that. Someone's got to contribute now, don't they?"

Mina suddenly felt guilty. "Yes, they do."

Leila squeezed Mina tight again. "It's good to see you," she said quietly. Then her daughter tugged at her and said she was thirsty and her son said he needed to go to the bathroom, and Mr. Johnson and Leila left Mina to attend to their children.

Mina sighed and picked up the tray again.

"Tell me, Mina Joon." Aunt Firoozeh came trotting over and pulled Mina by the arm. "Oh, put that tray down. Let me *talk* to you! Now, tell me about your studies. What is it you're studying again? Engineering?" Aunt Firoozeh's face lit up.

"Not engineering," Mina said. She felt as if she sounded like a ten-year-old when she spoke Farsi.

"Oh." Aunt Firoozeh looked disappointed. Then she brightened up again. "Is it law, then? Are you studying law?"

"Nope. That's Kayvon. He's the lawyer."

"Oh." Aunt Firoozeh studied Mina suspiciously. "Well, we all know Hooman is Mr. Doctor and you said you hated medicine, silly goose that you are. So what *are* you studying? I know Yasaman's niece in the U.S. is wasting her time on some phony art degree. Please don't tell me you're still doing that."

"Um, no. But I did do an art minor as an undergrad."

Aunt Firoozeh rolled her eyes.

"But I'm doing a master's in business now," Mina added quickly. "It's serious stuff."

Aunt Firoozeh started to clap and gave Mina a big smile. "Oh, goodie! At least that's something. Now then, tell me, Mina Joon, what you do for that degree. Tell me all about it."

Mina started to explain the core requirements for the MBA. Aunt Firoozeh hung on to every word as though she were a prospective student. While Mina rambled on in her fifth-grade-level Farsi, she noticed, out of the corner of her eye, a middle-aged woman with her brown hair in a big bun studying her carefully, looking her up and down. Mina knew that look. The woman was scoping her out as a prospective wife for her son/nephew/second cousin. Mina cringed. She moved Aunt Firoozeh in front of her, so her hefty body blocked Mina from the woman's view.

"So, you make all this on your computer?" Aunt Firoozeh asked. "Mina Joon, can you teach me the computer? I want to learn, but your uncle Jafar, he is so lazy, he says the computer is a ridiculous fad that will fade away, just like Polaroid cameras. He doesn't seem to understand all that I could do if only I had a computer . . ."

Mina nodded sympathetically, aware that the woman in the brown bun had shifted to get a better view of her from a different angle. She tried to ignore her and listen to Aunt Firoozeh's long list of all of Uncle Jafar's wrongdoings instead. Aunt Firoozeh checked off the professions she could've mastered if only Uncle Jafar had been supportive: a chemistry professor, a concert pianist, and/or a neuroscientist/brain surgeon.

"Wow," Mina couldn't help but say in English.

"You see, Mina Joon, it's all his fault. That's the problem. I was like that Madame Curie. I mean I *could have been*. But he never encouraged me. He should've encouraged me!"

Uncle Jafar appeared out of nowhere, holding a glass of tea. "Ah, I see you are talking this poor girl's ear off, Firoozeh Joon. Yes, yes, we all know that I am the reason you did not get your Nobel Prize. Yes, yes, go on, tell her, tell her all the things I've done wrong, give her the god-awful list. Did she tell you yet that she could've been a race car driver were it not for me intercepting her dreams?"

"I loved driving! I had talent! But how could I cultivate all my talents when I had to get up at five every morning to make Monsieur his tea? I could've been a lady doctor, you know!"

"Who's stopping you, Firoozeh Khanom? Go on, if you really mean it. Many people start university in adulthood. Go now, instead of nagging me all day long!"

Aunt Firoozeh's face turned purple. "It's too late now, isn't it? Who would make your many meals, Jafar, and who would take care of the house? Mina Joon, he'd probably starve if I wasn't around. In fifty years of marriage, he hasn't cooked the rice once. Once!"

Listening to them go on in that old familiar way, Mina marveled at where she was. She was here. Standing in front of Aunt Firoozeh and Uncle Jafar as they argued just as they had all those years ago. Aunt Firoozeh held her doughy hand to her cheek in outrage, while Uncle Jafar pleaded his case.

As they continued bickering, Mina slowly slipped away. She walked to the old yellow armchair in Mamani and Agha Jan's living room and sank into it. The seat still had the same lumps. That woolly almond scent of the velvet upholstery. Mina closed her eyes. Her mother's laughter floated in from the kitchen. From its pitch, Mina knew Darya was with Aunt Nikki. Darya only laughed like that when she was with her sister. The smell of basmati rice and fragrant herbs filled the house. Familiar voices from long ago chatted all around her. Mina rested her head back on the golden velvet and just listened. A bunch of children (her cousins?) shouted, "Marco!" "Polo!" She heard them run. Hadn't she and Hooman and Kayvon played this game in this very living room? She'd squealed past the adults of back then, past a younger Aunt Firoozeh and a dark-haired Uncle Jafar, as her mother laughed in the kitchen, then with Mamani, cooking the rice. Mina was lost in that sweet place between past and present. The memories of childhood games in this living room, at parties just like this one, meshed with the present sounds of laughter and chatter, with the smell of rice and *khoresh*, with the feel of the soft chair. She was here. It was as though they had all suddenly come back to life after being dead. No wonder she had felt out of place with Michelle and Julian Krapper; something was always just out of reach for her over there in America. All that time she had missed these people and hadn't even known it.

"Mina Joon, hello!"

Mina opened her eyes. Above her stood a tall young woman.

"Don't joke now. I know you remember me!" The young woman's dark eyes shone.

Mina looked up at her in silence. The woman placed her hand on her heart in mock disbelief, and her fingers triggered Mina's memory. Those long thin fingers, the unmistakable scar on the right hand from the cut when they tried to open a can of tomatoes in her mother's kitchen when they were nine.

"Bita?"

"*Baleh!* Yes! Welcome. *Koja boodi?* Where were you? Your place has been empty here!"

"But how did you . . . ?"

"Your mother apparently told her old friends to contact my mother to track me down. She knows how to do her research! I couldn't believe it when I heard you were back. You think I would miss your homecoming party? *Begoo, chetori?* Tell me, how are you? How on earth have you been?"

Bita took Mina's hand and laughed. Her laughter was both something from long ago, and something Mina had never stopped hearing. She knew that laugh. This elegantly dressed, sophisticated woman had the same laugh as the girl who had jumped on her bed as they danced to John Travolta in those days of war.

"I can't believe you came. You're actually here. *Bia bebeenam.*

Come and let me look at you!" Bita pulled Mina up into a semidance, semihug. She held Mina out at arm's length and regarded her.

"You're here," Bita said again. "You're really here."

DARYA HUMMED AS SHE PUT the last of the dirty *estekan* and plates into the sink after the guests had left. Mina still had the black spots floating in front of her eyes, but the chat with Bita had left her high. They had talked about old classmates and teachers and boys from the old neighborhood. This one's getting his master's in Canada, that one got asylum in Sweden, the tall one who teased them was a teacher in Tehran, and then there were those who went off to war and came back with fewer limbs or never came back, and the shy one who'd committed suicide. And Mrs. Amiri? A water aerobics instructor in Los Angeles now. Mina had listened to all of Bita's update as though in a dream.

Then Bita had made a statement toward the end of their talk that made Mina feel an unfathomable return of preadolescent excitement and nervousness.

"I'm having a party on Wednesday night. I want you to be there."

Later that night as Mina got ready for bed, she felt as though she'd just been invited to the royal ball at the queen's palace. Only, she reminded herself as she brushed her teeth, the king was dead and Queen Farah lived in a house in Connecticut and the crown prince was married to a lawyer somewhere in Virginia.

CHAPTER THIRTY

THIS IS NOT TIMBUKTU

mina and Darya shot up the silver skyscraper in northern Tehran in a shiny elevator equipped with a digital voice that called out the floors in Farsi. Darya had come to drop Mina off and to say hello to Bita's mother, her old friend.

"And remember to help," Darya said. "Make yourself useful. Don't just stand and watch. Help Bita prepare for the party."

The door of Apartment 3G was opened by Bita's mom, Suri. She looked almost the same—a poufy hairdo and red lipstick—except that her face was speckled with age spots.

"Well, look at you!" Suri said. "*Vay khoda*, my God!"

Darya and Suri kissed and hugged, then kissed and hugged again. Suri engulfed Mina in a big hug and kissed her too, then both Darya and Suri wiped lipstick off Mina's cheeks.

White leather couches flanked the spacious living room.

Bright paintings hung on the walls. Everything was hip and modern and fresh. Mina remembered a different set of furniture from before. Mina looked at the TV. Oprah was interviewing John Travolta. *Vay khoda* indeed.

"But . . ." Mina started. "What?"

"Come on, Mina, you must know that we watch everything you do in America. Satellite dishes are our friends! This isn't Timbuktu. It's *Tehran!*"

"I know . . . I never thought it would be . . . I mean, of course." Mina fumbled for the right words. "Oprah. Makes sense."

"Four times they've come and removed our satellite dishes," Suri said as she motioned for them to sit. "Four times we've been fined."

Darya shook her head in exaggerated empathy.

"Don't worry. We keep putting them back up. They want to forbid all contact with the rest of the world. But we're hooked up." Suri nodded proudly.

"You're hooked up all right," Darya said.

"We have CNN. We have BBC. We have—" Suri put her hands on her hips. "The Voice of America!"

Darya let out a whistle.

"Don't think we're all backward here, Mina Joon," Suri said.

Darya glared at Mina. Flicked her head just slightly to cue Mina to say something.

"Oh no, I didn't," Mina stammered.

"Let me help you with the food." Darya started for the kitchen.

"I won't let you touch a thing. You sit. I'll bring tea," Suri said.

"Come on, let me help."

After seventeen *tarof* back-and-forth statements with Darya insisting that they should help with the food for the "young people's party" and Suri insisting that as guests they should just sit and have tea and eat fruit and nuts and biscuits and some cake that she'd made just for them, a door slammed.

"*Salaam,* hello, hello!" Bita trotted in with a white towel wrapped around her head, and another towel wrapped around her body. Her face was red from her shower.

"Oh, Bita, get dressed before coming to greet guests!" Suri said.

"Well, hello, Khanom Beautiful, hope you had a good bathing time," Darya said.

"Thank you, thank you." Bita greeted Darya and Mina with shower-fresh kisses.

Bita pulled the white towel off her head. Dark hair dropped over her shoulders.

"Going to change!" she sang out. "Back in a sec!"

Because Darya was absolutely relentless in her *tarof* and would not take no for an answer, and because Mina pretended that she too really wanted to cook right then and there, Suri had no choice but to let them into the kitchen. Ceramic roosters stared at them from the kitchen shelves. On the glistening granite counter, they helped Suri put together a lentil, mint, and beet salad. Suri plucked leaves from the stems of washed mint, Darya chopped the mint into perfect pieces and added olive oil, vinegar, salt, pepper, and turmeric to Suri's cooked lentils. Mina chopped cooked beets into uneven clumps, the swirls on the pads of her fingers staining red.

A little bell sounded.

"That's my oven!" Suri pulled out a baking sheet filled with little sausages wrapped in dough.

"Oh!" Mina said. "Pigs in a blanket!"

Suri looked confused.

"Oh, that's just what they call it in the U.S.," Darya explained and gave Mina a look that said: There are no pigs in Iran.

"Oh, it's not actually pork, of course," Suri said. "It's beef. But it's quite good."

Mina only knew pork from going out with friends. Darya never served it. She made the kids order sweet-and-sour chicken in Chinese restaurants, never pork. Bologna sandwiches, if they ever had them at all, were beef bologna. The Jewish brands were Darya's favorites because "they are the closest to who we are." *The Persians and the Jews go way back*, Baba would always say. *Don't fall for this current political rhetoric. Heck, most of us WERE Jews and Zoroastrians before the Arabs invaded!*

"Don't work too hard, Mina Joon." Bita waltzed back into the kitchen wearing blue jeans and a sports bra.

"Oh, it's fine, it's no problem," Mina said. Mina had grown up in America while Bita had spent her adolescence in Iran shivering in basement shelters during the war, covering her hair with a headdress every day, and yet, in her presence, Mina felt like a dutiful, matronly lady servant. She felt suddenly very old-fashioned in her long, flowing, flowery dress that seemed *Little House on the Prairie*–ish next to Bita's casual wear.

Bita caught Mina looking at her outfit. "Don't worry, I'm going to change right before the party. I won't open the door with my bra on!" She bit into a non–pig in a blanket. "I wish it were real pork," she said. "I never had real pork till after the revolution, and then they said we couldn't have it. Now I eat it whenever I can. I like my pork roasted and spiced with chili flakes. I like it diced and salted. I like it on Thursday nights and on Friday mornings for breakfast." She grinned. "I loooove sausages!"

Suri stopped plucking. Darya stopped chopping. Mina looked at her beet-stained hands.

"Thank you, Bita, for sharing. Now grab a board and chop some onions," Suri said. "I've heard enough about your love of . . . *sausages.*"

Bita grabbed an onion and brought a knife down on it, hard. Mina mixed the beets into the salad.

"May this regime rot in hell!" Bita sang out and grabbed another non-pig, then swayed her booty in time with the onion chopping.

Suri, Darya, and Mina looked at one another and could do nothing but laugh. You couldn't stop Bita from being Bita.

JUST BEFORE 11:00 P.M., DARYA left with Suri so "you kids can have your space." Suri had arranged the food carefully on the tables and conveniently left the key to the liquor cabinet on the dining room table. Mina wondered if Darya would have gone to so much trouble for a party of Mina's in the States. But then, Mina didn't have too many parties. Baba and Darya were always worried about the possibility of drugs or alcohol being brought to their house. It was enough that their children lived in such a permissive culture. Baba and Darya erected boundaries wherever possible in order to maintain "decency." But in Bita's case, the opposite was happening. Her parents were going out of their way to help with her party and to ensure a good time for all. It was precisely because they lived in such a repressive country, with so much emphasis on the laws of "decency" that Suri compensated by giving her daughter free rein within the confines of their home.

Then the guests arrived. They came in couples, groups, some with their arms interlaced. They were all attractive and much hipper than Mina had expected. They had come for a good time, and at Bita's house, they knew they would have one. One girl pulled off her headscarf to reveal dozens of long thin braids glittering with beads. She came with a tall, green-eyed twentysomething man with a goatee. When the girl unbuttoned her *roopoosh*, Mina suppressed a gasp. She was wearing tight leather pants with a silver, shimmery, barely-there tube top. Her bare midriff showed off sixpack abs and a silver belly ring.

"You must be Mina. Bita has told me so much about you! You live in *New York*! I love New York!" the girl in braids said.

"If I can make it there, I can make it anywhere!" The greeneyed man in the goatee tipped an imaginary hat.

At that moment, Bita walked in—wearing a strapless black minidress with perfume and teased hair. She kicked up her legs, open-toed silver high heels piercing the air. "Da da da da dum, da da da da dum! It's up to you, New York, Neeewwww Yawk!" She grabbed the girl with braids and the man with the goatee and they joined her in an impromptu cancan. Soon the three of them fell over into a messy pile on the floor, arms and legs and spiky heels everywhere. They untangled from one another in a fit of giggles. When the man straightened up, he looked at Mina. Even though he was still laughing a bit, his eyes seemed sad. He pulled at his goatee. "Well, welcome," he said to Mina. "Welcome to Iran."

Bita untangled her arms from her friend's. "Mina, this is Lilly." She pointed to the girl with the braids and the belly ring. "And this," she said as she poked the man with the goatee in the stomach, "is her boyfriend, Massoud."

"I'm very happy," Mina said. "I'm very happy . . ." She faltered, not sure how to go on in formal Farsi. "I'm lucky to meet you," she said, trying to use the correct, polite formalities.

Massoud and Lilly looked puzzled and exchanged a glance with Bita.

"Oh, don't be so official and old-fashioned!" Bita said. "Come on, it's the *nineties!*"

They all laughed. Mina laughed too, but nervously.

"Do you think the guards are patrolling around here tonight?" Massoud pulled at his goatee, surveying the windows.

"Don't worry, I'll take care of them," Bita said.

Lilly high-fived her. "Hey, do you have Tupac's latest CD?"

"You bet. I'm not just going to play Madonna! You guys want some wine? Gin and tonics?"

Once they got their drinks, Massoud, Lilly, and Bita talked about music. Mina stood close and tried to join in, but she had nothing to say. She kept thinking about how Bita had introduced Massoud. Lilly's "boyfriend." Just like that. She thought boyfriends weren't allowed. Baba and Darya always said Persian girls didn't do the boyfriend thing. *Thou shalt study and work hard and get straight As, and then, once thou hast achieved thy college degree, thou shalt marry a Persian man who has a secure, respectable position in life, and thou shalt have babies and take care of thy husband, home, children, and career.* Baba and Darya's code of conduct seemed startlingly old-fashioned here. Mina felt ridiculous in her long floral dress. She felt like a nerd crashing the cool people's party.

Lilly and Massoud were kissing now. Mina awkwardly backed away from them toward the food.

"Oh, those two!" Bita shrugged. "Lovebirds! In their own nest of bliss. You know what I mean?"

"Yuppo," Mina said. She had a flashback of Mr. Dashti sipping tea at her parents' house in Queens.

THE GUESTS DANCED. THEY SWAYED to the rock and roll and sang the lyrics of the American Top 40. They were shocked that Mina didn't know all the lyrics. "But don't you live there?" they asked with baffled looks. "Wouldn't you listen to the Top 40 every day if you actually lived in America?" Mina shook her head. No, you wouldn't. Not necessarily. It's not like that. It's not like that over there.

Most of the guests were couples. Dating. Going steady. A few were single, like Bita, who had recently broken up with a man she only referred to as Silly Sassan.

Bita introduced Mina to a tall thin girl who looked like a model and used to be Massoud's old neighbor. She was now engaged to Lilly's second cousin. Mina nodded and smiled and tried to say the right things in Farsi. A pattern soon emerged. Upon hearing that she was Bita's old friend from the States, the guests' initial reaction was one of excitement and curiosity. But then, after a few moments of small talk, it became clear to the guests that Mina was a bit square. After a period of polite exchange, the guests inevitably tuned out and walked off, uninterested. The men's eyes would begin to roam, and the girls would look bored and move on. And soon, Mina stood alone by the food table, watching everyone dance.

"I know you know this song!" Bita yelled at Mina from the dance floor. "Come on!"

Mina walked over to her awkwardly. Bita grabbed her hand.

"I guess I just don't keep up with the top hits," Mina said, doing something in between a bounce and a prayer movement, trying to mirror Bita, but feeling utterly out of step.

Bita swayed her hips seductively. "You don't get out much, do you?"

"I'm usually . . . busy," Mina mumbled. "It's not like everyone in the States just parties."

Bita thumped her body to the beat. "If I were there," she said, panting, "I'd enjoy every single freedom-dripping moment."

A short chubby girl in a green leather dress started to dance wildly and soon a group of other dancing guests formed a circle around her. Bodies twisted, stretched, shrank. The guests made themselves into tight balls, lowered themselves to the floor, rose up again, jumped to the beat. They thumped and bounced, lost in the flow. Dirty dancing took over. Mina tried to keep up. Everyone around her knew the moves. The forces outside the apartment were being exorcised. They were sticking it to the Revolutionary Guards. Freedom was available, in short spurts, indoors. A fugitive dance.

The group grooved and thumped, closing in on Mina. The air was sexually charged. Mina began to nudge her way through the sweaty bodies. After pushing her way past elbows and flung arms and moving bottoms, she finally slid out of the cluster of dancers. She scurried to the wall, back near the table of food. It was too loud. It was too much. She was worried that a guard might burst in. She needed water. She went to the kitchen, the music pounding in her ears, black spots appearing in front of her eyes.

MINA FELT RELIEF ONCE INSIDE the oasis of Suri's well-lit kitchen, with its granite countertops and ceramic roosters. The swinging door closed behind her, and she leaned against it, closing her eyes as the sound of the blasting music diminished slightly. She took a deep breath.

Suddenly, she was flung across the room. She barely caught onto the counter's edge and tried to balance herself. Her flowery dress had ridden up her legs. Dizzy, Mina put her hand to her forehead to shield her eyes from the fluorescent kitchen lights. She tried to make out the figure standing in the door.

"Are you okay?" a man said.

Mina faltered for a moment and just stared. The man wore a blue dress shirt and khaki slacks. His dark hair was cropped short. He looked vaguely familiar, but she didn't know why. This man was the only other person here who wasn't dressed for a glitzy nightclub. He looked more Friday business casual. And he had spoken in English, with an American accent.

"I'm sorry, I didn't mean to scare you," he said, coming closer. "I didn't know anyone was behind the door. Are you—" He looked at the long flowing dress tangled between her thighs, and then again at her face. "Are you all right?"

"Yes, yes, of course." Mina felt her face redden. She gripped the hem of her grandma dress and tried to tug it back down, but it was badly tangled and she had to pull hard. "I'm just fine," she said, trying to look cool and composed as her dress finally fell into place. She looked up. He had a clean-shaven face and huge brown eyes.

"Good. I'm so sorry."

Mina stood extra tall to show him she was just fine. Even with the black spots still dancing in front of her eyes, she could see how handsome he was.

He pulled up one of the kitchen stools for her and held out his arm. Mina scooped up her long dress and hesitated, but then climbed up on the stool clumsily, holding on to him. He sat on a stool next to her.

"You must be Mina," he said, smiling. He had perfect teeth.

"How do you know my name?"

"Bita told me that her old friend was visiting from the States." He smiled at her long puffy dress, gathered near her knees. "That would be you, no?"

"Yes."

The ceramic roosters in Suri's kitchen looked at them. Muffled beats from outside the kitchen thumped away.

"And, um, where are you from?" She cursed at herself for asking a stupid question. Of course he was Iranian. She could tell from looking at him. But the perfect English. The lack of an accent.

"Connecticut," he said.

Just the word Connecticut made Mina suddenly homesick for the States. Clean grass, mochaccinos, and newspapers in English. Normality. As opposed to this strange mix of Hollywood/Soho nightlife in the midst of Islamic fundamentalism.

"I'm Ramin, by the way," he said. "Pleased to meet you."

"Pleased to meet you too," Mina said. When she spoke to him, it felt as if she were falling, sliding off the stool.

He extended his hand for a shake.

"Connecticut?" She shook his hand. It felt big and clean.

"Transplanted to. Iranian-Connectican."

They both smiled now. Mina felt at ease. Even though he'd thrown her across the room, he had somehow steadied her.

MINA SPENT THE REST OF Bita's party in the kitchen. Ramin told Mina about Connecticut and his job at an architectural firm. He had moved to America when he was fifteen. He was back in Iran now for just a week, visiting his sick grandmother, who was on the verge of death. He'd had to pay a hefty sum of *toman* to avoid being drafted into the army upon entry. Like many exiles, he hadn't served the mandatory army duty required of all Iranian males.

"You risked a lot by coming back," Mina said as she sipped the sherbet drink he'd made for her. "They could have drafted you."

"We were very close, my grandmother and I," he said quietly. "During the revolution, she lived with us. I knew it was risky to come, but I couldn't let her die without seeing her. My parents sent my brother and me to the States when I was a teenager because of the revolution. And that was the last time I saw my grandmother, and we never really got to say good-bye. We stayed with my uncle in California and thought we'd be back by the end of the summer. But sixteen years passed. So this time, I had to come."

He got up and took Mina's empty glass from her hand. He made them more sherbet drinks, using the cherry syrup bottle that Suri had left on the counter. Mina watched his strong hands swirl the syrup into the water as the dark red cloud rose higher in the glass. As Ramin sat next to her again, the music in the other room was momentarily muted, the dancing bodies outside that door temporarily forgotten.

Suddenly, the door swung open and Bita flew into the kitchen. Her hair was now puffed up like the mane of a lion. Her glittery makeup sparkled on her face.

"Mina? Mina!" Her voice was wobbly with too much wine. "There you are!" She stopped when she saw them. Mina and Ramin were perched on the kitchen stools, cherry sherbet glasses in their hands, talking with their heads close.

"Oh," Bita said. "Oh. You're fine. I see that you're fine." She seemed amused. She smiled as she walked out backward, tottering on her heels, twirling when she reached the door.

Ramin looked at Mina without saying anything for a minute.

"Seems like you're fine," he said, not taking his eyes off her.

Mina felt her face burn under the fluorescent kitchen light.

"Seems like I am." She raised her glass. Ramin raised his too. And there under the supervision of the ceramic roosters their glasses touched. And when they clinked, something scattered in front of Mina's eyes. In the tiny diamond of space where their glasses joined, the black spots in front of her eyes burst and split and finally broke away. With that *clink*, they were gone.

And she could see just fine.

DAWN SPREAD INTO THE GRAY night sky and aroused prayer callers. The guests quietly donned their Islamic uniforms, head-scarves, and coats and got ready to tiptoe outside. The colorful, laughing, dancing scantily clad girls all became veiled women, like a row of crows, marching on, driving on back home. The boys straightened themselves out and walked away from the girls they had been holding, touching, loving. They would walk or drive home separately. Mina watched as Cinderellas turned to paupers, as the magic coach turned back into a pumpkin. It was that kind of hour. It was that kind of transformation.

Later, when Mina and Bita sank into the pillows of Bita's bed, the necessary reflecting on the night began. Darya had liked the idea of Mina spending the night at Bita's and not having to worry about the hassles of returning home late. Now Bita updated Mina on new alliances forged through the party. She mentioned with awe the best dancers of the night. Mina tried to listen but all she could think about was the man from Connecticut. She kept replaying their evening in her head. As he had reached to take his coat from the hook in the foyer, he had thanked Bita and turned to Mina.

"Good night."

Mina had pointed to the slowly emerging dawn outside the window. "Morning."

They had stood awkwardly in the foyer. He put on his coat while Mina waited by the door. He had looked into her eyes one more time, and there was a pull, an energy that was almost tangible. And Mina felt herself falling again, falling down, down, down.

"Good morning, then," he'd said. And then she'd watched him walk out onto the corridor and into the elevator.

"So?" Bita nudged Mina.

"What?"

"Seems like you liked him?"

"Liked who?" It was a throwback to their school days, only

now they weren't talking about the crown prince and John Travolta.

"You know." Bita playfully hit Mina with a pillow. "The guy you sat with and talked to in the kitchen for the *entire* party."

"Yes, very nice, he was quite nice really."

Bita giggled into her duvet cover.

"He's not bad looking either! He's my friend Toofan's old classmate. Toofan asked if he could come along tonight." Bita snuggled under the covers. "A bit serious, though." She paused. "How come you guys who live in the States are so serious?"

Mina shrugged. She had no answer.

"I've already invited a huge group of my friends back for a breakfast get-together on Friday morning. I can ask Toofan to make sure to bring Mr. Dashti too."

"What?" Mina was suddenly sitting up in the bed, her staticky hair forming temporary antennas around her head. How on earth did Bita know about Mr. Dashti? "What did you say?"

"Mr. Dashti," Bita repeated. "You know, Mr. All-Night-Talking-in-the-Kitchen. Mr. Dashti."

"Is that his last name? We never even mentioned last names." Mina stared at her, shocked.

"Very American of you. Well, his name is Mr. Dashti. He has an architectural degree. Lives in Connecticut, as you know. Apparently his older brother is some hotshot with Kodak or something in Atlanta."

Mina plopped back onto the pillow and stared at the ceiling, then slid down under the covers. "Oh my God," she whispered. "Oh my God."

"What is it? You okay?"

Mina poked her head out from the duvet and nodded yes.

"You're all pale! I think you really like him!" Bita tucked the duvet around Mina. "Now go to sleep. You can see him again at the breakfast in two days." As she closed her eyes, Bita murmured, "He had the nicest teeth, don't you think?"

"Yes," Mina said as she prepared to lie awake. "The nicest teeth."

MINA DIDN'T SLEEP. SHE SAT upright in bed, as Bita snoozed peacefully beside her. Without her makeup, Bita's face looked more familiar. Mina thought of Ramin. She found herself smiling involuntarily, like a crazy person, remembering when she'd made him laugh. She felt a surge of energy every time she remembered her successful, witty comments. And she cringed at the moments when she'd been awkward or flat or silly. But still. *Still.* There had been more good moments, and their conversation had been so easy, and he had been so sweet. The thoughts raced round and round in her head, keeping her up, keeping her alert, keeping her busy. Then she remembered that he was a Mr. Dashti. What were the chances of her coming all the way to Iran and meeting Mr. Dashti's brother? How on earth could she not have noticed some resemblance? (The teeth! The teeth were exactly like his!) Did he even know she had met his older brother for tea at her parents' house? The questions swirled in her head as Bita snored on. Eventually, Mina made herself lie down and shut her eyes. But her mind was still humming. On top of all the other questions, one question stood paramount. With all her experience, her networks and research collated with Excel graphs, how on earth did Darya miss this bachelor sitting right next door in Connecticut? How could her mother, who had located attractive, intelligent men all over the U.S. of A. and beyond, have missed this quiet architect, with his blue shirt and khaki slacks, sketching away at a drafting table in Connecticut? *Oh, Maman,* Mina thought, as she finally started to give in to sleep. *If you only knew.*

CHAPTER THIRTY-ONE

BREAKFAST BY
THE KOI POND

Two days later, Bita and Mina carried the samovar out to the garden. Bita had insisted that the breakfast be held outdoors, since it was an unusually mild day for December. Mina had come early to help Bita prepare.

"Mr. Dashti should be here soon, but Toofan said they might be a bit late," Bita said, then launched into background information. "Toofan said Dashti grew up in America. He didn't go there with his parents. He and his older brother stayed with their uncle in California at first. He works in Connecticut now, and his older brother . . ."

"I've met his older brother."

"In New York?"

"Yes, in New York."

"You know him?"

"We've met."

"I see." Bita's expression implied that she'd ask a lot more questions later.

They put the samovar on a folding table. Mina arranged the fresh *lavash, barbari,* and *sangak* breads on a tray. She cut the feta cheese into thick slices. The jams were Suri's own—fig, quince, and sour cherry. Mina remembered the sour-cherry jam Mamani used to make, her cotton apron stretched around her thick middle, her sleeves rolled up in the summer heat, part of her hair stuck to her forehead as she stirred the contents of the copper pot on the stove. Mina would stand on her tiptoes and watch the cherries start to bubble. Darya had not met, did not even know, this younger brother. This younger brother with his kind brown eyes and perfect teeth.

Bita's parents' apartment complex had a small manicured garden in its courtyard. A blue-tiled koi pond complete with lily pads and goldfish was its centerpiece. The walls surrounding the courtyard were high and made of cement. This meant the garden was safe from outside view.

Soon, Bita's friends arrived for the breakfast get-together. Mina recognized some of them from the party. The guys wore casual jackets and jeans this time, and the girls wore jeans and brightly colored *roopoosh.* Some of the girls, including Mina and Bita, even pulled off their scarves, feeling safe enough in the courtyard from the eyes of the Revolutionary Guards. Apparently, there was an unspoken agreement among the apartment complex residents to not rat on one another. But they kept their scarves around their necks, ready to pull them on if necessary. Mina felt as if they could be in the States except she would probably not be hanging out with so many good-looking, fun young people in the States. This was the in crowd.

The folding tables were now covered with small gifts the guests had brought: baskets of fruit, a pink orchid in a pot, nougat candy. Sweet black chai steamed from small glasses. Frothy cappuccino spurted from Bita's dad's machine.

When Ramin arrived, he handed Bita's mom a bouquet of flowers, then came to greet Bita and Mina. Suddenly Bita remembered that she needed to go and do something and left Mina and Ramin alone. Ramin poured two glasses of orange juice and sat next to Mina on one of the lawn chairs. Mina told him about Professor Van Heusen and the time he called on her when she hadn't read the case. She told him about her decision to visit Iran. Ramin sipped on his juice and listened. Time slowed down. Other guests came and went in the background, carrying food, bringing back plates, throwing away used napkins, poring over newly developed photos from the party. Mina and Ramin stayed seated and talked. Black hair, dark eyes, light skin, bright clothing—two people pulled together. And, years from now, years and years from now, could they be sitting on two lawn chairs, their hair gray, their eyes faded with cataracts, their skin wrinkled—but still together, chatting away?

A few of the pigeons grew bolder and descended from the garden wall onto the ground near their chairs. An old couple. Old friends. Mina could see it. She downed her tea. She must be going nuts. Having all these Darya-esque thoughts, seeing into the future and imagining their hair growing light with age. It was just a breakfast. He was just an architect from Connecticut, visiting his grandmother. He was Mr. Dashti's younger brother, for goodness' sakes. He was not her future husband!

"He loves chemistry," Ramin was saying. "But business school opened a lot of doors for him, and Kodak was the perfect job. I missed him the last time he was in New York. He was there only recently, but I was away in the Midwest at a conference. I haven't seen him in a while." Ramin balanced his glass on the arm of the lawn chair. "So, that's my brother! Anyway, you have two older brothers? Are they in New . . ."

"I've met your brother . . ." Mina said abruptly.

She felt as if the pigeons had stopped and stared. Mina went on and recounted the day the older Mr. Dashti came to visit.

Ramin listened to the whole story, eyes twinkling. Mina was surprised at her own lack of self-censorship.

"And then he said thank you and drove away, and my parents and I put away the dishes," Mina finished. "So you see, I've met your older brother."

Ramin was quiet for a moment, his chin cupped in his hand. He grinned. Then he chuckled. He looked at Mina sideways and started to laugh. Mina bit her lip and started to snort and giggle. Soon they were both laughing.

"We have such beautiful traditions, don't you think?" Ramin said.

"Oh yes," Mina said. "Amazing ones that aren't embarrassing *at all*!"

Ramin laughed. "You've got to hand it to your mom, though. She does her research well."

"Not that well," Mina said shyly. "She somehow missed finding you all this time."

"Aha!" A crimson blush rose from Ramin's neck to his ears. "Well, I'm not that easy to pin down," he said. "My statistics are unlisted. I don't own too many suits. I don't drink much tea. And I'm not one for putting down roots."

The pigeons were at their toes now, nibbling on crumbs from their *naan*. A plane roared above. A piece of bark from one of the trees fell into the koi pond, and the water rippled in front of them.

"Did he wear his beige suit?" Ramin asked.

Mina looked at the pond and nodded. "He did."

"He loves that suit," Ramin said.

WHEN SHE REACHED AGHA JAN'S front door, Mina wasn't sure if she had actually walked up the steps just behind her. All the songs were true. Yes, believe it or not, I *am* walking on air. I swear, I know, I've never loved this way before. Yes, you *are* so beautiful to me. It *is* a wonderful world. Every campy lyric flew into her head and made sense. No wonder. No wonder those lyricists wrote those words, no wonder that man built the Taj Mahal ("for a *Persian* woman, he built it!" Baba always said), no wonder kings abdicated thrones. Was this the feeling? Because the world had just changed from black and white to Technicolor, the colors were colors she could taste, touch, *draw*. She jumped up the steps. She couldn't wait to see him again.

Darya opened the door, a glass of tea in her hand. "Mina, you look flushed. How was the breakfast? Are you all right?"

Mina kissed Darya forcefully on the cheek. She squeezed her tight. Her headscarf slid off before she was even inside the house. "It was so wonderfully wonderful, Maman Joon. You would never believe it! I had the best time with Mr. Dashti!"

She ran to the bedroom, having only enough time to see Darya's mouth in the shape of a perfect zero.

CHAPTER THIRTY-TWO

SCHEDULING CONFLICTS

Darya watched Mina fidget at lunch later that day. They were hosting the meal for their relatives, and Darya noticed Mina smile far too widely at people she didn't remember. Watched her tune out and stand mesmerized in front of Aunt Firoozeh. Darya sighed. So much of youth was attractive, agreeable, and made her long for it once it was gone. She saw Mina flip her hair and giggle at nothing for no good reason. But then again, much of the time, the young were so damn annoying. Darya poured herself another glass of tea. Mina was exhibiting all the signs of young love: the spaciness, the giggling, the la-la-land expressions. Let her live, she told herself. Let Mina have this. *To taste what I myself have had.* Isn't that what Darya had told her daughter? *To have a fraction of what I had in this life.* And to think Mina seemed smitten with Mr. Dashti's younger brother! How

Darya had missed Ramin in her U.S. research was beyond her. Her sources had kept the younger brother all to themselves and shoved the older one on her.

But now that Mina was finally falling for someone halfway decent and feeling so happy, Darya felt as if she didn't want her daughter to slip away. Didn't want to let her go. After all those spreadsheets and all those calculations, she suddenly didn't want to lose her.

"When can I see him?" Mina asked after the last of the lunch guests had left. "We're always so scheduled here!"

"My God, Mina, you just saw him this morning."

"I know, but the next few days are all booked up. When can I just have some free time?"

"We are here to see family. That's why we came. To see family in Tehran and, later, to sightsee in the other cities. We can't just . . ."

"I get it," Mina said.

Darya sighed. "Let me see what I can do. Maybe we can carve out some time and invite him over to tea . . ."

"Can I see him alone?"

"Alone where? Any place you meet him would be filled with relatives who either live there or come to visit you. There is no 'alone' here." Darya sniffed. "Not to mention that it would be inappropriate."

"Can we go out alone?"

"It's risky here, Mina. Nikki told me the guards have started a new round of crackdowns to rein in 'immoral' behavior. They're out on the streets in full force these days. They're even stopping opposite sex couples and asking them to produce a marriage certificate! You could get fined or even arrested if you're out together."

"We can't just walk in a park?"

"No, it's risky right now. Not to mention that we are booked solid."

It was true, they were snatched up for breakfast, lunch, and dinner by relatives who wanted to host them, feed them, see them again. The relatives spoiled them with fried eggplant and tomato *khoresh*, rice with fresh *sabzi* and fish, lasagna with béchamel sauce, fancy salads, and the very best kabobs. For dessert there was saffron rice pudding, rosewater ice cream, all sorts of cakes and pastries, and homemade apple pies. The relatives had spent their *toman* on the biggest and best fruit for them, kneaded dough and fried meat cutlets, dusted living rooms and beat Persian rugs for their arrival. Darya knew how much they were going out of their way for them and appreciated it. From the looks of it, Mina certainly appreciated it too, or at least the food. Every time Darya looked at her, Mina was eating. Rice dripping with butter, rice holding lima beans tight within it, rice with rich, fragrant hot *khoresh*.

"We're fattening up," Darya said. "All this food!"

"Can we just have one unscheduled morning?"

Darya sighed. "Fine. Monday morning after breakfast and before lunch at Aunt Nikki's."

Mina ran to the phone.

"There's no guarantee he'll be available!" Darya called out. "He's here to see his grandmother, remember?"

Mina came back a few minutes later, her cheeks flushed red. "He said yes. He can slip out on Monday at ten thirty, after an early breakfast with his grandmother and a few of her friends and before lunch at his father's oldest brother's house. He said to meet at the People's Park, by a big tree near the main gate."

"Okay, then." Darya felt her stomach sink. The crackdowns were getting worse each day. She didn't want Mina to risk it. But Mina looked so happy. Didn't her daughter deserve to experience a little old-fashioned courtship in this land? Why did the authorities have to make that so difficult? Why did they have to sap the joy out of everything? "I know the spot well," Darya said. She had spent her youth at that park. It was one of her favorite places in the whole city. "I can tell you how to get there, but you must be careful. You'll have to pretend you're a brother and sister going for a walk. No contact, absolutely no touching."

"I understand."

"I'm sorry, it's just the way it is. These are the rules and we have to abide by them. I don't want you raising suspicion. Remember, what is done cannot be undone."

ON THE MORNING THAT MINA was to meet Ramin at the People's Park, Darya watched her daughter try on several different outfits, even though whatever she wore would be covered by her *roopoosh*. She watched Mina style her hair carefully, the same hair that would soon be covered by a headdress. Mina insisted on wearing a green headscarf, she wanted some color around her face. There was a different energy about her; she seemed excited but strangely composed. Darya felt again the bittersweet knowledge that her daughter was beginning a new stage and that each new stage brought a greater distance from her. She closed her eyes and prayed to any God that Mina would remain safe. She'd wanted something like this for Mina, hadn't she? She was happy for her, of course she was happy.

Have fun, she said. Be careful, she said. Say hello to Ramin from us. Watch out for the Revolutionary Guards.

CHAPTER THIRTY-THREE

UNDER THE
SYCAMORE TREE

Mina left at ten o'clock. As she walked, she thought of Ramin standing in the doorway of Bita's apartment the night of the party, his arms crossed, looking as if he could both save the world and not give a damn about it.

She had seen her college classmates' architectural drafts on long sheets of paper. Ramin must make dozens of those designs. He probably used only blue or black ink, and Mina had spent her childhood dreaming of painting the world in color. But she was impressed by an architect's skills with a pen and paper. She wanted to ask Ramin more about his drawings. Even though she was on her way to a job on Wall Street, something about meeting him made her feel as if she could touch colors again. Touch them and taste them and maybe even create them.

As Mina approached the park, she remembered how he had

risked his career, his whole future, to come to Iran and visit his sick old grandmother. He had faced the authorities at the airport and stood his ground. He might have been drafted, detained, arrested. He could have lost everything he had worked for in America.

Mina looked to her right and to her left, took a deep breath, and entered the park.

HE WAS STANDING BY THE TREE, as promised, with a single flower in his hand. When she was near him, he gave it to her. A crimson rose. The exchange was quick, but she was painfully aware that neither of them was as adept as the regular citizens at navigating the threat of watchful guards. As instructed, they walked in parallel, about six feet apart, as though they were walking on invisible railroad tracks. Never too close. And never, ever touching.

Two children walked side by side, sucking on orange Popsicles. A boy and a girl. Mina remembered those Popsicles. She could almost taste the tangy sweetness as melted orange drops slid down the girl's chin. The girl and the boy skipped past them, arms now linked. They had not yet entered the danger age where their changing bodies rendered their connection unholy.

"It's good to see you again," Ramin said, just loud enough for Mina to hear him across the divide.

"Same here." She glanced quickly at him. He was wearing jeans and a light brown coat. His face was flushed. It was getting colder now. It had been a mild winter, but today she felt the chill.

"Are you cold?" he asked.

"No. Thank you for the flower. It's beautiful."

"My pleasure," he said quietly. "I figured I'd be like the poets.

Oh, let us drink some wine for there is no tomorrow and give thy friend from the U.S. a rose? Is that what Khayyam says?"

She burst out laughing.

"You have a great laugh."

"Thanks."

Was he blushing? She wished she could look at him long enough to tell. Instead, she looked down. All she could see from her peripheral vision were his legs from the knees down. His shins under the denim cloth. His feet moving in rhythm with hers.

"You know, Mina, I had such a great time at Bita's breakfast. And at the party the other night."

The sound of his deep voice soothed her. It made her feel as if she were all alone in the world with him, sitting close to him, even though they walked in a public park, trying to be unseen.

"Bita's a great hostess," Mina said. She crossed her arms to shield against the wind, the rose against her chest.

"She is, but that's not why. I mean, the reason is because, well, it felt serendipitous, but it was because we . . ."

They heard a car motor and a loud screeching of brakes. Ramin stopped in midsentence. They looked to their right. A green jeep had driven up to the edge of the park. Five or six bearded men in fatigues holding guns sat in the back. Mina halted.

"Keep moving," Ramin whispered.

Mina stared at her feet.

"Don't stop, Mina. Look straight ahead and keep going."

The jeep veered onto a lane and parked abruptly. *Run, Ramin,* Mina wanted to shout. *Run before they come to us.*

The guards tumbled out just a few feet away. Mina felt their eyes on every inch of her. She wished suddenly that she could turn back time, rewind the tape and be small again, have Ramin and herself shrink to childhood, where their stroll together would not be criminal. What was the offending age? Ten? Twelve?

One of the guards called out. *"Beeyan cigar een posht!"*

His voice was rough and startled Mina. He'd asked the other guards to join him for a smoke at the back of the jeep. Mina couldn't tell if he really wanted a smoke, or if he'd noticed Mina and Ramin and was saving them by distracting the other guards. Maybe he was empathetic to their parallel-line walk. Maybe he had his own girlfriend somewhere. Maybe he was just lazy and didn't feel like dealing with them right now. Mina wanted to think that the guard was helping them out. She wanted to believe that somehow she had an ally in that group, a young guard who knew that two people should just be able to walk together in peace.

Whatever the reason, the guards now stood in a cluster by the jeep. Out of the corner of her eye, Mina saw the flicker of a lighter, the burning of a cigarette.

Ramin motioned toward a tree nearby, a huge sycamore tree with branches reaching out to the sky and a trunk two feet wide.

"Behind it, stand behind it," Ramin whispered.

She scurried around the tree and stood behind its huge trunk. Her heart was beating so fast that she was sweating now despite the cold. Still gripping the rose, she suddenly realized how foolish it was to hold it. It gave them away. She let the flower drop to the ground and covered it with her foot but not before a few of its petals flew off, scattering around her like drops of blood.

Ramin leaned against the opposite side of the tree. She could hear his breathing. Mina remained hidden from the guards' view. All they would be able to see from where they stood was Ramin's lanky figure, just a young man relaxing under a tree.

"You okay?" Ramin's whisper was bold, concerned.

"Yes, fine." The dry December air filled her lungs as she took in a deep breath. "Are they watching?"

"Yes, they're looking right at me."

"Oh, God."

"It's okay, Mina." His voice had a slight quiver. He was, she knew, just as frightened as she was, but he was attempting to be calm for her sake. She wished she could just see his face. She wanted to comfort and be comforted by him at the same time.

"Don't speak, Ramin. They'll know you're talking to someone."

"They can't see you. And even if they see my lips moving, let them think I'm just another crazy guy talking to himself. God knows I'd have enough reason to be nuts here with all these rules they have."

She couldn't help but laugh, though she stifled it immediately.

"Did I already tell you that you have the best laugh?" he asked. His voice was more relaxed now.

"You did." They stood for a moment in silence.

"Do you like it here?" he asked softly.

"Well, I did until the guards showed up." Her heart still pounded. She rubbed her clammy hands against her *roopoosh*. She hated that the guards had this effect on her. But they always had and probably always would. Their presence had made the very air around the tree electric with danger.

"No, I mean, *here*."

She realized then that he was asking not about the park, but about the country.

"I do and I don't. From the minute I arrived, I haven't stopped thinking about leaving. Sometimes it's all too . . ."

"Different?" he asked.

"Yes," she said. "But I don't mean different from home, from the U.S. I mean . . ."

"Of course," he interrupted. "You mean different from before."

His deep voice carried understanding. With him, she didn't have to explain. With American men, 1979 was just another year. But Ramin knew. As with Leila and Bita, for him the year of the revolution was when the world was cleaved into Before and After. And even though the men who came over to tea knew that too, it never felt easy to talk to them. Like Baba, those suitors had worked so hard at "owning" their new lives in America that Mina sometimes felt they were afraid to even admit what they had lost, the price they had paid. But Ramin was different. From that very first time in the kitchen at Bita's party, he had had no problem cutting to the truth. With Ramin, she felt free to acknowledge the melancholy of loss. His wise, calm voice relaxed her even now as she hid under a tree in a Tehran park with the Revolutionary Guards' morality police nearby.

Mina leaned into the tree and let the bark dig into her back. Knowing that Ramin was on the other side made the trunk feel solid and reassuring.

"But I also love it at the same time," she said. "The food . . ."

"I know. I've eaten more in the past few days than I do in weeks back home! And the trouble everyone goes to for you . . ."

She smiled. Even as the cold air chilled her hands and face,

Mina was beginning to feel better. Talking to him lifted her fear and filled her with warmth. "They go to so much trouble that sometimes it's overwhelming. Every meal is like a feast. But . . ."

"It's all so good," he finished the sentence for her. "It does feel good to be spoiled."

Mina looked up at the leaves in the branches of the tree. They were pale yellow, deep red, some still green, a few orange. "The other thing I've been struck by," she said, "is all the color here." At her feet lay a coppery carpet dotted by her crimson rose petals and a few other flame-colored leaves. She thought of the sparkling mosaics on the buildings in south Tehran, the turquoise-blue koi ponds all over the city, the intricately woven colorful rugs in homes and shops. The mounds of saffron, turmeric, and sumac in the bazaar and the kaleidoscopic designs of flower beds in the parks. "Nobody tells you about the colors."

"I know. Since I left it's as if I always remembered my life here in black and white. But there is so much color here. I'd forgotten just how much I missed it."

Exactly, Mina thought. She imagined him leaning against the tree, looking up at the same flame-colored leaves. She leaned more heavily against the tree trunk, as though it could bring her closer to him. The timbre of his voice, the sound of his words made her feel safe. Her heart had stopped pounding now, the adrenaline that had fueled her when she first saw the guards was ebbing. Even though she knew the guards were watching, even though they held guns, she found that as long as he was on the other side of that tree, talking to her, she did not want to be anywhere else. She ran her hands against the peeling bark. The air was dry and cold, but the trunk of the tree seemed to emanate warmth. That morning, she had bathed with rosewater soap. She had carefully washed and dried her hair. He could not see her hair, could not smell its fragrance. He could not know how much she wanted to be next to him.

"Sometimes, I wish I never had to leave," he said.

"I know," she whispered. "But I suppose we have to get back to our lives."

Our lives. Even as she said the words, she imagined racing through the hallways of the business school. She thought of taking her exams and graduating and hanging on to a strap in a New York City subway car on her way to work. She had things to do. Goals to accomplish. He had meetings to attend, projects to finish, deadlines to meet. *Our lives.*

"What I wanted to say was that when I saw you in the kitchen at Bita's, I . . . well, what I'm saying is that I think it would be good for us to . . . I just thought that . . . what if we could keep in touch?" he finally asked.

A few crimson and yellow leaves floated past Mina's face in the breeze. "Of course," she said with relief. "We'll keep in touch." She stared at the rose on the ground. "I wish we had more time. I wish this hadn't all been so rushed."

"We'll have an even better time back home."

She could hear his feet on the dry leaves, adjusting his position. The air smelled of damp leaves and roasted nuts. Suddenly, she felt suspended, just the two of them, under that tree, and the rest fell away. She was free of both the past and the future. They were here now, together. As each moment ticked by, as each delicious lazy forever moment stretched out under that tree—it could not be undone. It was theirs.

"When do you go back?" he asked, bringing her back to reality.

"In a week. I can't believe I'm already halfway through my trip. We're going to visit a few other cities."

"Let me guess, Shiraz and Isfahan?"

"Yes."

"I have great memories of Shiraz. The land of the poets. What is it they call it? The 'Land of Love'! You have to visit Persepolis while you're there."

"That's the plan. And you? When do you go back?"

"Tomorrow."

The wind made the branches shake, and a few more leaves fell to the ground. She wanted to stop time and make this moment last. Despite the danger, she longed to reach around the tree and touch him. The guards were watching. She had spent most of her life balancing between cultures, never really quite at home. But with him, right here, under this vast, beautiful tree, she was home. With him, she felt she finally belonged.

"I leave early in the morning."

"Oh."

"But we'll call. Yes?"

A group of mothers and children walked by, and their voices interrupted Ramin and Mina's conversation. She leaned her head against the rough bark and closed her eyes. It was reassuring to think that this tree had stood in this park for a hundred years. It predated the guards. It predated the current rulers and the Shah before them. How many other couples had stood under this tree? How many other conversations had it known?

She opened her eyes and looked up at a slate-colored sky between the branches. A few more people walked by. If anyone thought they looked like lovers, they did not care. The guards only cared because they were paid to care.

The sounds of passersby stopped after a while, and it was just the two of them again, alone.

"It's cold," she said.

"I wish I could give you my coat."

She smiled. "Do you think it'll snow?"

"Give me your hand," he whispered.

She heard the rasp of fabric against the rough surface of the trunk. "No, Ramin, please. They'll see," she hissed.

But with her heart pounding, Mina slid her left arm around the tree. Her fingers walked along the bark, searching for his. She felt for his hand, a hand that she'd only touched once when they first introduced themselves with a handshake at the party, and found it reaching for hers. His fingers were warm, his skin was so soft. Slowly, gently, his hand entwined with hers. Both of them knew that they should not be doing this. But once they touched, nothing felt more natural. Is this what Darya had been talking about? Is this the happiness that she wanted to find for Mina?

"It is so beautiful here," she said.

They talked then for a while more, about the snow he saw on the peak of the Alborz Mountains every morning from his grandmother's window, and the difference between kabobs here and in the U.S. He asked for her phone number and she told him, and he repeated it several times so he wouldn't forget it. All the time, their hands were intertwined.

And then it started.

First one flake and then another as thin as a dream. They landed on her eyelashes, her tongue, they dusted her hand in his.

The snow filled in the crevices between their fingers, binding them as a unit, no longer two separate things.

Leaning against that tree, swathed in cloth from head to toe with the guards only a few feet away—she felt surprisingly free. His deep voice carried and caressed her, making her feel as if she were floating. Years and years from now, she would remember this moment. She had fallen in love, right then and there. This much she knew. But was this all they would have? Would they really keep in touch? Her life would go on, her schedule was full. His life was busy with work. But no one could undo this moment. No one could make what had happened not happen. When their hands touched, the risk they'd taken to be here was all worth it.

"It's getting late," she said. As she spoke, a feeling of loss enveloped her. She was with the only man she'd ever truly wanted, and she had to leave. But lunch obligations waited. Their respective families were expecting them. "We have to go."

He squeezed her hand one last time. "I'll call you in New York," he said.

Slowly, reluctantly, she let go of his hand. She heard his footsteps receding, his feet rustling in the snow-wet leaves. She shivered. He would now walk past the guards and back to his grandmother's house so he could go to the airport so he could get on a plane and so he could return to his normal life. God willing. There was still the exit from the country to worry about; sometimes exiles were detained at the very last minute before departure. Mina's knees felt weak. Whether she was shaking from the cold or his touch or his footsteps in the snow—she did not know. "Good-bye," she whispered to the emptiness.

As she stepped away from the tree, her headdress snagged

in its bark. She tugged at it, dislodging the cloth at last, but then turned to see a tiny coil of green thread still clinging to the trunk.

The guards were still smoking by the jeep, on their third or fourth or twentieth cigarette now. A few of them passed a walkie-talkie back and forth. One of them glanced up as she walked by, and his gaze took in all of her, his eyes finally locking on her face. Did he know? Had he seen Ramin against the tree, had he guessed? Mina walked faster, still scared but feeling more alive than she'd ever felt. The people she walked past could not have known that she was dissolving into someone else, that she had just felt her life reshaped by love.

Mina thought of the tiny coil of thread from her headscarf, hanging on the tree. Would it still be there after the snow stopped falling? Would it be there after storms and rainfall, after the seasons changed, after the guards grew up, grew old and died? How long would the coil of green hang there, wedged into that timeless tree? Mina wanted it to stay there forever. She wanted that coil of thread to mark for all time the moment when her world was cleaved into a whole new Before and After.

CHAPTER THIRTY-FOUR

POETS, PRAYERS, AND PERSEPOLIS

"M ina, pay attention!" Darya waved a map as they sat in the plane. "See, the cat's left ear borders Turkey and the right ear touches Azerbaijan. Its belly sits on the Persian Gulf. The right side rubs against Afghanistan and Pakistan."

"I know." Mina had seen cat-shaped Iran on a map a hundred times.

"Right here is the shared bloody border with Iraq," Agha Jan said.

Mina looked out the plane window and thought about Ramin. Whenever there was a big life question to be answered, Mamani would fish out her Divan book by the fourteenth-century Persian poet Hafez, open the book to a random page, and read the top right corner. There lay the answer to her question.

Mina wished she could ask Hafez whether she and Ramin would actually keep in touch. Who was to say if once they got back to the U.S. they could keep up a connection or even a conversation? Their moments in Iran had seemed suspended from reality. Could the love that Mina had felt under the tree in People's Park really be sustained?

"You will love Shiraz!" Darya squeezed Mina's hand. "Some of our country's most famous poets are from there. Shiraz is known for its literature, its wine . . . its *romance*! And once there, we will visit Persepolis, the site of the famous ancient ruins. From there, we'll go to Isfahan, one of Iran's most historic and beautiful cities."

The plane rattled on in the sky. The flight attendant winked as she passed by. Agha Jan snored in his seat. Mina wondered if Ramin had arrived in Connecticut.

SIGNS PAINTED WITH SEVENTIES-STYLE BUBBLE letters told them where to exit the Shiraz airport. The signs looked as if they hadn't been updated in decades. Mina, Darya, and Agha Jan wheeled their luggage behind them and walked out onto the street. Agha Jan hailed a taxi, and they drove past large boulevards lined with trees, beautiful buildings that stood behind reflecting pools, gardens filled with colorful flowers. At their hotel, a man with a bulbous nose and white stubbly beard was introduced to them as their guide. They washed up quickly and got ready for their first sightseeing spots: the resting places of the famous poets Saadi and Hafez.

Saadi's marble tomb was at the end of Boustan Boulevard in a peaceful blue room. His verses were inscribed in the sea-blue tiles of the walls.

"He died around 1290," Darya said. "They say he was over a hundred years old then."

"Did you know your very own Ralph Waldo Emerson was a fan of our poet Saadi?" Agha Jan said to Mina. "Touch his tomb and say a prayer."

The marble was cold and smooth when Mina touched it. She closed her eyes and saw Ramin. She prayed that he had gotten back to the U.S. safely.

Their next stop was Hafez's resting place, a mausoleum that lay in a private pavilion in a lush garden. Mina had grown up learning lines from Hafez's famous *ghazal* verses, listening to Mamani recite his wise words. Hafez's tomb had a mystical, magical feel and Mina thought of Mamani and how she must have come here several times. Tourists walked around, holding cameras. A young woman placed her lips on the poet's tomb. Mina wondered what Hafez would think of his country today. She also wondered what he would think of someone storing their artwork under their bed and working on spreadsheets day and night.

Mina went to the garden outside the mausoleum and walked by its shimmering pool. A new feeling had blossomed inside her ever since her time with Ramin in the People's Park. It was a feeling that made her think she should grab what she wanted out of life, rather than keep doing what she was told was her passion. She shouldn't have stopped reading Persian poetry. She shouldn't have stopped a lot of things, like drawing and painting.

That night in the Shiraz hotel, Mina dreamed that Hafez was

doing the backstroke in the rectangular pool near his tomb. Saadi was drinking tea with Darya and laughing. Mina was dressed in a flight attendant's uniform, floating in the sky, arms outstretched. She called out, "I'm in love! Love!" Saadi and Darya continued to chat, ignoring her. Hafez just said, "But is he?" then emptied out the water in his goggles and stretched out in the garden to tan.

"SURPRISE!"

Mina, Darya, and Agha Jan sat in the lobby after lunch the next day and stared at Bita standing in front of them with a duffel bag.

"Just came for one day and one night! That's all the time off I could get. But we can see Persepolis together! You haven't gone there yet, have you?"

Mina was delighted and stunned to see Bita in the lobby. She had told Bita about their itinerary, but she had never expected Bita to just show up. Women were not supposed to travel without chaperones.

"Bita Joon, did you come here alone?" Darya asked.

"I told the guy at the airport that my brother was joining me. I took care of him," Bita said.

"Paid him a bribe?" Mina asked. Bribery had become such a common way to get around the stringent rules that Mina wouldn't have been surprised if Bita had taken part in it. But still. It just felt like something that Bita shouldn't have to do.

"When do we go to Persepolis?" Bita asked, giving her duffel bag to a porter.

WARNING

Important Note

It is informed to all respected visitors that touching
or displacing stones in the site is forbidden and any
kind of moving scratching, writing memories and so on
will make the ofenders liable to prosecution.

"You would think they could use correct English spelling!"
Mina said as she read the sign near the entrance of Persepolis.

"It's the best they can do," Darya said with a sniff.

Their guide had taken the afternoon off, and a taxi driver had
brought them here and said he'd wait for them in the car. No tour
guide was needed for Persepolis when they had Agha Jan, who had
been a professor of history at Tehran University. His passion and
life's work was the history of ancient civilizations. As soon as they
entered the grounds, Agha Jan took on a professorial tone. "Welcome to Persepolis, *Takhte Jamshid*! You now stand at the famed
ruins of palaces that Darius the Great built more than twenty-five
hundred years ago!"

Mina felt dwarfed by the decorated columns that towered
majestically above her. Everything was bathed in sunlight. The air
smelled of dust and time.

Agha Jan pointed to a sculpture of men in procession carrying
carpets, chairs, vases, and bowls. "These are delegations from various nations going before the Achaemenian ruler."

Mina ran her hand across the carvings of the men, lingering

on the curls of their long hair. Was she imagining it, or did one of the men look just like Ramin?

"Please don't touch," Agha Jan said.

Huge columns reached into the sky. Some of the columns had broken over the centuries and were now small stumps. Bas-reliefs carved with intricate details ran into gaping holes of empty space. Mina took a photo of Bita by a sculpture of two huge bulls with human faces. Bita's head barely reached the bottom of the bulls' feet. It was liberating and humbling to be so tiny against the vastness of this past. Mina took more photos. People walked by in hushed silence, stopping to stare at a pillar or remnant walls of a palace. The requisite group of guards stood at a distance near the bottom of the plain.

Mina walked through the fallen city, careful not to disturb any ancient stone.

"It took over sixty years to build this part," Agha Jan said. "This here is Achaemenian sculpture, not Assyrian. Why?"

No one answered.

"Because in Assyria the bulls have five legs, whereas the Achaemenians gave them only four!" Agha Jan said.

"Of course!" Bita hit her forehead with her palm.

"That's where the King of Kings received his visitors. And that's the Apadana staircase," Agha Jan continued.

Mina remembered learning about the Achaemenian dynasty and Darius the Great in school. The Achaemenians had ruled pre-Islam, when Iran's main religion was Zoroastrianism, the three pillars of which were "good thoughts, good words, good deeds." Many Iranians were proud of their Zoroastrian past, and to this day Agha Jan wore a pendant of its main symbol—a human emerging from a winged disk.

Bita looked up with wonder on her face. "To think of the people who designed and sculpted all this. It's amazing what artists can do! Right, Mina?"

"Right," Mina said. The way the columns fell into the saffron light made Mina's fingers ache for a brush, the smallest blob of paint, anything to render this on a canvas.

Maybe she could spend the night here. Brush her teeth underneath the Apadana staircase. Feel the sculptures against her nightgowned back. Maybe she could stay for a while. Live here and paint, drink sweet tea by the columns in the morning. Ramin should be here. Taking it all in in his calm way, climbing to the top of the staircase at night with her. Any kind of moving scratching, writing memories and so on will make the *ofenders* liable to prosecution. The stones wouldn't crumble under their bodies. Before her, people had made love here. When the walls were filled with music, when the cups overflowed with wine, when the platforms spilled with laughing guests. Women in jeweled robes had walked on these stairs. Enormous feasts had been held inside these walls.

They took a short break for lunch: a picnic of *kotelet* sandwiches in *lavash* bread with pickles and tomato slices that they had brought from the hotel, and tea from Darya's thermos. After lunch, they explored more. When the sun began to set, it bathed all of Persepolis in a golden haze. A gust of wind swirled around them and it was suddenly cold. The ends of Mina's headscarf lifted in the wind.

Darya looked at her father with concern. "Baba, you've walked all day. You must be tired. Come with me. We can have tea in the taxi." She turned to Mina and Bita. "You two can look around for just a little more, but come to the taxi before it gets too late."

"We won't be long," Mina said.

Darya led her father away, and the two of them got smaller in the distance. Mina turned to Bita. "I'm so glad you came."

"I figured I'd make the most of our time. Once you go back to Tehran, you'll be so busy with your relatives those last few days, and then you'll be off to the U.S.! Who knows when we'll see each other again?"

Mina didn't want to think about that.

Bita stopped walking. "The best way to experience this place is with the wind in your hair," she said. Then, as calmly as when she'd removed the towel from her wet hair on the day of her party, she reached up and removed her headscarf.

"Bita, are you crazy? Put it back on right now!" Mina pointed to the group of guards standing in the distance.

It wasn't long before the thumping of boots made Mina freeze. A guard appeared next to them.

Bita's hair flew in the wind, highlighted by the golden rays of the setting sun.

"Khanom," the guard began.

Mina looked at his lanky arms and legs, took in his thick eyebrows. He looked like Hooman. He could've been her brother.

"Yes?" Bita answered innocently. "Did you say something to me?"

Mina's stomach fell. Her arms were suddenly numb. Nothing had changed since the day Bita had identified the whiskey bottle in Mrs. Amiri's class.

The guard glared at Mina. He would not look directly at a woman who was exposed.

"Do you have any business with me?" Bita repeated in a high angry voice.

He reddened at her words. Bita had detracted from his authority by addressing him in her intimate tone, using the singular "you" in Farsi, instead of the more formal plural pronoun for "you." Mina stared at the gun that hung from the guard's belt. Next to his gun was a walkie-talkie with which he could alert all the other guards. Mina's heart hammered against her chest.

"You are under arrest," the guard growled at the ground. Then he looked directly at Bita. "Come with me right now, you whore."

Anger rose in Mina like a wave that worked its way from the bottom of her sneakered feet all the way to her own covered head. His tone, his righteousness, his treating Bita as if she were subhuman made her scream, "You should be ashamed for bullying a woman! No one was here. She was just standing here alone with me. Go. Just leave us alone!"

Bita stared dumbfounded at Mina.

The guard looked stunned for just a moment. But then his face hardened into fierce resolution. Mina's insults had crossed the line. He no longer looked like Hooman. "I can," the guard said slowly, "arrest both of you right now. And then we will do what we want with you. Do you understand?"

Mina could feel the adrenaline running through her arms and legs. Without thinking, she pivoted on her left foot. She lifted her right leg, bent her knee, flexed, and aimed. With every atom of her being, she kicked. It all happened in a matter of seconds. Side Heel Thrust Kick. The kick she'd practiced almost all her life. Her kick hit him in the "precious place," as Kayvon had referred to it in her karate lessons. The walkie-talkie snapped out of the guard's belt and landed a few feet away, near Bita.

"Take it!" Mina screamed.

A bewildered Bita paused, then grabbed the walkie-talkie.

"*Run!*" Mina yelled.

They ran as if their lives depended on it. They ran past the sculptures of ancient gift-bearers for kings, past the staircase of King Darius, past the broken pillars whose stumps ended in mid-air. They ran past the gray-golden remains of long ago—past the glory and the fallen grandeur. They ran in the opposite direction of the rest of the guards, who still stood in a cluster, unaware that their comrade was writhing on the ground, kicked in the balls by a girl. They ran and ran, their *roopoosh* flying in the air, their sneakered feet thumping on the ground, their breath loud and deafening, their hearts beating faster than they could ever remember. They did not stop till they reached the taxi parked on the side of the road and then they vaulted in and slammed the door.

"What happened?" Darya looked scared.

"What on earth . . ." Agha Jan mumbled.

"*Go!*" Mina yelled at the driver.

The driver jumped, startled. He turned on the engine and stepped on the gas so fast that Darya's tea spilled all over the backseat.

"Go, go, please!" Bita cried.

He went fast. He broke every law. He raced past the plains and sped onto the highway.

Darya gave up drinking any tea. Agha Jan bounced in the backseat of the car, crumpled and confused. There was no time for explanations. As they zoomed past the outskirts of the city, Mina rolled down the window and threw out the guard's walkie-talkie.

Once they were back in the center of Shiraz and the car slowed down in the city's streets, Bita took Mina's hand and linked her pinky finger with hers.

"Thanks," Bita whispered. "I just . . . get carried away sometimes."

"I know." Mina squeezed Bita's pinky. "I know you."

CHAPTER THIRTY-FIVE

HALF THE WORLD

Bita left the next day, back to Tehran, to her job at the advertising firm where she was the head of the department for highway billboards. Mina, Darya, and Agha Jan continued on to the city of Isfahan, glad to leave behind Shiraz and Mina's kicking of the guard.

"He could have chased you and then where would we be?" Darya's forehead vein throbbed.

"He couldn't chase her because she had rendered him helpless," Agha Jan said. He turned to Mina. "It was truly dangerous what you did," he said, not for the first time, but Mina couldn't miss the note of pride in his voice.

When they arrived in Isfahan, they checked into a grand old hotel with a red carpeted staircase and Persian rugs strewn across its large rooms.

"Isfahan is called Nesfe-Jahan, 'Half the World,'" Agha Jan said over a lunch of kabobs and rice. "Go see the synagogue. Go see the mosque. Darya, go show this girl half the world."

While Agha Jan took his afternoon nap, Darya took Mina to Isfahan's main square. Horses and carriages lined up for tourists. At one end was a huge bazaar, at another was the main mosque with its glittering minarets. All around the square were handicraft shops. Darya wanted to spend time at the bazaar, but Mina was eager to explore the artisan shops.

They agreed to split up for an hour and then meet for tea.

Mina walked by the shops, occasionally stopping to take photos of the ancient buildings around her. *He would call once they were back in the U.S., why wouldn't he?* She clicked her camera at the turquoise minarets and onion-shaped dome of the mosque at the end of the square.

In the window of one of the handicraft shops, a *khatam* box painted with delicate, colorful strokes in the style of old Persian miniature paintings caught her eye. On the box was the face of a young woman being kissed on the cheek by a man in a turban. The woman's expression was one of bliss. Mina couldn't take her eyes off the box. She stared at it for a few minutes, then went into the shop.

Inside it was dark and smelled of metal and glue and paint. Mina heard a tap-tapping, the banging of a small hammer onto something. As her eyes adjusted to the dim light, she saw a man bent over a table. He seemed to be in a trance, hammering at a metal tray. On the wall behind him were dozens of silver and copper trays and plates with patterns etched into them. Mina made out scenes of birds and deer, storks and flowers. The man's hands flew, cutting the air with a rasp.

"Sit, rest, relax."

She was surprised at his familiar tone. He'd used the singular verb conjugation of "you" in Farsi, as though she was family or a friend.

She went closer and was able to see that he was hammering out a rose. Like the one Ramin had given her in the park.

"Go on, sit down." His gray eyes peeked out over round spectacles. Steel-colored tufts of hair stood out on either side of his head. His shirt was open at the top, revealing more steel-wool tufts on his chest. He wore gray suit pants with white plastic slippers.

Mina climbed onto a wooden stool near the table.

"Visiting?"

"*Baleh.* Yes."

He etched out a bird next to the rose. "Where from?"

"America."

"Ah." He gave the bird wings. "Lots of you come back."

Mina had only seen hands move so fast once before, when Uncle Jafar played the sitar for them when she was a child.

The man strummed out the body of the bird. He didn't ask, Why did you leave? When did you leave? How do you like it here? He seemed too busy.

"Forty-five years," he said after a stretch of silence, as if responding to a question Mina had asked, even though she'd said nothing. "That's how long I've been doing this. Longer even, if you count my time as a child."

A proud and beautiful bird emerged from his etching. Its chest was round, its wings spread out.

"Every day," he added, as though Mina had just asked him

how often he did this. He looked up and smiled. "Except Fridays. That's God's day." He held up the finished tray.

"It's fantastic," Mina said.

"We artists," he said. "Have to do our work. No?"

Mina wasn't sure what to say. *We artists?* "Does the government tell you what you can and cannot make?" she asked.

"They tell me what I can and cannot *sell*. Display." He cleared the filings off the table. "But nobody can affect what I can or cannot *make*." He cleaned his hands on an old rag and stood up.

"Come," he said. "Let me show you something." The artisan moved to the back of the shop where a black sheet hung from nails hammered into the wall.

A cautionary voice that sounded just like Darya's warned Mina not to follow strangers behind black curtains. But Mina rose and followed the artisan. The artisan swished the sheet aside.

Behind the curtain was a large storage room. From floor to ceiling, shelves were crammed with etched trays, decorated ceramics, and mosaic boxes. Piles of copper plates, painstakingly engraved, towered on one shelf. Mosaic *khatam* boxes in gold and blue and every possible color sat in groups on the floor. Leather canvases adorned with fancy calligraphy and dozens of paintings covered every inch of the walls. Scenes of lovers in embrace, men and women dancing and lounging under trees, dizzied Mina. One large painting stood out. It was of a long-haired woman in a purple robe, leaning against a tree, playing what looked like a small guitar. A man in flowing robes looked up at her. Mina recognized the woman's face. It was the same one she'd seen on the box in the shop window. The woman had the same expression of bliss.

"You like that one?" The artisan walked up to the painting. "It's one of my favorites. Come," he said. "Let's have some tea."

"Oh no, I can't . . ." Mina said.

"Please. Don't *tarof*." He went to a samovar set on a small table near a cot. Mina hadn't noticed the cot before. A framed photo of a young man hung above it.

"I take my afternoon nap here." The artisan handed her an *estekan* of tea and sat on the cot. "I heard that in America, you don't take the afternoon nap. True?"

"People don't usually . . . have cots at work."

"Why not? Not so wise to skip the afternoon nap. It's good for your heart." He tapped his chest with ink-stained fingers. "As to your question about what the government allows me to make, please know, my friend, that governments come and go. We artists continue our work. Every day."

She sat on a chair next to the cot and they drank their tea. She should have felt uncomfortable sitting in a storage room with a strange man, but she felt as though she were with a kindred soul, a spirit from another world.

He drained his tea glass, then got up. "Back to work," he said matter-of-factly.

As they walked out, Mina took one last look at the painting of the woman playing the guitar, a man by her side, under the tree. She drank that image in.

With a swish of the black sheet, the storage room disappeared and they were back in the shop. The man slid behind his table, picked up his hammer and a nail, and within seconds was drumming out the legs of a stork.

"I'd like to buy the *khatam* box in the store window," Mina said suddenly. "The one of the man and the woman." She got out her wallet.

"My gift to you. Please."

"No, no," Mina insisted and put the money on the counter. "And thank you for the tea."

He went to the window, got the box, and wrapped it in newspaper for her. Mina was at the door, her hand on the doorknob when he said, "My son died in the war."

Of course. The photograph above the cot. The young man's face.

"My wife has the most terrible of afflictions now. *Afsordeghi.* Depression. That's her face on that box you're holding and in that painting you liked. That's her when she was happy."

"I am so sorry," Mina said.

"Our son was the light of our eyes. My wife is my soul. When I paint her as she was, she comes back to me," the artist mumbled. "Go, then. May God protect you."

"*Khodahafez,*" Mina replied.

She swung the door open and was once again in the glare of the square. The sun was blinding. The shops, the horse-drawn tourist carriages, the sounds and smells of the outside world engulfed her. She thought of the artisan, bent over his table, hammering out his images.

She realized that she wanted to capture every angle of the minarets and ancient buildings, Bita by the Persepolis sculptures, the grocer with his boxes of onions, the young people dancing in the living room of the apartment building. She never wanted to forget the tree in the People's Park, the way the leaves fell as she listened to Ramin talk, the snow that landed on her hand in his.

How could she stop these images from slipping through her fingers? Why hadn't she painted? When did she stop doing what she loved?

The camera wasn't enough. It never was.

She knew what she had to do.

DARYA WOVE HER WAY THROUGH the alleyways of the bazaar, stopping to sift spices through her hands, smelling the cardamom and cumin, feeling the rough edges of dried limes. Men called out to her, advertising their wares, and she walked on, pushing through the people who filled the lanes of the bazaar. She felt so far away from her job at the bank and math camp and her Spreading Spreadsheet Specs class. What on earth would Sam do in a place like this? He wouldn't even know where to look, what to say. Then again, being such a "laid-back dude," he would probably find a way to navigate these alleys, and before long, he'd be relaxed here too. He was that kind of person. So at peace. Which, she knew, was what made him so attractive to her. She loved his calm.

But the truth was, she missed Parviz. All that time in the U.S. she had missed Iran and now here she was back in Iran, and everything made her think of Parviz. He would have loved to see everyone again. He would have sat at the kitchen table and talked Agha Jan's ear off. He and Uncle Jafar could have argued about music and philosophy again. She missed Parviz's loud voice, even his self-help mumbo jumbo. She missed his action-oriented, goal-setting, life-seizing, triumphant leaps in the air. Everything in Iran reminded her of him. Hadn't they been young together here? Hadn't they had their courtship here?

What is done cannot be undone.

They had raised three children together. They had moved to a new continent and started life over together. Parviz was a part of her.

So, while she had enjoyed the attention from Sam—his smiles, his no-fuss ways, his quiet words during the breaks of their spreadsheet class—it was never going to be anything more than that. Ever. And now she knew she had never even wanted it to be.

Darya was so caught up in her thoughts that she walked right into a group of chadored women. "Excuse me," she mumbled in English. The women frowned and walked off. So her reflexes were in English now. Darya tried not to bump into any more people and focused her attention on a bright silver tea set displayed on woven tapestries.

She was relieved when she looked down the alley of the bazaar and saw Mina walk toward her. Just seeing her daughter made her happy. Here was her daughter who didn't know how beautiful she was, who could never know just how much she loved her and how her own world, Darya's, had been reshaped by Mina's presence in it. Here was the daughter she had raised with Parviz.

Darya slipped her arm through Mina's. "Let's go, Mina. Let's go and have together tea."

SHE WANTED MINA TO APPRECIATE the beauty here—she wanted to give her a taste of everything—but they had so little time left. She took her to a teahouse that she remembered from years ago near the Bridge of Thirty-three Arches. The door was tucked away under the bridge and steps led down to a cozy room where tea was served. Darya was delighted to find the teahouse as she remembered it. People sat shoeless on Persian rugs, leaning against crimson and burgundy carpeted cushions. Men smoked *ghalyoon*, women relaxed drinking. Darya showed Mina where to stow her shoes. She motioned to the waiter and they sat. How many tea bags bobbing in lukewarm water had she put up with in the States? But here, they would have real tea with leaves meticulously selected and mixed in just the right proportion. The brewing, the *dam-avardan*, would be supervised with care. At the right time, the tea would be poured into *estekan* and served with hacked-off pieces of sugar. Darya couldn't wait to put the sugar between her teeth, to feel it slowly dissolve and melt in her mouth as she sipped.

When the waiter brought their tea and chunks of snow-white sugar on clear saucers, Darya decided the time had come to ask Mina.

"So," she said, clearing her throat. "Are you a lover now?" She used the poets' words. *Eshgh*/love. *Ashegh*/one who's in love/lover.

"I beg your pardon?" Mina's arm holding the tea glass froze in midair.

"Oh please, I can tell when a girl's in love. And it's not fair that I barely know anything about him. I know he has nice teeth. As if that means anything!"

"You've met his brother," Mina said. "Graphed him. You know of the family."

"Your father and I don't know anything about *him*," Darya said. Yes, she knew of the Dashti family because of the previous research for the older brother. But that did not feel like enough anymore. "I mean, who is he, even? What's he *like*?"

"He's . . . well, in the few times that I've seen him, he's been quite thoughtful."

"Is he kind?" Darya asked. "Because, Mina, there's a lot to be said for education. And a profession. And family history. And, well, looks. But if there's one thing that matters, it's character. That's the only thing that lasts. Degrees can lose significance, jobs can be lost, a family's past really shouldn't define a person, and as for looks . . ." Darya sighed. "Well, looks fade for the best of us. But character, Mina, is what lasts. Kindness will carry you through the ups and downs of life."

"He is kind. Very."

"Well, that's a start."

"But really, ups and downs of life? It's not like we're going to get married or anything!"

"No, of course not. That's not what I'm saying at all." Darya sipped her tea. "Wait, why not?"

"Because I barely know him! Plus, he's in Connecticut. Long distance never works."

"It's only an hour away, Mina."

"Who knows what will happen?"

"Everything works out if it's the right person."

"Can you just please promise me that we're done with the spreadsheets and suitors? No matter what?"

Sitting in this teahouse near the bridge, with the sound of the water lapping overhead and the feel of the rug against her toes, Darya felt embarrassed by those spreadsheets. She had tried so hard to find the perfect formula for her daughter's happiness when really there was no way she could control her daughter's future. She'd always known that, even if she hadn't wanted to admit it. Those spreadsheets felt far away, like something she'd done in another life.

"You know what, Mina? I'm beginning to think there is no one right person. No predestined soul mate. There's no formula. Or if there is, a lot of different combinations can give you a right answer . . . or a right person." Darya realized as she said this that she finally believed it. True, she'd spent her entire adult life with Parviz and been happy. What if Mamani had picked someone else? If Darya had married one of her other suitors, who was to say she wouldn't have been just as happy? There was no magic value for the formula to work. Different variables fit into the equation. For example, in another lifetime, under different circumstances, she and Sam could have maybe been a wonderful couple together.

Mina sighed. "I have something to tell you."

"You're not going to get married, I know, Mina. Let's just see how it unfolds. No pressure. I'll stop . . ."

"No, it's not that. I'm quitting business school."

"Excuse me?"

"I have to. I want to paint. I don't want to look back years from now and regret not giving it a shot."

Darya was starting to feel dizzy. "Mina, remember your promise? That if we came on this trip, you'd actually go back and buckle down and focus on business school for a change, without constantly thinking you should be doing something else? Remember that?"

"I do. But I had no idea the power that this place would have over me. The problem is I've been doing the wrong thing. I need to be committed."

"Yes, committed!"

"But committed to *my art*, not to Wall Street. I need to . . .

devote the time. It won't happen by itself. I have to focus. Quitting business school is the only way."

As her daughter talked, Darya leaned against the carpeted cushions, exhausted. This was the power her children held over her. They could walk into a room and just the sight of them would make her heart soar and then the next minute, they could open their mouths and say absurdities that rendered her helpless. What was she to say to Parviz now? This trip that Darya had championed against Parviz's better judgment was not supposed to make Mina quit business school. It was supposed to keep her more firmly in it.

Where was Parviz when she needed him? Where was he to just talk sense into this girl?

What had this trip done to her daughter?

CHAPTER THIRTY-SIX

DUAL EXISTENCE

most mornings in her Broadway apartment, Mina got up early. She dressed in workout clothes and went for a run in Riverside Park. Then she came home, showered, and gathered her materials. Paints. Brushes. Not computers. Not calculators. She'd finally ordered the brand of oil paint that the artist from Marblehead, Massachusetts, had recommended on the website she'd been surfing when Professor Van Heusen called on her in finance class.

Ramin had called. They'd spoken a few times on the phone. They kept saying, "We should get together." But he had deadlines and she had exams and, well, they were busy. It wasn't like that moment under the tree. Mina wanted it to be, she wanted that magic again, but she felt as if she were just having conversations on the phone.

She painted. She used canvas, a rough, textured canvas that held the paint well. She had a routine. Every day. Every day except Fridays. She got up early and painted. The ritual helped free her mind from Ramin while at the same time reminding her of him, and she realized that she wanted to both forget and remember that moment in People's Park.

It was hard at first. The canvas remained blank. Her painting muscles were out of shape. She had no idea where to start. But then she'd remember the artisan in his shop in Isfahan, or the way the arches of the bridge fell into one another, or the columns of Persepolis, and the images moved her to action. She'd start with just one stroke. And on good days, before she knew it, her arm took over. Her hand moved. As if it already knew the shapes and colors she wanted to make.

While the rest of her building still slept, Mina painted. And then her watch beeped. That was part of the ritual. It beeped and it was time to pack it all up. She'd put the colors away. Then she'd take off her paint-splattered jeans and change into clean slacks and a crisp shirt. She'd comb her hair into place. Drink a cup of strong coffee.

And gather her finance notes.

And before long, she was in one of her business school classrooms, typing on her laptop, solving problems.

She had been sure that she would quit. They'd returned to Tehran from Isfahan, and Mina had vowed, over and over again, to quit business school and just paint full-time when she got back to New York.

But Bita had come over on her last night in Iran. Mina had just finished packing. Other guests were in Agha Jan's house, saying their last good-byes to Darya. Tea was being served.

"Let's go to the roof," Bita said. "Come on, for just a few minutes. You have to see Tehran at night, from the rooftop. Remember?"

Countless summers Mina had spent on the rooftops of Tehran. Countless summer nights they'd slept up there to escape the heat. Before the bombs.

Once they were on the roof, Bita lay down on her back and looked up at the sky.

"You know, when we were younger, I always thought that you'd grow up to be an artist," Bita said.

"Yeah, me too," Mina said. It stung. She hated that she'd given up. That she'd disappointed friends like Bita. She couldn't wait to announce that she was no longer going to run away from what she loved. She would make Bita proud, and she would show everyone that she was ready to be serious about her art once and for all. Mina sat up. "You know what, Bita? I'm not going to put it off anymore. I'm going to actually be true to myself once and for all. And true to art. When I go back, I'm going to quit!"

"Quit what?"

"Business school. I'm just going to paint. I'm not a business person! I was just doing it for my mother. Plus, I'm tired of the dual existence. The dual life! An artist in business school."

Bita was quiet for a while. She lay on her back and stared up at the sky. Then she said, "It's funny that you say dual existence, Mina. You know my party? You know the dances we have, my friends and I? We go wild. Inside my house I'm the crazy party girl. Outside, on the streets, I'm just another covered woman who can't open her mouth. Talk about dual existence! We have one life indoors, another outdoors. We say one thing with our friends, another thing out in public. Because we get arrested if we say what we really want to say. But Mina Joon. Business school? Painting? That's not a dual existence. That's just . . . life."

Mina stared at the Tehran lights. She looked out at rooftop after rooftop after rooftop and thought of all the people in their homes—what they watched, listened to, said inside. What they could never admit to watching, listening to, and saying once they were in public under the watchful eyes of the guards.

"Mina," Bita continued gently, "you should finish what you start. Don't you know? You are *there*. You are *free*. Quit? Why on earth would you quit? Pick up your paintbrush and paint if you want. But please don't waste the opportunities you've been given there."

"I just don't want to waste any more time."

"I'll tell you about waste, Mina Joon. I will become an old woman here. I won't stop fighting in the tiny little ways that I can. I'll do it for as long as it takes. I'll die protesting on the streets one day if I have to. Who knows what it will take for this country to be free? Maybe you and I will live to see it, maybe we won't. But, Mina, your life is there. And you should live it to the fullest." Bita sat up then. "Who said it has to be either business or painting? Do both!"

Bita got up then and walked over to the very edge of the roof. She leaned against the railing. When she spoke again, her voice was quiet. "Do it for me, then. Do it all. Be everything you can possibly be. Paint for me, Mina. Get your master's. Do your work. I won't lose touch with you this time, I promise. I'll fight here. You live your life there."

Mina watched as Bita slid her hand along the railing of the roof.

"Some nights I go up to our roof. I stand there and look up at the sky and I scream. I scream at the top of my lungs. I yell to God, to anyone, to the world out there. *Please please hear us over here!* I beg for the world to hear me." She turned to Mina, and her eyes were filled with tears. "You think I don't know how ridiculous my dual existence is? You think I'm not aware of the emptiness of those parties? If I had a smidgen of true freedom, I'd give up all those parties just to *live*. To walk down the street, to say what I want, to be myself. To be free." Bita's voice was quiet, but steady. "Sometimes I think God hears you better over there in the U.S. Don't quit, Mina. Go back and paint and get your business degree and work and get married and have kids and live! *Boro*, keep going! We're not the type to be suffocated. Right?"

Mina walked up and joined Bita at the railing. They leaned out over the rooftop with the lights of Tehran shimmering around them. Mina knew she'd hear Bita's screams all the way back in New York. She'd think of her friend, over here, standing on the rooftop, and screaming out for the world to hear.

"Paint us if you don't know what to paint," Bita said. "Show them we exist."

IF SHE FELT TIRED, SHE forced herself to get up; if she was exhausted, she kept going. Some days when the alarm went off, Mina did not want to paint, but when she went to her computer and saw an e-mail from Bita, she was suddenly less tired. She stopped resenting her classes and started applying herself. She read and studied the assigned cases diligently. Professor Van Heusen called on her, and she actually knew what she was talking about. Day after day, her paintings took shape. She caught Bita's dark, shining eyes. She drew the lights from a Tehran rooftop. She painted the cucumbers in Hussein Agha's little shop and blue-domed buildings in Isfahan square. She smeared burgundy for the cushions at the teahouse. She drew a woman in purple, her face beaming. She painted pomegranates, and she even managed to capture Mamani's face when she'd been young.

She told Ramin on the phone that she'd started painting again, and he sounded genuinely happy for her. But it wasn't the same. She could tell they were both working too hard to come up with things to say to each other. Mina began to see that she had been wrong all this time. The whole thing was nothing, and Mina had mistaken it for love. It saddened her to realize she had thought they had something when really all they had was a day in a park.

CHAPTER THIRTY-SEVEN

SPREADSHEET GOOD-BYES

Sam leaned in after class. "I want to hear all about it. That trip of yours. You want to go to Starbucks?"

Darya was silent. The two-week trip had taken a lot out of her. And put a lot back into her. Miranda Katilla had been puzzled at first to hear where she'd been. Slightly annoyed, it seemed, at all the Spreading Spreadsheet Specs work that Darya had missed. She'd given Darya piles of handouts to help her catch up.

And seeing Sam again? Seeing him in that basement room, sitting on the tennis-balled chair? Yes, she still felt like a silly schoolgirl when he smiled. Even if she had just come back from a place that felt more like home than Queens ever would. Even if the clothes that had been in her suitcase still smelled of dried Persian limes and dust. Smelled of pain and loss and grief and pride.

"I do not have time for coffee," was all she could say. "I do not have time . . ."

"I'd never waste your time with coffee." He smiled sheepishly. "But I know you love your tea."

"I can't." She had to end this flirting. She had her Parviz.

"You can. It's really not that complicated."

Darya gave in because it was, after all, the last day of class, and she would never see this man again and she was fiftysomething and not a child or a teenager and there was nothing wrong with having tea/coffee/lemonade or even whiskey with your classmate from your Spreading Spreadsheet Specs adult education class. There wasn't. Not one thing wrong at all.

They went to the coffee shop that Sam knew, the good one, the one he'd wanted to take her to all along. It was crowded and warm inside, yet Darya wished that she'd brought a stole or a pashmina or a chador she could cover herself with so that no one she knew could see her sitting there with Sam.

You couldn't have two lives at once. You couldn't be married to Parviz Rezayi, be mother of Hooman the doctor, Kayvon the lawyer, Mina the . . . Wait, what was she? Business school artist? Artist/student? Whatever. Mina would turn out to be whatever she wanted to be, this much Darya now knew. In any case, you couldn't be all those things and flirt with Sam Collins and think about what might have been. You couldn't reach over and touch his hair and pull him in and kiss him.

That's not how it worked.

Sam returned with Darya's tea. It came with a china cup and saucer and an iron Japanese kettle with real leaves inside.

"Thank you," Darya said.

She poured the tea and watched the steam rise from the cup. She inhaled the vapors and tried to clear her head.

"It was a great class," he said.

"It was," she said. And now he would be gone. Gone from her life starting next week, no more sitting next to him in that basement, no more scooching her chair up to his, no more shared breaks under the starless city sky. None of that. Back to their own separate lives. Him with his young guitar students and her with her math camp, job at the bank, honeyed milk for Parviz, and her kids who were taller than she was.

What is done cannot be undone, Darya thought. I have my life. She sipped her tea.

"It was really nice to get to know you during these past six weeks," Sam said. "I feel like . . . like I would have loved to get to know you better."

Darya choked on the hot tea, her eyes teared, her skin felt hot. A few other patrons turned to look at her. A large young man got up announcing, "Certified in the Heimlich!" and headed for her, but Darya waved her hand and smiled at everyone and sputtered, "I am fine, thank you. I am fine, thank you so much. It is nothing."

"Are you okay?" Sam had gotten up and was leaning over her. Bergamot, soap, Samishness. She inhaled it all. "Are you sure?"

"It was nothing." Darya looked up at him and smiled. "I'll be okay."

They would sit here and she would have tea and he would have coffee and they would say good-bye. That's how it worked. She would put an end to this flirtation once and for all. She could not do this to herself. Or to Parviz. Or to this kind Sam man in front of her. She had her Persian pride.

Sam sat back down across from her. "Parviz, right? Your husband? We ran into each other. When you were away. At Starbucks. Anyway, he's a great guy. We just chatted and he said . . ." Sam paused and smiled shyly. "His exact words to me were, 'Hey, Mister Sam, how's your instrument?' "

Darya made a mental note to kill Parviz when she got home.

"I told him it's in very good shape. We talked music for a while, and he told me he's always loved the guitar. I said that I play here occasionally, at this coffee shop. They have local musicians' night on Saturdays." Sam paused. "So maybe you could come sometime? Both of you, of course. Performance times are posted on the bulletin board."

"Oh. Yes, of course," Darya said.

"I taught myself"—Sam looked down at his chord-strumming hands—"a Persian folk song. I think you'd like it." He looked up at her shyly. "So drop in on Saturday night. Have a listen."

"I will . . . we will," Darya said. She wanted to hold him. He had taught himself a Persian folk song. She was moved at his kindness. She had a favorite folk song that went well with guitar, and she used to sing it when she was young, back when anything seemed possible. She wanted Sam to have picked that song.

They were quiet for a while. He leaned back in his seat and stared at her. Then he said, "Isn't life just . . . something else?"

"Something. Else," Darya said. "Yes, it is." Her eyes were filling with tears, and she felt dizzy and slightly nauseated from the tea. She was hot and sweating now. Kavita would've sounded the alarms of menopause. But she knew that wasn't it.

They sipped from their cups and looked out the window. "It was great to meet you," he finally said.

She pretended to fuss with the tea leaves in the kettle. He busied himself with the bill and his wallet. When they were ready to go, he got up and pulled out her chair. It scraped loudly on the floor. There were no tennis balls on this chair.

"Good luck with everything," she said.

It's just how it was.

CHAPTER THIRTY-EIGHT

HOME

On warmer days, Mina painted in Riverside Park. The open air and the sun and the sounds of the river were so welcome after all the cold days of winter. She staked out a spot on the grass by the river. She leaned against a huge oak tree there and did her work.

She adjusted the canvas and tried to remember the People's Park. She mixed the oil paints on a separate palette, trying to get just the right shade of green. It had been weeks since her final dismal conversation with Ramin. She needed to forget him, move on. What they had experienced on their trip did not remotely apply to their real-world lives. She struggled to push him out of her mind, but no matter what she did, she couldn't forget the *place*. It helped to try and paint that scene, if nothing else to get the details of the sheer physical beauty of People's Park. She'd worked for weeks at getting the tree on canvas.

She had been painting for almost half an hour, lost in her work, when she heard rustling, and someone said, "You've managed to capture it perfectly. Amazing."

Mina's hand froze. The voice from behind the tree had the deep timbre that had once warmed her, even as she stood in the cold against a rough tree. She whipped her head around but stopped herself from looking all the way around the tree. She just felt her heart pound and had to grip the paintbrush in order to keep it from falling to the ground.

"I hope it's okay that I came here."

"I never expected . . . how are you?" she said finally.

"Oh, Mina. This shouldn't have taken me so long. I finally just had to see you. To tell you in person."

"Tell me what?" she asked.

"That—I am so sorry, Mina. I blew it on the phone, I know."

"There's no need to apologize—" she began, but he interrupted.

"Mina, please . . ." He came around the trunk then and stood in front of her. If a moment ago she had despaired over their stilted phone calls and his not coming sooner, she was now rooted to where she sat in the grass. Because one look at him standing there, his feet apart and the way he crossed his arms across his chest like a teenage boy, made her melt again. She did not want to come undone. Then she looked into his eyes and saw the sadness.

"What's wrong, Ramin?"

"My grandmother passed away a few weeks ago."

His face was raw with pain. Mina knew the look of grief all too well, could recognize it in a person's eyes. She felt again that sinking, sick-to-the-stomach feeling of loss. It was something that was accessible to her within a second, a taste that came back as if it had never left. "I am so sorry," was all she could say.

Mina looked up at the branches of the tree, at the leaves that looked like a canopy. She remembered the other tree they'd stood under, in that other world—the flame-colored leaves and the cold air on her cheek. The guards that stood by, waiting. "It's good you got to see her, at least. It was worth all the risks."

"Let's just . . . let's sit, Mina."

He came to her side and slid down the trunk till he was sitting right by her. He smelled of mint and she wondered if she smelled like paint and turpentine. She tightened her ponytail in an attempt to look less scruffy. He leaned against the tree, his knees drawn up to his chest. He smiled at her. "You're painting."

"What about my painting?"

"No, *you're* painting. I know you told me you were, but it's different to actually see your work. You're so talented. Quite frankly, I love that you are painting our tree."

She felt her face burn a little. "Yes, the tree." She wanted to say "our" but couldn't just yet. She sat straight up. "How did you even know to find me here?"

"I called your parents' house. I spoke to your dad, by the way. We had a nice chat about my brother and how he's doing . . ."

Mina cringed. "Oh no."

"No, it was fine," Ramin said. "And then your dad gave the phone to your mom, who told me where you go every morning. Took me a while to find you, though. Lots of trees here."

Mina smiled. "My mom likes to know my routine. Even if it involves art."

"Oh, she sounded very proud of you."

"She did?"

"Yes."

Mina looked out at the park in front of them. An older couple walked their dog. The air smelled of freshly cut grass and jasmine. Spring with all its renewal and new possibilities hung in every tree, from every leaf. She wanted to hug him. To tell him again that she was sorry about his grandmother and that it would get easier with time. She wanted to hold his hand again.

"It is just so great to see you again," he said quietly.

The bark dug into her back and the sleeve of his shirt almost touched her arm. "It's great to see you too," she said. She pulled her knees in and cocked her head and looked at him. "I don't like the phone," she suddenly blurted out.

He laughed. "I'm not a huge fan either."

"You never know if it's a good time to call, if the other person is in the middle of something . . ."

"If they really want to talk . . ."

"If they're busy . . ."

"And we're both so busy, right?" He looked at her sideways with a grin.

They both laughed then. Mina leaned her head back against the tree and felt the rough bark through her hair.

"Mina, I've missed you. Look, I know we saw each other, what, three times? On a trip halfway across the world. But I can't stop thinking about any of it. I know it sounds strange, but every time I was with you in Tehran, it was just so comfortable . . ."

"Comfortable? Like an old sofa?"

"Yes. No. I mean comfortable in a really good way." He bit his lip, a little flustered. "You know, Mina," he said, his voice quiet. "People always say I'm so lucky because I can fit in anywhere. I've lived in such different places. In California, in Tehran, in Connecticut. But the truth is, to this day, I feel like an outsider in America. Then when I went to Iran, even though it was great to be back, I was an outsider, a foreigner there now. Sometimes I think to belong everywhere is to really belong nowhere. Which is maybe why, so far"—he sighed—"I've been reluctant to put down real roots. But then I met you." He looked at her, and his face was no longer sad.

Mina stretched her legs over the bulky, bumpy roots of the tree. How long had she floated precariously on that hyphen that separated the place where she had her childhood and the place where she now lived? How long had she hovered, never feeling at home on either side of that hyphen? Now she remembered what Ramin had given her. What had made that day under the tree in the People's Park feel so timeless, so otherworldly. With him, she finally belonged. "I know," she said.

"How about we start again? In person? Do you think maybe we could pick up where we left off at the park?"

"We are in person . . . now." Mina looked at him.

He inched a little closer. His arm felt solid and strong next to hers.

"I missed you too," she said. She slowly rested her head on his shoulder. "It feels so . . ." She looked up at him and winked. "Comfortable."

He just smiled, looking relieved.

They sat like that under the tree. After a few minutes, he found her hand and held it. It felt as if she'd come home.

"Let's try again," he said.

The leaves in the branches trembled in the breeze. Her canvas teetered on the easel. Oil paints lay strewn around their feet.

"Let's . . ." she started to say.

But before she could finish her sentence, he drew her in and held her face in both his hands. Then he kissed her—a long, slow kiss in the park, under the tree, for all the world to see.

CHAPTER THIRTY-NINE

LOCAL TALENT AT
THE COFFEE SHOP

When does Sizzling Sam show up?" Kavita patted her hair.
"Why is Parviz late?" Darya looked at her watch,
then at the door.

"He plays sitar?" Yung-Ja asked.

"Not sitar. Guitar," Darya said.

They had finished math camp and their samosas and kimbap
and were at the coffee shop where Sam was to perform. Parviz had
even agreed to attend, though he had hesitated at first, but then
he'd said that it would be rude to not come and hear Sam sing the
Persian folk song he'd promised to play. After all, he had learned
Farsi for it.

Kavita squealed when Sam walked onto the makeshift
stage. He was wearing jeans and a flannel shirt. He sat on
a stool in the middle of the room as the audience sipped on

cappuccinomochafrappeblanco—whatever it was they were drinking. Darya was a little put off by the large vessels from which the people drank. Why did they have to drink out of cups that were practically bowls? She breathed in her tea. Where was Parviz?

The manager of the coffee shop introduced Sam, said he was a local gem, and mentioned the names of some musicians who had apparently influenced Sam when he was young. He said Sam was available for lessons. Then he left the stage, and Sam picked up his guitar.

At first, he just strummed out the notes. Darya's heart fluttered when she heard the introductory verse to the folk song she had loved all her life. Sam's hair fell over his face as he looked down at his fingers on the guitar. Then he lifted his head, smiled, and began to sing. His voice was deep but soft and mellifluous. Each Farsi word in Sam's American accent sounded like honey. The audience grew quiet, and the only sound was Sam's music. Darya sat perfectly still. When he took in a breath, she held her own. Then when his voice soared again, she felt undone.

"Beautiful." Yung-Ja leaned in. "He is good!"

"I am *transported*," Kavita said. "I am besotted!"

Darya looked around the coffee shop and saw that Sam had given the gift of her favorite song to every person there, handed it out like a present. She loved him for it.

Halfway through the song, the door opened and there was Parviz in his suit. He must have come straight from the hospital. He found Darya, and she made space for him next to her, and together they sat as Sam's voice filled the room, and Kavita closed her eyes and swayed while Yung-Ja's eyes stayed locked on Sam. Near the end, Sam looked directly at Darya, and paused. Before he hit the climax, his face was completely at peace. And then, he went for the highest note, the note that always made Darya melt, the one that had always moved her. Sam held that note with delicacy and love. The audience hovered in the air with him, not wanting the moment to end, not wanting his voice to stop.

Darya quickly wiped her tears away and reached for Parviz's hand. How many husbands would take this in stride? How many men would be so Parviz-esque and put away their pride and jealousy and come to a coffee shop to hear Sam sing a song that everyone must know he had prepared for her? She was thankful for all of it: for her good friends Kavita and Yung-Ja sitting with her, for the people listening rapt in the coffee shop, for the symmetry of numbers that helped her cope with the asymmetry of her life and always would. She was thankful for the husband who tapped his foot to the beat, no matter what, and for Sam who had taught himself a Persian song and had sung it from the heart.

THE AUDIENCE BROKE INTO APPLAUSE at the end of Sam's performance, and a few people went up to congratulate him. Darya and Parviz and Kavita and Yung-Ja inched their way to the group of people gathering on the stage.

"Well done, my good young sir!" Parviz slapped Sam on the back a little too hard when they reached him. He then moved aside and brought Kavita and Yung-Ja in front of Sam. "Have you met these Lovely Ladies of the Mathematics?"

"Brilliant barely describes the beauty of your ballad." Kavita shook Sam's hand.

"Very good." Yung-Ja bowed her head.

"Thank you," Darya said quietly. She was sad that it had to

end, that she had to go. She might never see him again. But above all, she was so proud of him.

Sam smiled at her and thanked them all. He was then engulfed by more audience members congratulating him.

They walked to the parking lot. Parviz had come straight from the hospital in his car, and Darya had driven from home in hers. After Kavita and Yung-Ja said good-bye, Parviz and Darya were left alone.

"Thank you for coming," Darya said.

"It was a nice performance," Parviz said. "I give him credit. His Farsi was almost spot-on."

"I give *you* credit for being so . . . so . . ."

"For being an open-minded gentleman who tolerates the crushes of musicians on my wife?"

Darya laughed. "See you at home."

"Don't run off with him! You're not going anywhere. You're mine!" Parviz kissed her, then walked to his car.

That night, Parviz set the table while Darya prepared dinner. They watched an episode of a nature show devoted to coral reefs. Parviz ate his pistachios, and they both had honeyed milk before bed.

And Darya fell asleep, still hearing Sam's song, in the arms of the man who had helped her climb over the rough and rocky places on all those past mountain hikes and beyond.

CHAPTER FORTY

JUST THIS

The house was scented with heaps of crimson and purple flowers. Darya's hair was blown and styled, the gray waves bobbed up and down as she rushed about the house, rearranging pieces of furniture. Sometime after her return from Iran, Darya had stopped using hair dye. She no longer felt the need to have red hair to prove that she was free. Today, she wore a gold dress lined with silk that she had sewn at her old sewing machine. The dress ended right below her knees, the three-quarter sleeves would've pleased Jackie O. Most important, the cut and style befitted a mother of the bride. Darya fluttered from room to room putting velvet cushions at just the right angle on the fat sofas, straightening the fringes on the Persian rugs, sifting through her fingers the burgundy and yellow *Esfand* seeds, and scattering orange rinds on a tray so they could finish drying in the afternoon sun for her *Shirin Polo* dish.

Her sister, Nikki, polished the large oval wedding mirror. It had been difficult and expensive for Nikki to get the visa, but after their reunion in Iran, the women had vowed to keep visiting each other. Darya was determined to see her father and sister and all the rest of the relatives regularly now. Nikki would be coming to the U.S. more frequently, even if it meant going to Dubai and waiting for months for her visa clearance. Darya dusted the colored eggs that they had dyed in greens and blues. The idea of grandchildren floored Darya, but one day, Mina would know that first flicker of movement inside her belly. One day, Darya could hold against her cheek the soft face of a new baby. Darya stopped her thoughts. She was thinking ahead too fast, too soon. She didn't want to jinx it all.

"He seems like quite a good man," Nikki said.

"He does. He is." Darya arranged the eggs in a bowl. "My sources told me about the older brother, but said nothing about the younger one. You don't think it was deliberate, do you?"

"*Chemeedonam.* I have no idea. The point is . . . Mina found him. May God give them a healthy, long, and joyful life together. May their children grow up safe under their parents' shadows. May they always have each other," Nikki murmured and prayed as she polished the wedding mirror.

Parviz walked in, his arms loaded with more flowers.

"I was the first one at the Chelsea flower market early this morning!" he said. "Because he who wakes up early is he who accomplishes!"

"Put them in the kitchen, Parviz, I'll have to organize them," Darya said. "Oh no, this one's wilted!"

"Everything in the universe is as it should be, Darya Joon,"

Parviz said. "Nothing can be perfect. You just have to work . . . in your circle of energy!"

"I'll work on my soup is what I'll do, thank you." Darya went into the kitchen and dropped stalks of leek into the food processor. All week she'd browned beef, chopped *sabzi*, sautéed vegetables, prepared desserts. The food at Mina's wedding would be her own; she would have none of that catered stuff. Hooman's wedding had been in a rented hall, with catered food and soft music. The bride's family had arranged everything. It was perfectly American. But Mina's wedding—at Darya's home, with her food, her friends, would be Persian.

At exactly 11:15 a.m., Mina returned from the hairdresser. Her black hair was slightly trimmed, blow-dried straight—but not at all specially styled.

"Mina Joon, just this, *hameen?*"

"Just this," Mina said.

Darya forced herself to say nothing more about the sleek hairdo that was no hairdo at all, about how being a bride comes but once in a lifetime (God willing), how her hair ought to be teased, sprayed, propped, pinned, perfected.

"Just this," Mina repeated and threw her wind slicker on the armchair.

As she watched Mina go up the steps, Darya suddenly felt the impulse to rush up, grab her, and whisper, "Mina Joon, you don't have to get married. You can stay right here, in this house— who needs it, the meals you'll have to cook, the screaming children you'll have to deal with, the nights next to him while he snores, who needs it, Mina Joon! Just continue to be my little girl, always."

But instead she heard her own voice tell Mina to hurry up and get ready because the guests would be arriving soon.

In the kitchen, Darya put on her apron and found reassurance in her pots and pans. The cast-iron Dutch oven, her stainless steel sauté pan from Iran. Darya boiled and sautéed and fried. She ground walnuts for the sauce for her sweet-and-sour *fesenjoon* dish. She tucked raisins and dates between mounds of saffron rice. She sprinkled sliced almonds on the top.

She heard movement upstairs. The water pipes gurgled. She remembered her own wedding.

That small square window with the ugly yellow light in Mamani's bedroom. Darya had sat at the vanity table, rubbing rouge into her cheeks as she cried. For one moment she'd considered contorting her body into a shape that could squeeze out that tiny square window and escape. All the guests had already gathered in the living room. She had been able to hear her parents being congratulated. But Darya had been nineteen and not ready for the gift that Mamani had given her. And Parviz—all gangly and nervous, the white flesh of his skinny wrists peeking out below his shirtsleeves, a scattering of acne barely faded from his face. Darya had walked out of that bedroom ready to die.

But instead she had lived. And created more life. Parviz had proved to be kind and tender and sweet—tending to her every need, resurrecting her dead dreams. Her mother had not failed her.

Darya picked up her rubber spatula and spread icing on the sponge cake she had baked earlier in the day, swallowing the lump in her throat. Mina loved her sponge cake. On this, her unofficial last day in that house, she would have her mother's sponge cake. Darya would give her that.

THE GUESTS CAME IN DRESSED up, laughing, excited. Ramin came with his parents and his older brother, Mr. Dashti. Greetings and kisses and congratulations were shared. After Ramin's family, the Persian wedding officiant arrived. Darya retreated to the kitchen to finish cooking.

From the open kitchen door, as she dropped the dark burgundy barberries onto her *Shirin Polo*, Darya caught a glimpse of Ramin. He sat at the dining room table, his friends surrounding him—college friends and colleagues probably, as he talked and they listened. One particularly tall blond woman clapped in glee as Ramin recounted his date with Mina at the People's Park.

There he was. Darya patted her *koofteh* meatballs into the Pyrex dish, making room for the grilled vegetables. Where was she?

Darya whizzed through the living room, grazing guests on the shoulder and giving them quick smiles as she hurried upstairs. Where was she?

Upstairs, in Darya's bedroom Mina sat on the bed, dressed in white. Lisa, Hooman's wife, and Deborah, Kayvon's girlfriend, fluttered about her. Yooni was pinning the bridal veil onto Mina's hair, and Pria was fussing with the bouquet. For a fleeting second, Darya had an image of having tea with her married daughter. Maybe she would be one of those women in stores and restaurants with their grown daughters, the ones she used to see when they first came to America, the ones that had made her miss her own mother. She realized then that it wasn't the end. Hadn't Darya relied on Mamani even after she was married? She and Mina would still have each other. When Mina got back from her honeymoon, Darya and Mina could go out for "together tea" and talk about Mina's work plans and where to buy the best moisturizer. It was a huge relief to realize that her daughter would still be hers.

"You look beautiful," Darya said.

DARYA CAME DOWN THE STEPS first, to happy cheers. Baba stood with the other guests gazing up at Darya descending in gold, then at Mina coming down in her bridal white. As Mina came into view, everyone broke into applause. Cheers filled the room. Darya reached the bottom of the stairs and turned and looked up at Mina as if to say, "Mina Joon, this is for you! You are the star."

Then she stepped aside.

THE HEELS OF MINA'S PEARL-COLORED pumps sank into the thick carpet with each step. She had to concentrate on her balance. With one hand, she lifted her wedding dress and with the other she held tight to a bouquet of roses. The cheering grew louder and louder as Mina descended the stairs. When she walked down the final step, the guests exploded in applause. Ramin sat on a tiny bench near the silk bridal *sofreh* spread on the floor, waiting for her. Men and women whistled. Mina took it all in. She could see the pride on Darya's face. Baba had never looked more optimistic. Hooman and Kayvon whistled and did a shimmy together. Mina looked out and saw Aunt Nikki. She saw Yung-Ja and Kavita, laughing and clapping hard. She saw Mr. Dashti. He stood there in his favorite beige suit, his few strands of hair combed strategically across his head. He wiped a handkerchief across his forehead with his doughy hand and smiled. Next to him stood a petite Asian woman, his girlfriend.

If Bita had been there, she would have cheered the loudest for Mina. Aunt Firoozeh would have cried and Uncle Jafar would have shushed her quiet. Leila would have been proud to be there, her children could have been the ring bearer and the flower girl.

And Mamani. If Mamani had been there, she would have stood quietly next to Darya, her dark eyes shining with pride, her soft, feathery face wrinkled with the largest smile.

Last, her eyes rested on Ramin, waiting for her by the *sofreh*, in his crisp clean suit, his kind eyes smiling up at her. Mina's body started to shake. A tickle worked from the bottom of her toes all the way up to her face. Baba jumped up and down. Darya's hazel eyes filled with tears even as she smiled. Her brothers stood tall in their shirtsleeves, clapping as hard as they could.

And Mina was made of laughter.

THE BRIDAL *SOFREH*, A *TERMEH* CLOTH that Mamani had sewn by hand for Darya's wedding years ago, was spread on the living room floor, its gold and silver threads glittering in the sunlight filtering through the windows. It was at once strong and soft, covered with significant objects for this occasion. Darya and Aunt Nikki had spent days preparing and arranging them:

A mirror at the head of the bridal *sofreh* lit by candelabra on either side, positioned so that when Mina sat on the bride-and-groom bench, her reflection in the mirror was all Ramin saw.

A tray of spices to guard against evil spirits and the evil eye, arranged in different colors. *Esfand* seeds carefully sprinkled to ward off negative energy and bad thoughts. In the upper portion of the tray, Darya had spelled out "*Mobarak Bad*—Congratulations"—in grains of wild rice.

Lace napkins in the shape of doves carrying in their beaks candy-shell almonds in pastel blue, pink, and white.

A large flat *sangak* bread with the blessing "*Mobarak Bad*" spelled out with cinnamon seeds, garnished on the side with feta cheese and green herbs.

A bowl of colored eggs to symbolize fertility.

Bowls of sweets and small Persian pastries prepared by Darya—sugar-coated almonds, rice cookies, chickpea cookies, almond cookies, and baklava.

A bowl of honey to ensure the sweetness of their future.

Two cones of sugar to be used during the *Aghd* ceremony.

An open Koran by the mirror surrounded by jasmine and rose petals.

On the corner of the bridal *sofreh*, Mina had added the *khatam* box with the painting of the long-lashed woman and the man in profile kissing her. A reminder of her journey.

MINA TOOK HER SEAT ON the small bench next to Ramin in front of the bridal *sofreh*. The bench was small, so that the two of them touched. A piece of white silk cloth was held above their heads. Tradition called for women who were happily married to hold up either end of the cloth. Darya held up the side closest to Mina's head, and Aunt Nikki held the other. Ramin's mother, a tall, elegant woman, with her hair in a sophisticated bun, rubbed two cones of sugar above the white silk cloth. The sugar was to rain down happiness and sweetness on the bride and groom.

"I vood like to velcome evehreevon to dees ceremony," the wedding officiant said with his strong Iranian accent. "Vee are here today to join in marry-age dees man and dees voo-man."

The officiant then proceeded to translate what he'd just said into Farsi.

Mina sighed. This would take a while.

As the officiant continued to talk, explaining everything in two languages, he also added Arabic prayers. Mina didn't understand a word of those. She wanted to reach and tug Darya's skirt as she had as a child so that Darya would tell the officiant to hurry up and get on with it.

As if reading her mind, Ramin slid his hand across to Mina and held her hand in his. As the officiant droned on, Ramin lifted Mina's hand and kissed it.

Mina squealed in surprise.

The officiant faltered for a minute, but then went on more loudly. "And you see, deh veddeeng eez for the man and voo-man to expehress der deevoshun!"

Ramin squeezed Mina's hand.

After what seemed like a very long speech, the officiant finally asked, "Veel dees voo-man, Mina Rezayi, agree to marry dees man, Aghaye Mohandess Ramin Dashti?"

Mina said nothing.

"She went to pick flowers!" Aunt Nikki called out.

"She's picking out sweet jasmine!" Darya said.

"She went to the library!" Baba cried.

Mina stayed silent, not saying yes the first time, as Persian tradition warranted.

The officiant asked again. "Does she accept eet? Does she vant to join him in marry-age?"

"She's busy!" Hooman called out.

"She's got a million things to do!" Kayvon said.

"She has tests to study for!" Yung-Ja called out, catching on.

Mina stayed quiet, playing along.

"I veel ask again," the officiant said. "Does this laydee accept dees man's hand in marry-age?"

Mina looked up from behind the bridal veil, threw it off, and shouted, "Yes!"

Baba jumped into the air. Hooman and Kayvon whistled. The room burst into applause and cheers. Aunt Nikki flapped one hand against her lips and made a loud cheering sound *"Looo loooo loooo looooo!"*

After Ramin said yes the first time (as was deemed the tradition for grooms), they exchanged rings. Hooman and Kayvon handed Mina her ring, Mr. Dashti handed Ramin his.

The white cloth above their heads dropped behind them amidst cheers and music. Darya bent down to where Mina and Ramin sat on the bench and held out the bowl of honey. Ramin and Mina each dipped a pinky finger into the honey and then, at the same time, inserted the honeyed finger into the other's mouth. Ramin sucked the honey off Mina's finger, and Mina sucked the honey off Ramin's. For sweetness. For life.

Then Ramin sucked the rest of Mina's fingers. The crowd went wild. The officiant turned away.

Darya was the first to give them her gift—a gold necklace that Mamani had given her on her wedding day. One that had belonged to Mamani's mother. Women came up to Mina and handed her boxes of jewelry. Some of the boxes were new, American. Tiffany's and Fortunoff's. But most were wrapped in tiny ancient velvet pouches—gold and silver owned by grandmothers and great-grandmothers. Guests went up to Ramin and kissed him on either cheek, then kissed Mina's cheeks. Mina and Ramin were engulfed in hug after hug. Mina hugged Ramin's mother as Aunt Nikki clasped another necklace around her neck. Someone, Mina didn't know who, slipped a bracelet around her wrist. Soon Mina's and Ramin's feet were surrounded by boxes and boxes of jewelry.

Darya bent down to put the boxes away, to keep them organized in a tidy pile. The guests continued to come up to congratulate the bride and groom. Before long, Ramin was dabbing at his eyes, and Mina was doing the same. Darya gave them tissues. Mina started to laugh, then cry, then laugh again.

The *Mobarak* wedding song with its lyrics wishing joy for the bride and groom started then. The guests began to dance, couples and groups joining in a circle. Mina and Ramin got up from their bench and walked around the room, shaking hands and kissing everyone.

"The bride and groom must dance!" Baba yelled.

Slowly, Ramin raised his hands in the air like a flamenco dancer. He stomped his feet on the ground and moved his eyebrows up and down at Mina. Mina hesitated for just a moment, then she attempted her best Persian dance. Together they moved to applause. As the song ended, Mina saw Baba rush to the DJ as though on a mission.

"Baba, no, please don't!" Kayvon yelled.

But it was too late. Within minutes, the familiar first notes of ABBA's seventies' classic filled the room.

Baba pointed at Mina. "You are the dancing queen!"

In a half cartwheel, half jump of joy, Baba joined Mina and Ramin on the dance floor. After a few minutes, Hooman and Lisa, Kayvon and Deborah joined them too.

DARYA WATCHED HER FAMILY DANCE. She watched Parviz jump with Mina and Ramin. Watched Lisa—Hooman's sensible, pediatrician wife—and Deborah—Kayvon's kind, creative girlfriend—dance with her sons, the sons she had feared would die on the border of Iran, whose future she had been determined to shape without participation in a war. Her mission to protect her children had been successful. Though America would never be home for her, on a day like today, she could deeply appreciate the great gifts she had been able to give her children.

"Dance with us!" Mina called out to her. "Come on, Maman!"

"Come on, Daryoosh!" Ramin called out to his brother.

The older Mr. Dashti hesitated at first, but then jogged onto the dance floor with his petite girlfriend. They both started to do furious disco moves. Everybody cheered and clapped.

They had made it, Darya thought. The bombs hadn't killed them, the Revolutionary Guards hadn't imprisoned them, their home hadn't been confiscated, and their family had left alive. Almost all alive.

As she walked to the kitchen to get the cake out, Darya was acutely aware that Mamani's place was empty tonight. But the joy in her home outweighed the loss. For that she was supremely grateful.

KAVITA AND YUNG-JA HELPED DARYA place the cake on the same dining room table where they had solved equations together for years. Mina and Ramin posed as Kayvon took photos, and it was then that Darya realized she had forgotten to bring out a cake cutter. Before she could get it, Parviz marched out of the kitchen brandishing a huge black plastic spatula.

"It's her wedding cake, for goodness' sake!" Darya tried to stop him.

But it was too late. Mina plunged the spatula into the cake, laughing, and cut big uneven chunks.

Darya cringed as the lopsided slices were handed out. Ramin delicately placed a bite in Mina's mouth as Mina scooped up some cake for Ramin, crumbs dropping all over his beautiful shirt, both of them laughing through the mess. Darya told herself to let it go. Real life was messy. It would never add up, it would never be perfect.

It didn't need to be.

LATER, IN THE KITCHEN, MINA walked in and flung her arms around Darya's neck.

"Oh, Maman!" she said as Darya tried to balance saffron pudding on a tray. "Everything was so delicious! Thank you! The cake was a hit . . ."

"You should have used the cake cutter," Darya said, not for the first time.

"This is all I wanted. Just this," Mina said.

Darya wobbled on her feet. She was exhausted. She had

worked her fingers raw. Stayed up nights preparing the bridal *sofreh*. She put down the tray and steadied herself against the kitchen counter.

"You know what?" Mina swept a piece of hair from Darya's face. "She's here. I know it. Mamani is here tonight." Mina's eyes were filled with tears. Darya blinked back her own and nodded. She was relieved when Mina drew her in and hugged her tight.

"Come on." Mina took Darya's hand and led her out of the kitchen. "You've toiled enough. Come and dance with me, Maman."

"No, Mina Joon." Darya resisted.

"Yes," Mina said.

When they reached the middle of the living room, Darya and Mina joined the rest of the dancing guests. Darya mirrored Mina, swaying her hips and twirling her hands. She remembered teaching a three-year-old Mina these very moves, patiently playing the music over and over. The joy on that three-year-old girl's face was right in front of her now. Only her daughter was now a bride. It had all happened in a minute.

When the song finished, Mina stopped, and Darya was relieved to catch her breath. The rest of the guests bounced to a new beat.

Mina stood still in front of Darya. She opened her mouth as if she were going to say something, then closed it again.

"What is it, Mina? Are you all right?"

"You know, Maman," Mina said quietly. "I haven't thanked you."

"You just thanked me. In the kitchen."

"No, I mean I haven't thanked you. Really ever."

The music blasted around them. People danced, lost in their own worlds.

Mina rested her hands on Darya's shoulders and paused for a minute. Then she said, "Thank you, Maman, for everything. Thank you for the bridal *sofreh*. For the food. For all your *zahmat*, your efforts these past few weeks. Thank you for everything you've given me. For all your hard work through all these years. For all that you've done for me."

Darya felt then that everything she'd ever lived was worth this moment. She saw herself reflected in her daughter's eyes. She would say those very words to Mamani if she could.

She did, in her heart.

Acknowledgments

Years ago Leonard Michaels told me to write this book. It took a while. Lenny, how I wish you were still here.

I want to thank my editor, Lee Boudreaux. She is a dream come true. Her skill, exuberance, and good humor made working on this book a pleasure. A huge thank-you to her assistant, Karen Maine, whose expert eye and endless talents helped this project so much. Thanks also to cover designer Allison Saltzman, production editor Tamara Arellano, copyeditor Georgia Maas, and the entire amazing team at Ecco.

I am grateful for my wise and wonderful agent, Wendy Sherman. It is because of her belief in my characters that this book found a home. And my deep appreciation goes to Jane Rosenman for her excellent advice.

A few teachers can't be forgotten. Charles Muscatine encouraged me to become a writer. Chuck Wachtel was my MFA thesis adviser. E. L. Doctorow's novel class provided lasting guidance. And Alexander Chee is not only a gifted teacher but one of the most generous writers of our time.

Thank you to my peers who provided feedback on early drafts: Courtney Angela Brkic, Cara Davis Conomos, Susan Carlton, Victoria Fraser, Lisa Liberty Becker, Lee Hoffman, Charity Tremblay, and Lara J. K. Wilson. And a big thank-you to Linda K. Wertheimer, who met with me over many a tea and made sure I never gave up on this book.

Charles Baxter's lecture on "what's done cannot be undone" at the Bread Loaf Writers' Conference helped me form Darya's thoughts. Najmieh Batmanglij's cookbook *New Food of Life* was a great resource for traditional Iranian wedding items. And Grub Street's inaugural Launch Lab provided much-appreciated knowledge and camaraderie after the book was done. Thank you to all my fellow Launch Labbers and to Lynne Griffin and Katrin Schumann for being excellent coaches.

Photographer extraordinaire David E. Lawrence braved a freezing fall morning at Walden Pond to work his camera magic. His skills are second to none. Thank you to both Lawrence families for their friendship. And thank you to Marjorie Travis for her perspective and many chats.

My sister, Maryam, encouraged me to write essays, in English, when we were children in Iran. She gave me the classics to read. I am grateful that our bond has weathered war, revolution, and several continents.

My mother's love and her belief that I could be successful at anything I pursued has been a driving force in my life. Her endless energy and strength in the face of many hardships inspire me. It is her dishes that I cook, her tea that I brew, and her soul that is mine.

My father's wisdom and calm have encouraged many, always. Despite decades of a debilitating disease, many surgeries, and constant pain, he has retained his optimism and excellent humor. My love and respect for him know no bounds. He is my kindred spirit.

I owe the greatest thanks of all to my husband, Kamran. Throughout the journey of this book, he has been my biggest supporter and truest friend. His love has sustained me. And he's really good at thinking of chapter titles. Thank you, Kamran Joon, for everything.

A big thanks to my children, Mona and Rod. Your creativity, joy, and mischief have enriched my days in ways I could never have imagined. It is my hope that you reach for your dreams and fulfill your potential. Even if it takes a while.

And to my grandmother, Mamani. How I wish we'd had more time.